MW01135871

Beauty and the Horseman's Head

By Holly Kelly

Published by Clean Paranormal

Other Books by Holly Kelly

Cursed by the Fountain of Youth (An Unnatural States of America Book)

Rising (book 1 in The Rising Series)
Descending (book 2 in The Rising Series)
Avenging (book 3 in The Rising Series)
Raging (book 4, in The Rising Series)

Beauty and the Horseman's Head

ISBN-13: 978-1978492851
ISBN-10: 1978492855

Edited by: Tamara Hart Heiner
Cover Design by: Holly Kelly

Clean Paranormal
Spanish Fork, Utah 84660

HollyKellyBooks.com

Beauty and the Horseman's Head

Chapter 1

The smell of musket powder mingled with the sound of cannon fire. Hope's legs burned with exhaustion from the long journey. The British had arrived, bringing death and destruction.

She wrung her hands in her worn skirt as she stumbled to keep up. Her thoughts flitted to the state of her clothing. They were in dire need of repair. It wasn't that she didn't have thread to mend her clothing, but that thread was reserved for knitting together the wounds of the patriots. Mary thought her idea was ludicrous. But if stitching held fabric together, why not skin and flesh? The captain didn't exactly forbid her to try, but he did have a look of disbelief on his face when she described what she wanted to do.

It would work.

She was almost positive it would. And the condition of her dress was significantly less important than the lives of others.

The sound of musket fire caused her heart to leap into her throat.

"Hold back," Mary said at her side as she stopped.

The other nurses did as they were told and scrambled behind wide trunks to block any stray musket balls. Hope hesitated a moment, wondering if they might be too close to the battle. A sharp crack accompanied a branch exploding above her. Splinters rained down on her head. Hope dove behind the nearest tree, her heart pounding as she sat with her back against the trunk.

"Hesitating will get you killed, Miss Lowhouse."

"We need to move back," Hope said. "We're too close."

"We are fine where we are," Mary said.

Hope's heart pounded at the sounds of conflict surrounding them. She tried not to think about her father, there in the thick of battle. Each shout, each boom, each blood-curdling cry could be him.

Blinking back tears, she steeled herself. He raised her better than that. She was not brought up by a soft, maternal hand. Her mother died giving birth to her. Her father taught her to be strong, to not give into her weaker female emotions. She was as tough as any man, and real men didn't cry.

Hope jumped at the next shout. That one was close. *Is the battle moving toward us?* She looked over at Mary. Her jaw was tight, her fingers dug into the earth as she sat motionless.

Another shout, even closer. It *was* coming toward them!

Shouldn't they be retreating away from the battle?

Mary did not move. She did not even have the sense to prepare to move. She sat as still as a stone statue.

Hope turned onto her knees.

"Miss Lowhouse, you stay put," Mary hissed, all the while not moving.

"The battle is drawing near," Hope said.

"That is just your imagination," Mary answered.

"I *never* entertain fanciful thoughts," Hope said, her temper rising. "They are truly moving this way."

"You will stay in place, Miss. Lowhouse!" Mary looked at the other girls, some of whom looked ready to bolt. "You will all stay in place."

"But they *are* getting closer!" another voice hissed.

"You are just panicking," Mary said, finally moving. She slowly peered around the trunk.

A sharp crack pierced the air, and Mary stiffened. Not a moment later, she tipped over. Her open eyes stared into the sky. A red dot the size of a pine tree shilling dimpled the center of her forehead.

Screams erupted from the girls as they scrambled, racing through the clearing like a herd of frightened deer—only much slower and more erratic.

"Wait!" Hope shouted. "Keep to the trees!"

Another shot thumped into the ground nearby, and Hope decided it was her time to run. She did her best to keep behind the trunks as she moved from tree to tree.

The battle sounds faded. She'd lost sight of any of the other girls. In the distance, she spotted a fat oak tree with branches spread like a canopy. The trunk looked to be three feet wide, the perfect place to hide. She sprinted, breathing a sigh of relief when she finally reached it. A surprised face popped into view behind it, and she squeaked a cry. The barrel of a musket raised and pointed at her forehead.

He's not wearing red. That thought calmed her heart just a bit, as much as it could while having a musket pointed at her.

"Hope?" a familiar voice said. The musket lowered.

Hope raised her eyes to a handsome face that made her stomach turn. "Eli? What are you doing out here?"

A look of guilt flashed across his features just before he composed himself. "I'm waiting in ambush, of course."

"But our troops are between us and the red coats. Do you hope to ambush our own men?"

"Of course not. You don't know what you're talking about. But then, you are a woman. I wouldn't expect you to understand such things."

"I understand plenty." Hope raised her chin.

Eli stepped closer to her. His clothes were clean and expensive—very unlike most patriots, who were gruff and not afraid to get dirty. He seemed more like he belonged with the red coats, with their pressed jackets and fine wigs.

"What I don't understand," he said, "is why a proper young lady like yourself is showing so much of her womanly attributes." He fingered the fabric at her chest.

Hope looked down in horror at her bodice. It had torn, revealing the swell of her breasts. She slapped her hand against her chest as she took a step back.

"Don't cover yourself on my account," he said, smiling as he stepped toward her again. "I truly don't mind. It's a nice distraction from the battle."

"Curb your wicked thoughts, Eli." Hope narrowed her eyes and clenched a fist. "Or I'll curb them for you."

He chuckled. "Feisty mares are much more enjoyable to tame."

"You'll never tame me."

"Is that a challenge?" he asked, amused.

"It's a promise." She held his gaze, unwavering. "Now I think I should let you get back to your ambush."

He shook his head. "I need to see to your safety first."

"I don't need a keeper."

"But I insist." He stepped forward and took her by the arm. His fingers cut into her.

"Ouch," she gasped as pain shot through her. "Stop. Let go!"

"Am I hurting you?" he asked, amusement in his eyes.

"Yes, you idiot!" Hope shouted, her anger rising as fear crept into her heart.

"Sometimes pain is a good thing. It teaches one her place."

"Where are you taking me?" She squirmed, trying to break free from his grasp.

"Somewhere we can be alone."

"We're already alone."

"Somewhere we cannot be interrupted," he said.

Hope's chest constricted so tightly she could hardly draw a breath. She knew exactly what was in his wicked heart. Her father had warned her about men like him.

"I know just the place that will afford us privacy." He looked down at her as he dragged her along.

"You would not dare," she growled as she struggled.

"Oh, now, don't sound so appalled. You are of age, and I am in need of a wife. I have already spoken to your father, and he has given his support. Who will ever know but you and I if we know each other intimately before we wed?"

"God will know. And I will tell my father."

He scoffed. "You will give him all the details? I think not. Once I have had you, no one else will want you. And you will not say a word."

"You are a depraved man. I would rather die than lie with you."

"One day you will be begging for me to come to your bed. You just don't realize how lucky you are. You will find that out in the years to come."

They neared a thick grove of trees with an opening in the thicket.

"If you touch me," she said, her voice shaking, "I—

"You will what?" he challenged. "Fight me? I am twice your size. It'd be like a fly trying to fight an ox." He proved his words when he pulled her roughly forward and smashed his lips against hers, pressing his body into her.

It took all Hope's might to push him away. She smashed her knee against his groin, and Eli howled and dropped to the ground.

Hope had barely taken a breath when a flying blur blindsided her from the right, colliding with her. And then she was tumbling down the hill in a tangle of limbs and bodies. She was periodically crushed by an incredible weight, only to have that weight tumble off her as she continued her descent down the slope. She could hear Eli shouting in the distance. She finally came to a stop at the bottom of the hill, sprawled across a bare, muscled chest.

Every part of her ached, but mostly her head. She was relieved that nothing seemed broken. Raising her eyes, she searched out the face of the cause of her fall. Icy-blue eyes stared widely at her. He shook his head. She caught sight of his ears and sucked in a breath. They were pointed!

She blinked in disbelief, and when she looked again, the points were gone. His ears looked wholly human now. The fall must have addled her brain.

She gasped out, "Who are you?"

"You are human, right?" he asked as he raised up on his elbows. Hope slid down his chest and scrambled back.

"What else would I be?" she asked.

"What else, indeed." He frowned, then looked up at the sky and shouted, "You can't trap me here forever, Haryk!"

"Trap you?" Hope said. "How can you be trapped outside in the open? Where did you come from? Who are you?"

"You are full of questions, aren't you?" He stood and brushed the leaves off his oddly tailored brown pants and high, black leather boots. A leather strap slung across his heavily muscled bare chest, from shoulder to adjacent hip. His nearly white blond hair hung near to his waist, pulled back with a leather tie.

Despite having hair as long as a woman's, there was absolutely nothing feminine about him. He literally oozed masculinity. He cleared the crushed leaves away and straightened to his full height.

"Hope!" Eli's voice rang out as he made his way down the hillside.

She stumbled back, putting the stranger between her and her would-be assailant.

The stranger narrowed his eyes as he looked from Hope to Eli.

Eli came up short, his eyes widening as they looked at the stranger. "And who might you be? A redcoat who's lost his coat?"

"A red what?" the stranger asked.

"Red. Coat." Eli enunciated each syllable.

"I own nothing red," the stranger said.

7

"As if I would believe you." Eli raised his musket. "Step away from my betrothed."

"I am not your betrothed," Hope growled. "I will never marry you. You have an evil mind and wicked intentions."

The stranger raised an eyebrow. "Wicked intentions, huh?" His gaze lingered on her throbbing lips and then lowered to her ripped bodice.

Heat rose in her cheeks as she clasped the ripped fabric and held it together to cover herself. She looked up at the stranger's face and was surprised to see anger in his eyes.

He turned back to Eli. "I may not be the most noble of creatures. I have no qualms about seducing women. I care not who they are or what circumstances they are in. If they are easy to look on and willing, I will not hesitate. But a man who would force himself on a woman is a coward and a snake." At those words, he waved his hand, and Eli was gone.

"Wha…?" Hope said, stunned. "Where did he go?"

"From his dress, he was obviously a soldier, and I can hear the sounds of battle in the distance. I sent him to do his job."

"You . . . sent him? But, how?"

He smiled, his eyes twinkling as he said, "Like this."

And then he was gone.

"I definitely hit my head too hard." Had the stranger been there in the first place? Was it all a hallucination? The uncertainty unnerved her. What if it was real? It sure seemed so.

Hope thought about what the stranger said. A man who would seduce women was obviously not righteous. But he'd saved her from an even more wicked man. Perhaps good and evil were not black and white. Perhaps there was both darkness and light in everyone or variant shades of gray.

"Or perhaps your brain was damaged, Hope. That seemed the most likely scenario," she grumbled to herself.

The boom of a cannon brought her back to her senses. What was she doing standing here? She had much more important things to concern herself with. She had lives to save.

Without hesitation, she ran toward the sounds of battle.

Chapter 2

Hope's heart sat heavy in her chest as they trudged through the rain. She hoped they would find a place to camp soon, but so far, all they found was thick forest with no good place to pitch their tents. If only they'd won the battle, they could have stayed put and set camp.

An older man fell into step at her side. "Where on earth did you learn such methods?"

She knew exactly what he was talking about. Her sewing had gained the attention of everyone—well, everyone who was still alive. She shrugged. "I saw it back in New York. I was assisting a man who had to amputate a leg. The doctor used a needle to stitch the skin together over the stump. The man's wound healed without infection. It got me thinking, why can't we stitch together other wounds? That way they would not remain open to allow filth to enter."

"Ah, you're one of those!" the man exclaimed.

"One of what?" Hope said.

"You think that dirt brings disease."

"Not just dirt, filth. Haven't you observed that the cleanliest of people live the longest?"

"That's just a coincidence."

"I don't put much stock in coincidences. Back home, there was a woman who claimed that boiling water would kill all diseases. She would only drink and bathe in water that had been boiled and then cooled to the proper temperature."

"That's ludicrous."

"She's eighty-six years old. Do you know any other who has reached that age?"

"How much can you know? What are you, sixteen?"

Hope raised her chin. "I'm twenty."

"What does your husband think about a wife with such independent thought?"

"I'm not yet married."

"What?" the man gasped.

"My father has allowed me to decide whom I will marry. I've not found a man worthy of me, as yet."

"Now I see where you get it. Your father is a strange one— allowing his daughter so much freedom. It's one thing to allow you a say, it's another to allow you to remain unmarried at such an ungodly age."

"We are fighting for freedom, are we not?"

"Freedom from British rule, not common sense," he said.

"My father knows I will be the one who has to live with the consequences should I choose a less-than-worthy husband. I'd say it shows his confidence and trust in my judgment. "She looked up. The troops spread out as they entered a clearing. "Finally!" she couldn't help exclaiming.

"Good luck on finding a husband," he said as he stepped away. "You'll need it."

Hope joined the other women as they set up their tents. As always, they avoided talking to her. She'd tried to solicit friendship, but she had a difficult time relating to them. They were much younger than her, and they seemed to only want to discuss who was the most handsome, unattached soldier. Then they would spend the remainder of their conversations complaining about how the war had disrupted their lives.

Hope found the war not an inconvenience, but a noble cause. Her work nursing injured soldiers gave her a sense of purpose and a satisfaction she did not get from the mindless frivolities the other girls missed so much.

"Miss Lowhouse?" a deep voice petitioned from behind.

Hope turned to find a young soldier with sympathy in his eyes. Her stomach dropped. She was very familiar with this expression—devastating news always followed. "Yes?"

"Your father wishes to see you."

"My father?" Hope said, as her mind raced over his condition when she last spoke to him hours before. He had looked well for someone who had just been through a major battle. He had favored his right side just a bit but claimed he was fine.

Hope raced, stumbling on occasion, through the camp as she followed the young man. Her father's tent came into view. A crowd surrounded the opening. She was so worried, she pushed her way through, forgetting all politeness.

What she saw when she got inside made her heart faint. Her father lay on his bedroll, his face white, a sheen of sweat on his brow. He looked to be on death's door.

Hope collapsed to her knees beside him. "Father? What happened? I thought you were well."

"I didn't want you to worry, child," he said, his voice hollow.

"Let me see it," she demanded.

Her father pursed his lips as he gave a nod.

She pulled his shirt up and gasped at the sight. Blood flowed from an inch-wide wound in his belly, mixing with bowel excrement. All the knowledge she'd gained, all the training she'd had, would not save him. Her father was dying. Tears sprang to her eyes and a sob rattled her chest.

"Oh, now what have I said about tears?" he asked.

"They help nothing," she said and sniffed.

He nodded. "There is one thing I want you to do before I die."

"Anything."

"Eli André has asked for your hand. I will not die and leave you uncared for."

"But Father—"

"No. Please, just listen to me."

The desperation in his voice caused her to pause. Hope snapped her mouth closed and turned her gaze down on her hands, clasped in her lap.

"I've always tried to protect you from the realities of life," he said. "Perhaps in doing so, I have been remiss in my responsibilities. Now, I must leave you and without me to care for you, you will be destitute, homeless, or at best, forced into servitude. As a father it is my duty to make sure you are provided for. Eli is a good man, and he has means to care for you. The minister has vouched for his honorable intentions. He will treat you well. Please. Hope…, look at me."

She raised her gaze to meet his eyes and her heart broke at the tears swelling in his eyes. Her father never cried.

"Please, do not let me die and leave this undone," he said. "My heart could not bear it." One tear broke free and trailed down his cheek.

How could she put this burden on her father as he lay on his deathbed? She couldn't possibly. As he wished to protect her, she would do the same for him, even if it meant stretching the truth a bit. "Okay, father. I'll marry him."

The relief on his face was overwhelming as guilt pressed down on her. She had no intention of following through on her word. Any kind of life, even that of servitude, would be better than being married to a monster. Still, lying went against everything she stood for. Lying to her father was even worse.

Eli sauntered in, a triumphant look in his eyes. He stepped forward and knelt beside her. "I will care for your daughter as I care for my own life. I swear it."

"Thank you, son," her father said.

"Are we ready to begin?" Pastor Davis's familiar voice spoke at her back.

Hope whipped around as a gasp escaped her lips. "What? Now?"

Eli put his hand over hers. "Let's put your father's mind at ease."

"That is very thoughtful." Her father turned to her and said, "I only wish I could walk you down the aisle."

Hope bit down on her bottom lip to stop the protest threatening to spill from her mouth. Her mind raced to figure out an escape from this nightmare. It was bad enough that her father would be joining his maker soon. How could she make vows to such an evil man? If it were just her, she could resign herself to a

14

life of misery to please her father. But Eli would want children. How could she let such a wicked man raise her children?

To Hope's horror, the pastor spoke the first words of the wedding ceremony. Before she could prepare, he was asking her, "Do you take Eli André to be your lawful wedded husband?"

Hope sat for several long moments with her jaw hanging.

"Answer the minister," her father said.

Hope mumbled, "I do." She cleared her throat and added under her breath the word, "not." She really hoped God heard it. He had to. He heard everything.

Her heart turned to lead in her chest when she heard the words, "I now pronounce you man and wife."

Eli leaned down to kiss her. Hope had to force herself not to push him away. She endured the brief kiss and turned away, feeling nauseated.

No one congratulated her. It seemed everyone could tell this was not a day of celebration for her.

Hope felt physically sick. *I'm not married. I said, "I do not."* She kept repeating the words in her mind. She was not married. God knew she wasn't, even if the rest of the world thought she was.

"I'll leave you with your father, to say your goodbyes, Mrs. André," Eli said.

She swallowed bile. Perhaps she should let nature take its course and vomit on the vile man

Her attention stole away when her father took her hand. His cold fingers clutched her weakly. "Thank you, child."

Hope nodded, tears once again falling. Eli left and the others followed, closing the tent flap behind them.

"You can't die," she said.

"Oh, now, you are an intelligent young woman. Much more intelligent than your addlebrained father. You know how this ends."

A sob shook her chest. She crawled forward and laid her head on his shoulder. "I love you, Papa."

"I love you too, child," he said as he brushed his hand over her hair. His breathing labored as he continued to stroke her. "Would you sing for me? I wish to hear an angel's voice in my last minutes on earth."

Hope nodded, and sung softly, a bright hymn that her father loved. She sang for countless minutes. His breathing relaxed. Still, he continued to stroke her hair. She did her best to focus on the words and tune and not her father slipping from her. Eventually, his stroking hand dropped away, and his breathing stilled. She had no idea how much time had passed when she heard a voice.

"Mrs. André?"

Hope looked up to see young Gwenyth standing in the doorway.

"Mr. Andre has drawn a bath for you. He bids you come."

"But, my father…" Hope said as she sat up and turned toward him.

His eyes were closed, his chest still. His lips were stained blue.

"He's gone," she said gently.

Hope gave a shaky nod as she sat, unable to look away.

"Mrs. André?"

Hope swallowed. Her eyes were dry. Her mind numb. Her father lay dead at her side. Still, she didn't move. She felt nothing. Not sad. Not happy. Not anything in between.

A warm hand on her arm brought her back to her senses. She nodded and rose to her feet.

"Come on. It's cold in here. Let's get you that bath. Your husband was even kind enough to heat the water for you."

"It's cold in here?" Hope asked.

"Yes. But the bath is warm."

"But my father. He might need another blanket." She scrambled to find more bedding. She opened his trunk and pulled out an extra wool blanket. It was worn and threadbare, but it would help. She brought it over to add to his blankets.

"But, Mrs. André. Your father is—"

"Cold. He's very cold." She pulled the blankets over him, tucking them up under his neck.

"He's dead."

That word shot like a dagger through her heart as she shook her head. "He can't be."

"Truly, he is," Gwenyth said as she tugged on Hope's arm.

Hope followed. "No. He'll be fine. He just needs to rest."

"Come on," Gwenyth said. "You need your husband."

"But I'm not married."

"Yes, you are."

"I lied to the minister. God knows I'm not married."

"Come. You're not thinking right. A nice warm bath will help."

Hope didn't protest more. She followed obediently, bathing and dressing in a white sleeping gown as Gwenyth assisted her.

17

She was surprised to see an unfamiliar green dress hanging in her tent. Was this her tent? It looked different.

"Where am I?"

"This is your husband's tent. Isn't it nice? He was even able to get proper clothes for you to wear tomorrow."

Hope looked around. This tent was large, with several trunks next to a wide cot. How did he transport so much stuff?

Hope must have spoken out loud, because Gwenyth answered her question. "He has a large, sturdy wagon. Didn't you notice? And several horses. You are a lucky woman to have a husband with means."

Hope pursed her lips. *He's not my husband.* She really needed to tell the minister. She couldn't keep perpetuating the lie.

"Where are my clothes?"

"Well, he could only find the one dress and nightgown. He said you would be traveling to his home in Boston as soon as your father is buried. I'm sure you'll get a whole new wardrobe there."

"No, I mean, where are the dress and underclothes I was wearing earlier?"

"Those old things? But they were covered in your father's blood."

Hope frowned. "I can wash them."

"Your husband had them burned."

"He burned my clothes?" Hope's voice rose.

Gwenyth nodded, obviously stunned at her anger.

Hope forced herself to calm down.

"Should I get your husband?"

"Why? Don't you think he's done enough damage for now?"

"He asked me to fetch him as soon as you were ready."

"Ready for what?"

"Why, your wedding night, of course. You have wifely duties to attend to."

Chapter 3

Hope's jaw dropped. "But," she said, "my father just died."

"I understand," Gwenyth said, "but life does not stop when others pass on."

"This isn't just any other person. It's my father, my only kin."

Gwenyth frowned.

"Couldn't you tell him I've taken ill?"

"I don't know."

"Please, just tell him that I've been sick and am not fit for fulfilling my wifely duties."

"But that would be lying."

What's a white lie in the face of fornication? Which was what Hope would be committing if she allowed a man who truly wasn't her husband into her bed.

"Haven't you ever lost a close family member?" Hope asked.

Gwenyth's expression clouded. She nodded. "My twin sister. Two years ago."

"How do you think you would feel in my situation?"

Gwenyth sighed. Hope obviously had gotten to her. "Okay, I'll tell him. But please, don't ask me to lie again."

"I won't. I promise."

As soon as Gwenyth left, Hope put on the new dress and slipped on the shoes sitting beside it. They were a tad too big, but they'd have to do. She simply had to get things straightened out. Cracking open the tent door, she peeked out. No one seemed to be about. Now in which direction did the minister pitch his tent?

Hope slipped outside and kept to the shadows. She had no idea what the hour was, but it seemed late. She must have spent a long time in her father's tent. Her heart ached at the thought. She should be mourning him, not sneaking about the camp. If her father could see her, he'd give her quite the lecture.

Finally, she found a tent with a brown cross sewn into the canvas—the minister's tent. She crept up to the door. "Pastor Davis?" she whispered.

Hope heard someone moving about, and then the tent flap opened.

"Mrs. André?"

"I need to confess something. I didn't really say I do. I said I do not. Apparently, you didn't hear me properly. But I know God did. I am not truly married."

Pastor Davis shook his head. "I am the spokesperson for God. I am his eyes and ears in this camp. If I didn't hear it, you didn't say it. You are married, Mrs. André. Now I think your husband may be missing his wife."

"But…," Hope said, her heart pounding out of her chest. "I can't be married to him. That man is wicked. He attempted to steal my virtue from me just earlier today."

"That *is* concerning," the pastor said. "But be grateful he didn't succeed. Then he would have had a grievous sin on his conscience. And isn't it a grand thing that your husband finds you so appealing?"

"No," Hope said. "It isn't a grand thing. Doesn't the Bible say that for a man to look on a woman with lust in his eyes is committing adultery in his heart?"

21

"Neither you nor Eli were married at the time. Adultery was not possible for either of you. Besides, it's obvious his intention was to marry you. It's only natural for him to have feelings for you."

"I think you're missing the point!"

"Mrs. André do not raise your voice to me. It is apparent that you are in the wrong. Now, return to your husband, or I will have to drag you to him myself."

Hope was rendered speechless. This pastor was completely out of line! But the last thing she needed was to be taken to her husband—no, he was not her husband. It didn't matter what the pastor said. She absolutely was not married!

Still, if she did end up in the vile man's tent, he *would* rob her of her virtue. Of that, she was certain. He was much larger and stronger than her. She wouldn't stand a chance. It was obvious what she had to do next.

She had to leave.

"I'm sorry," she said as a plan formed in her mind. "I guess I'm just a bit nervous. I probably have nothing to worry about."

"I'm sure you don't, Mrs. André. And it's only natural for you to be nervous on your wedding night."

Hope nodded and turned to leave.

"Oh, and Mrs. André," the pastor said, "tell your husband thank you for the generous donation."

Hope bit down a retort. "I will," she said and smiled sweetly.

So, that's why he was so unreasonable. Her pseudo-husband bribed the pastor. Hope lost all respect for the so-called man of God. A pastor who could be swayed with money was guilty of priest craft. He was in no place to judge her.

And she was not married!

Hope moved quietly about the camp. There was one stop she needed to make before she set out on her own.

Her father's tent.

She crept around the side and peered around to the front. There didn't appear to be anyone about. Silently she stepped forward and peeped in. The moon cast just enough light to see the silhouette of her father. It looked like someone had covered his face. She entered and pulled the flap shut behind her.

It would be difficult to find what she needed, but she had to do it. And quietly. No one could know she was there. She shuffled over to the old trunk and felt her way to the latch. Flipping it carefully, she cringed when it made a loud snap. *Oh, please don't let anyone hear.*

She stood unmoving for a long time, waiting for someone to come and investigate, but no one did. Relaxing, she lifted the lid. It creaked, and she held her breath again. If this kept up, she'd be here forever. Carefully feeling her way in the trunk, she found her father's bag and lifted it out. The next thing she searched out was the little wooden box that held her family heirlooms—her mother's simple wedding ring, a lock of Hope's baby hair, and love letters her mother and father had exchanged.

She blinked back a tear and glanced toward her father. At least he and her mother were together again. There was so much Hope wanted to tell him, but she needed to hurry. Anytime now she could be discovered missing.

She stuffed the box in the bag and then pulled out the patchwork quilt from the bottom of the trunk—a quilt that was too precious to actually use. It was made with fabrics that held great meaning for her mother: pieces of her wedding gown, her grandmother's Sunday dresses, and even extra fabric she'd held back from Hope's infant gowns. She stuffed the quilt in the bag and reached for another blanket—one as worn as the one she'd laid over her father less than an hour ago.

And then she found his coin purse. It held all the money her father had in the world. Which was not a lot by many standards, but it should be enough to get her established into a new life.

Finally, her bag was packed. She crept toward the door just as a light pierced the crack of the tent. Hope held her breath, hoping it would move on. Instead, the door ripped open, and Eli's face appeared, lit by a lantern in his hand. He looked composed, but there was a spark of anger in his eyes.

"I thought I might find you here." He looked down at the bag she carried. "Are you going somewhere?"

Hope shook her head, her heart ramming against her chest. "I'm just collecting my belongings to bring back to our tent."

He scowled. "You have no belongings, Mrs. André. All things once owned by your father are now mine. Though I doubt he had anything of real value."

Hope forced back her reaction and nodded amiably.

Eli's eyes wandered over her body. She felt exposed, as though she stood naked before him. She pulled the bag over her chest.

"That dress looks much better than the rags you were wearing before."

"It's beautiful. Thank you."

His anger seemed to cool at her words. "It looks like you are feeling much better."

Fear shot through her as she realized her excuse for postponing their wedding night had disintegrated. He would now expect her to come to his bed.

"My stomach is still a bit weak, I'm afraid."

He chuckled. "Don't think another rescuer will appear. I could have you charged with witchcraft, you know. Summoning the devil like you did."

"What are you talking about?" she asked, feeling a bit light-headed. She had been sure her mind had been playing tricks on her.

"You know exactly what I'm talking about. Though I do not hold it against you. I have a bit of the devil in me too. We'll make a perfect team."

"I'm no witch."

"Of course, you aren't," he said and winked at her. He stepped toward her and pulled her up against him. His hand caressed her face, and then his eyes lowered to the swell of her breasts. "As for your weak stomach, I have the perfect cure, Mrs. André."

Hope's heart pounded against her chest. "Are you trying to seduce me while my father lies dead not three feet away?"

"Husbands do not seduce their wives. They take what belongs to them."

"Then I guess it's a good thing I'm not your wife."

He narrowed his eyes as he frowned. "What are you talking about? We spoke our vows only today. Have you gone addlebrained?"

"You spoke your vows. I said, I do *not*. It seems no one heard me properly."

Eli stepped back, stunned. Then he narrowed his eyes and raised his hand. His hand flew, and pain exploded in her cheek.

Hope found herself gasping on her hands and knees as she tried to get on top of the pain.

He'd struck her!

Never in her life had anyone laid a hand on her. And the man who vowed to love and cherish her, of all people. She blinked back tears, determined not to give him the satisfaction of crying. Raising her eyes, she realized she was only inches from her dead father.

If only he'd known what kind of man Eli André was. He never would have insisted she marry him. His weathered fingers peeked from under the blanket where they clasped something—his musket.

"You will never speak such lies to me again," Eli growled. "We are married, and you will show me the respect I deserve."

Hope nodded. "Yes, I will." She snatched the musket, turned, and thrust the handle at Eli. It hit him directly between the legs.

His face turned red as he clutched his groin and dropped to his knees.

"And that is exactly what you deserve," she said as she grabbed the bag and then scrambled her way out of the tent.

Heads were poking from their doors and gaping at her as she sprinted toward the forest. She'd only just made it to the trees when Eli began shouting.

They would be coming after her.

She ran through the woods, splashed through puddles, and ducked under branches as she continued to run, the moonlight guiding her way. The shouts and commotion eventually faded, but still she ran. She ran until her lungs burned. She ran until her legs weakened so severely, they scarcely held her up. And when she was too weak to run, she stumbled through the woods.

When daylight warmed the sky, she found a thicket, squeezed her way in, and collapsed in exhaustion. Sleep overtook her quickly, but nightmares plagued her with images of horror, pain, and despair. At last, her dreams were brightened by icy blue eyes framed by blond hair and pointed ears.

Chapter 4

Conall stood at the place where he'd entered the human realm, searching for the shimmer of light that would reveal the opening. He paced back and forth, his eyes sweeping the area.

Nothing.

It was gone.

Growling, he slammed his fist against a nearby trunk. Haryk was overreacting. Conall had only stolen a kiss, and it was only in play. He had no real interest in Edwina. Still, angering his brother had been foolish. Since he'd been crowned king, Haryk had lost his sense of humor.

It was truly a sad thing. They'd once found such joy in jokes, pranks, and other frivolities.

Should he have heeded his brother's warnings? Haryk had repeatedly told him to cease his foolishness. But what was the fun in that?

Though, perhaps Haryk was right. Maybe he did cross the line when he'd kiss Haryk's betrothed. But Haryk couldn't possibly intend to banish his brother to the human world forever. Haryk despised humans. Banishing Conall here was a particularly sharp insult.

"Haryk, you son of a goblin!" he shouted to the sky. "Open the door!"

He waited for a response. The old Haryk would have said something like, *if I'm the son of a goblin, what does that make you, brother?*

Instead, his response was silence. It was beginning to unnerve Conall.

He waited a full day for his brother to calm down and open the door. When that day passed, he left to forage for food and came back to wait once again. There were other doorways to Faery and others knew where to find them, but Conall didn't frequent the human world. He had no idea where to look for them. If he remained much longer, he'd have to set out in search of one. There wasn't an abundance of food to be found, and he was already feeling weak. Not to mention, the night had turned cold, and he had no blanket or even a shirt on his back.

Three days later, Conall had to admit defeat. His stomach cramped in hunger, and his magic was so far diminished that it was all he could do to maintain his glamour. It looked like his brother's anger would not cool down quickly. He needed to seek out a human's help.

It shouldn't be too difficult. Merith came here all the time. He said humans were easily manipulated and seducing them was fun.

Conall's mind went back to the human woman he'd tumbled down the hill with. She was easy to look on, with her fiery brown eyes, curly brown hair, and curves in just the right places. If all women were as appealing as her, he might find his time in the human world enjoyable.

Trudging through the forest, he came to a beaten path and followed it. Hopefully a home stood at the end of it. He found the occasional berry along the path, but nothing substantial enough to stifle his aching hunger.

The sky darkened as he journeyed. He had maybe an hour before it became too dark to continue. The scent of smoke filled the air. There had to be a human nearby. He kept to the path as the

29

darkness deepened, but the scent of burning pine kept him moving forward. Finally, he found the glow of a lighted house through the trees.

The house was little more than a one room cabin. Still, his stomach would not allow him to turn back. He heard someone moving about as he approached the door. He raised his fist and knocked. All activity within ceased, and he stood there in silence.

The door creaked open. He had to stifle a gasp at the face that peered at him through the crack. Her sharp, angular face was plagued with warts sprouting course hairs. This woman held nowhere near the appeal as the last human he'd met. In fact, she was downright hideous. Still, he caught the aroma of something delectable coming from inside.

"Hello?" she said. "Can I help you?"

"Hello, my dear," he answered smoothly. "I'm afraid I've become rather lost and am in need of a place to stay."

Her large, crooked teeth bit down on her bottom lip. "I don't know. . .." she finally answered.

He gave her a pleading look. "Could you ask your husband?" He glanced behind her.

"Oh, no. I'm not married. So, you see why it wouldn't be proper for you to sleep under my roof. I mean, we would be alone . . . together." She looked him over, her eyes lingering on his bare chest.

He turned on the charm. "I promise to be the perfect gentleman. Your lady's virtue is safe with me." Oh, how true that was!

She stood in silence, debating in her mind for a moment. The wind picked up, chilling his back. She shivered and sighed.

"All right. But you'll have to sleep on the floor. I do have a bed roll that will soften the hardness of the floor for you." She gestured him to come inside, and he did, allowing the warmth of the room to seep into his chilled skin.

"Are you hungry?" she asked. "I have some stew. I was just about to sit down to eat."

"You're very kind. Yes, I could eat."

They sat down to a meager meal of vegetable stew, and he practically inhaled his food.

"You *were* hungry," she said, smiling. She pushed her bowl toward him. "You're welcome to have mine."

He mumbled a thank you and made quick work of her bowl also. When he'd finished, he was still hungry, but at least he was no longer famished. If he weren't immortal, he might have been worried about starving to death. But as it was, hunger was just a torment to his stomach, not a threat to his life.

When he was finished, he rose to his feet as she gathered the dishes.

"Let me just get these washed," she said, "and I'll get you your bedding." She left him alone to step outside.

Conall looked around. This was an exceptionally small house, but it was clean. Perhaps he should stay here for a time. That was, if she would prepare more food for him and give him a warm place to stay. Perhaps he could glean some information that might give him a direction to seek out another doorway.

It wasn't long before she returned. She went straight to her trunk and pulled out a roll of blankets. "I hope this will be comfortable enough for you."

"I'm sure it'll be fine," he said. It had to be better than sleeping on the cold, hard ground.

Conall crawled into bed and was asleep in seconds.

*   *   *   *   *

The sound of sizzling meat awoke Conall, bringing a smile to his face. He could get used to this. He looked over at the human as she busied herself by the fire. He cringed when he saw her face. That was something he could never get used to. It seemed more warts had sprouted overnight and her nose...was it larger? It looked like a stork's beak.

She turned and smiled. Conall shuddered inside as he forced himself to smile back.

"Are you hungry?" she asked.

"I'm famished," he answered.

"Well, then come join me at the table. This time I made plenty."

Conall's stomach shouted for joy at the large banquet spread out before him.

"Listen," she said as he ate. "I'm sorry I was so suspicious of you. You were a perfect gentleman last night. And I was wondering . . ."

Conall looked up when she hesitated.

"Are you married?" she asked.

Conall chuckled. "No."

"Well, you look a bit lost. And I do have means."

Conall looked around at the tiny cabin. He wouldn't consider *this* means.

"I know the cabin is small," she said. "But I own fifty acres of land. That is no small piece of property. And I am a hard worker, a good cook, and will take care of your every need." As she said those words, her eyes brushed over his body.

Conall felt a bit sick when he realized what she was saying. "Are you offering yourself to me?"

She nodded, her eyes now on the floor. "Only if we properly wed."

Conall couldn't hold back his reaction. His laughter bellowed, reverberating off the walls.

When he finally composed himself, he looked up to see anger burning in her eyes. "I apologize," he said. "I just . . . well, first of all, I don't even know your name. Second of all, I couldn't bring myself to look at your face for the next fifty years—or however long you humans live—much less bed you."

Conall was surprised to see her anger melt into amusement. His heart skipped a beat as unease settled in his stomach.

"I *knew* you were more than just a man." She was now smiling widely. Something was definitely amiss.

She stood, leaning over as she cupped her hand in front of her face. Before he could guess what she was going to do, she blew. Green dust billowed around him and Conall gasped, inhaling a good amount of a bitter-tasting herb.

His mind went hazy as he looked at the witch. How did he not know what she was? Her face transformed before his eyes from hideous to beautiful.

"I think it's time I introduced myself," she said. Her face swam in his vision. "I'm Lavinia, and I'm happy to welcome you to hell."

*   *   *   *   *

"Carry that trunk to the wagon," a woman shouted, snapping Conall awake. "And don't drop it!"

The sound of clatter and footsteps caught his attention. He tried to look around, but his face was covered in fabric. He tried to lift it only to find he couldn't move his arms. In fact, he couldn't feel them at all.

Lavinia. That was her name. The witch.

What did she do to him?

"Witch!" he shouted.

Her footsteps neared and the cloth was ripped from off his face. "And the elf finally awakens." She snickered.

Conall tried to look around only to find he couldn't even budge his head. "What did you do to me?"

She smiled triumphantly. "Something no other witch has ever been able to do in the long history of witchcraft. And my mother thought I wouldn't amount to anything."

"What did you do to me?" he repeated in angry, clipped tones.

The sound of lumbering steps entered the cabin and Conall looked over, his breath stealing away in shock. A headless body was walking in the door. But not just any body—his!

"Isn't it amazing?" she said in awe as she looked at his headless form. "I just knew it would work. I only needed a faery," she turned to him and winked, "or an elf to pull it off. That was a bit of a stumbling block. I mean, how many of those does one meet in a lifetime? But then you just showed up on my doorstep. It must be fate."

"You don't know who you're dealing with. My brother is king of the Elven court. He will have your head. And believe me, witch or not, when he cuts off *your* head, you will die."

"Strong words for someone who has no body. Now, shut your pie hole or I'll stuff a sock in your mouth. I have to move. There is a town that deserves retribution, and now I have the means to deliver it."

"So, you mean to use my body to harass the humans?"

"Just the ones who deserve it."

"What town do you intend to inflict it upon?"

"Tarrytown, in a little glen called Sleepy Hollow."

35

Chapter 5

Eight Years Later

"How many chambers does the heart have?" Hope said as she finished the diagram on the chalkboard and turned around. Young, eager faces looked at her, many with their hands thrust in the air. Racheal lifted her hand tentatively. Hope's eyes widened as she suppressed a smile. The young girl was making progress.

"Racheal," Hope said.

"Four?" Racheal said quietly.

"Good! Yes, there are four chambers. And what is the heart's job?"

"It pumps the blood," Racheal said.

"Very good."

Hope began a new drawing. "The first person to tell me what organ this is will only have to do the odd problems for arithmetic."

She'd only drawn a small portion of the picture when a hand shot in the air. "Yes, Kaleb?"

"It's the kidney."

"Excellent."

"Mrs. Jones," Constance said with her hand raised.

"Yes?"

"Why are you teaching us about what's in the body? My mother says it's worthless information."

"Hmm, that is a good question." Hope put down the chalk and turned to the class. "How many of you are fond of your bodies?"

Everyone in the class raised their hands.

"Are not you even a bit curious about what's inside?"

Heads nodded all around.

"The Bible says, 'Fools despise wisdom and instruction.' I think the more we learn and understand, the more we become like God. Don't you think that is a good thing?"

Constance shut her mouth. That would put an end to the debate. The pastor's daughter would not dare speak out if it sounded like she was speaking against the Bible.

Hope turned to erase the board and began writing arithmetic problems in neat, even rows. "Don't forget, you older children will have a test on long division on Friday. I expect you all to do well *if* you've been practicing at home." A hum of groans filled the room, and Hope turned and frowned. At her glare, the room fell silent, and everyone returned to their work.

Almost an hour later, the children had finished and gone home. Hope corrected the children's work and replaced their slate boards on their desks. Gathering her coat and bag, she headed out the door and nearly ran over Mr. Yule.

"Pardon me, Mrs. Jones," he stammered. "I was hoping to accompany you on your walk to the inn."

Hope smiled even as she cringed inside. Mr. Yule stood before her, hunched over—she had a clear look at his scalp. Tufts of hair were making a last-ditch effort to hang onto his balding head. Mr. Yule was becoming an annoyance. How many hints did she have to throw at the man? "I do have to hurry, Mr. Yule. I need to get dinner going or the boarders will have no supper."

"I don't know how you do it. A woman as fragile as you, working so many hours. Cooking and cleaning at the inn and then the hours you put in teaching school."

Holly Kelly

"I am not as fragile as I look. I am quite fit, Mr. Yule."

He looked her over. "That you are."

His cheeks tinged with red. *Oh, good grief!*

"Which is why it is so surprising," he continued, "how long you've been widowed and not yet remarried."

And here he goes again.

"I am a man of means. I could take care of you. You are not too old to bear many children. We could yet have a houseful, and you would not have to lift a finger."

A houseful of children and not lift a finger? That would be a miracle.

"I am sorry, Mr. Yule," Hope said, "but I cannot see myself married to another. My heart still belongs to my late husband." Hope spoke the lie easily. She'd been saying it for years, and no one had ever questioned her. Any other woman might have married and moved on, but according to the law of the land, she was already married. Hope had resigned herself to the fact she could never marry. She would be forever alone. But still, she had her students and she gleaned joy from teaching them.

"I commend your loyalty to your deceased husband. But God would not expect you to remain a widow."

"I appreciate your opinion, but you will not be there when I face my Maker. That I must do alone."

They stepped up to the inn. It was lit up brightly, and there was a lot of commotion. Sounded like it was full tonight.

"Here's where I bid you goodbye," Mr. Yule said. "Just keep my offer in mind. If you ever change your mind, and I haven't found someone else, I will be willing to accept you as my wife."

38

"Your offer is very generous, but I am afraid I will not be changing my mind." A thought struck Hope. There was perhaps a way to stop Mr. Yule's unrequited solicitations. "I did notice, however, that Florence has been watching you with admiration." Hope was not telling a lie. Florence was on the hunt for a husband. She looked on every available man with admiration. .

His eyes lit up. "She has?"

"Yes, she has."

"She's not as comely as you." He rubbed his chin. "But she does have fine breeding hips."

Hope coughed to cover her laugh. "Yes, she does. I am sure she could bear you a dozen children."

He nodded eagerly. "I bet she could."

He rushed away after he offered a quick goodbye.

Hope gave a big sigh of relief and opened the door.

There was a crowd, and they were dressed in fine clothes. She sure hoped they kept their grabbing hands to themselves. The rich seemed to think they had the right to grope a woman at their pleasure. Hope kept her wooden spoon handy for such situations.

She picked up her skirt, turned, and nearly fainted.

There in the corner of the room, in deep conversation with two other men, stood Eli. She hadn't seen him since she'd fled on their wedding day. Sinking back toward the door, her mind raced.

What should she do? She had a life here. She was happy here. Why did he have to show up and threaten to ruin everything?

Perhaps he'd moved on. He may very well have remarried and wanted no one to know they'd ever wed—well, sort of wed.

If he were smart, he'd have accepted her denial of the marriage and gotten an annulment. She *had* to find out. But he could not see her.

Slipping out the front, she made her way around the house to the back door. As soon as she entered the kitchen, Elizabeth's eyes widened. "What are you doing sneaking in through the back?"

"Shh!" Hope hissed and gestured for her to follow her back outside.

Elizabeth looked around worriedly and followed.

"What is going on?" Elizabeth asked.

"You remember when I told you about…" She looked around suspiciously. "…you know who?"

Elizabeth's brow crinkled in confusion. "Who?"

"My husband," she whispered.

Her eyes flew open wide. "Oh, my heavens. He's here, isn't he?"

Hope nodded and swallowed the lump in her throat.

"What are you going to do?"

"Well," Hope said. "First of all, you'll have to do the serving. He absolutely cannot see me."

"And second of all?"

"I need you to find out if he had our marriage annulled."

"How am I supposed to do that?" Elizabeth asked.

"I don't know. Act like you are interested in him."

"My husband would kill me."

"I just need to know if he's moved on. I wish I could ask him myself, but I cannot take the chance. He may try to drag me home with him."

Elizabeth nodded. "I understand." She frowned. "I will see what I can find out."

Hope breathed a sigh of relief. "You are the best friend a girl could ever have."

"Yeah, I know." Elizabeth turned and left through the door.

Hope stepped over to the iron cauldron hanging over the fire and peeked in. A lamb's hindquarter was simmering in liquid surrounded by vegetables. From the looks of it, it had about fifteen minutes to go.

Curiosity pulled her to the door. It creaked as she cracked it open and peeked through. Elizabeth was speaking with Eli. He looked serious and then nodded his head and said something. If only Hope could hear what they were saying!

Elizabeth continued to talk. And then Eli said something that upset Elizabeth. She visibly paled. She said a few more words, gave a weak smile, and left the table. When Hope realized she was heading her way, she closed the door and waited.

Elizabeth rushed in and shut the door. Leaning against the frame, she pressed her hand over her heart.

"So, what is it? Is he still searching for me?"

"Oh, yeah. He's still searching."

"Then he *is* claiming I am his wife."

Elizabeth shook her head adamantly. "No, he's had his marriage with you annulled."

"Then why would he be searching for me?"

Elizabeth's eyes raised to hers, her expression frantic. "You are to hang for the murder of your father."

Chapter 6

"What?" Hope screeched.

"Shh!" Elizabeth hissed. "You don't want him to hear you, do you?"

"How can he say I killed my father? My father died from a gunshot sustained in battle."

"He said there's three witnesses who saw you pull the trigger. And when he confronted you about it, you attacked him and fled."

"He's lying."

"You don't think I know that?" Elizabeth asked. "You could not shoot your father any more than I could shoot mine. No, this man is vindictive. He looks rich and proud. He probably could not accept the fact that there was a woman who did not bow down at his feet and worship the ground he walked on."

"They cannot hang me without a trial," Hope said. "Maybe I should turn myself in."

"Are you crazy? With witnesses, including your husband's word, it'd be an open and shut case. He's right, you would hang."

"So, what do I do now?"

"You have to leave."

"What? Why can I not just wait until he leaves?"

"He's here for *you*. Someone recognized you here in town and told him where to find you. I told him you did not work here any longer, that you had moved on, but I don't know if he believed me. You must leave. Now."

"But I have nowhere else to go!"

Elizabeth's brows pressed together as she took a deep breath. "I have a cousin in Tarrytown. Just tell her you are a friend of mine, and I know she'll help you."

"Tarrytown?"

"It's in Westchester county, on the eastern side of the Hudson river."

Hope nodded, her heart crumbling away in her chest. Elizabeth gave her all the details, and Hope committed them to memory.

"Now," Elizabeth said, "take the back steps and go get your things."

"Now?"

"Of course, now." Elizabeth nudged her. "Go."

Hope turned to leave, but stopped when Elizabeth whispered, "Wait."

She turned around and Elizabeth threw her arms around her. "I may not see you again. I am going to miss you. You've been such a good friend."

Tears streamed down Hope's face. "I will miss you too. You are the sister I wish I had."

"I feel the same." Elizabeth blinked back her own tears. "Now go, before someone tells the snake you are here."

"Do you think they will?"

"I don't think so. Everyone out here knows and loves you. No one in this town would believe you capable of murder. Still, the risk is too high. You must go."

Hope nodded and rushed out the door. She packed up all her belongings. Her mind felt numb, and it seemed she had a black hole in her chest where her heart once resided. Who would love and inspire Racheal now? Her parents certainly wouldn't. Who would encourage Kaleb to follow his dream to become a doctor? She was needed here! But she could not help her students if she were dead. She finished packing all her possessions—which weren't much. She'd always told herself she did not need worldly belongings. All she needed was a good heart, strong body, and good friends. Now she left her good friends behind.

Hope slung her heavy bag over her shoulder and slipped out the door.

Nightfall had settled over the town, and there were few about. Hope avoided the main road. She did not want to provide Eli a trail to follow. She just needed a ride. Hope knew a number of men who would be willing to take her wherever she asked. Most of them wanted to court her. This was a small town, with few prospects for a wife.

But only one man had a heart of gold and no false hopes of pursuing her.

She walked over a mile out of town. The full moon guided her to a little farmhouse. She knocked on the door. A skinny old man opened it and smiled widely.

"Hello, Mr. Henry."

"Blimey, young lass," he said, his accent coming through strongly. "What are you doing sneaking about in the dark alone?" He curiously eyed the bulging bag in her arms.

Hope's smile faded away. "I am in need of a ride to the next town."

He frowned at the request, then turned and grabbed his musket. "Who do I need to kill to keep you here?"

Hope shook her head. She was almost certain he was not serious. "I don't want you to kill anybody. I am afraid my past has come to take retribution out on me. And it's in mine and everyone's best interest for me to leave."

He opened his mouth to argue, but she quickly said, "There is no other way. And don't ask me specifics. The less you know, the better off you are."

Mr. Henry scowled and then sighed. "I always knew there was somein' you were hiding. But I also know a good soul when I see one." He shook his head. "May your tormentors die with worms in their guts."

Hope chuckled. "I am really going to miss you, Mr. Henry."

"We don't have to say our goodbyes yet, Mrs. Jones. So, where ya headin'?"

"I need to get to Tarrytown."

"Hmm. That is a full day's journey. We'll be needin' ample supplies."

"I cannot ask you to take me the whole way."

"You don't have to ask me, I am volunteering. You think I would drop a young innocent off in a strange town to fend for herself? What kind of man do ya take me for?"

"I didn't mean anything by it. I just didn't want to inconvenience you."

"It's no inconvenience. Mable could do with the exercise, and I could do with the company."

Tears welled in Hope's eyes as her heart filled her chest.

Mr. Henry turned a scowling face at her. "Now, you know I cannot abide tears." She blinked them back. "I wasn't crying."

45

"I certainly hope not," he said, turning back to gather salted meat, cheese, and apples from his cupboards.

Hope helped him load the wagon, and Mr. Henry got Mable from her stall. She was a stout, older horse and Mr. Henry's best friend. Hope held the lantern while he attached the harness. When they were ready, Mr. Henry assisted her into the carriage and then followed. Lifting the lamp, he opened the glass and blew the flame out.

"Why did you do that?" Hope asked.

"We don't want anyone to see us on our travels, do we?"

"We might if it means not colliding with another carriage."

"Mable has her bells on, we will be fine, Missy. Besides, look at that full moon. Providence is with us."

"I sure hope so," she said.

Hours into their journey, Hope was jostled awake. She lifted her head from Mr. Henry's shoulder and straightened up. "I am sorry," she mumbled when she realized she'd been sleeping against the old man.

He chuckled. "No need to apologize. Do you know how long it's been since I held a beautiful woman while she slept?"

"How long is that?" she asked, holding back a smile.

"Never you mind." He scowled at her with a twinkle in his eye.

Hope brushed her hair back from her face and straightened her skirts. "How long have we been traveling?"

"Sun's been up for close to an hour. You are welcome to some meat and cheese."

Hope's stomach growled in response to the mention of food. "Thank you. I cannot tell you how much I appreciate your help."

"Oh, now. I will hear none of that. I was feeling a touch of cabin fever anyway. You are doing me a favor."

Hope pulled out the food sack, broke off a piece of cheese, and nibbled. "How much farther is Tarrytown?"

"I would say we are nearly there. I was hopin' you would stay asleep until we got into town."

"You dreaded my conversation that much?"

"Oh, now shush! You know I did not mean it that way."

Hope chuckled. "I know. I was just teasing."

"It's not right to tease an old man."

"You are no old man," she said.

"I have got boots older than you, Missy."

"Somehow I doubt that."

"It's true. The boots we got in the king's army were sturdy pieces of work."

"You fought in the king's army?" Hope's eyes widened in surprise. Images of her dying father filled her mind.

"I *was* a red coat, but that was before the Revolution." He turned his narrowed eyes on her. "Don't think me a loyalist. I saw the way the colonists were treated. I retired from the king's army decades before and stayed to make my home here with my Abitha, God rest her soul. When the war broke out, I was an old man, but I did my part to help my fellow colonists."

"I never doubted you did."

"Oh, now, lying's a sin." He raised an eyebrow.

47

"Maybe I was surprised to hear you were a redcoat, but I never doubted your kindness and integrity."

"Now don't be going overboard. I ain't kind. I am a crotchety old man."

"Who is willing to drive a young lady a full day's journey to assist her." Hope patted his hand.

He shook his head. "Like I told you. Mable and I needed the exercise."

Hope smiled and glanced around at the deeply wooded area, with wildflowers sprouting in abundance. "Well, this is beautiful country. What better place to get your exercise?"

"It is lovely country, though it looks like the folks here are wasteful people."

"How do you know?"

He gestured toward the road. The remnants of a rotting, smashed pumpkin was strewn across the dirt path.

"That is very large," Hope said, shaking her head. "That could have made several fine pies." Seconds later, the squash was further destroyed under the wagon wheels.

Unease settled in Hope's chest as they continued. Trees towered over them like a canopy, and a covered bridge came into view. The disquieting feeling increased as they neared. Nailed to the bridge entrance was a weathered, wooden sign with the name Sleepy Hollow painted in white.

Chapter 7

The darkness inside the cavern of the bridge seemed especially thick, and Henry moved a hair's width closer to her, as if sensing her unease. Hope caught movement from the right, and her heart took a leap. A lanky, shadowy figure disappeared into the trees at their approach. Perhaps they'd startled the man.

Neither she nor Henry spoke. It was as if they did not want to awaken the spirits who resided there. Hope pressed her lips together. Her imagination ran rampant. She knew better than to entertain such thoughts. Ghosts did not exist. When one died, they went to their Maker or to the fiery pits of Satan. They did not inhabit glens and covered bridges.

It was several minutes before her spirits lightened once again. As they continued, they passed a small church and several small houses, smoke billowing from their chimneys.

"So where does this friend of yours live?" Mr. Henry asked.

"It's actually Elizabeth's cousin. She said she lives in the center of town, in the largest house on the main road."

"Doesn't sound too hard to find."

In minutes, they pulled up to a very large, extravagant home. The clapboards were painted bright white, the shutters the color of bluebells around wide windows.

Hope straightened her gown and patted down her hair. Mr. Henry accompanied her to the front door, and she knocked. A woman opened the door. She looked to be close to thirty years of age, with dark brown hair and a rounded belly heavy with child.

"Rebekah?"

The woman nodded. "Yes? Do I know you?"

"I am a friend of Elizabeth. My name is Hope, and this is Mr. Henry."

"Oh, Elizabeth, my favorite cousin!" Her countenance brightened. "Is she coming?"

"No, I am sorry. She's not. She told me you could help me."

Rebekah's brows pressed together. "Are you in trouble?"

"Something like that. I need a place to stay while I get settled."

"Here, come on in. You and your friend make yourselves at home."

"Thank you." She sat down on a sofa, and Henry took a seat in a sturdy wooden chair.

"You are planning to remain here in Tarrytown?" Rebekah asked.

"Yes, I am," Hope answered.

"Is your husband following?"

Hope shook her head. "I am widowed. I will be looking for lodging and work."

"Work? Well, we find ourselves in need of a school teacher. I don't suppose you have experience teaching."

"I just left a teaching job in—" She stopped herself before giving out too much information. She should have thought up an acceptable story.

"She's a fine teacher," Mr. Henry said, rescuing her from her blunder. "The whole town was heartbroken when she had to leave."

"Did you like instructing children?"

"I adore it."

"Perfect. And with this kind gentleman's recommendations, I am sure you'll be an answer to many a prayer."

Hope felt a great measure of relief. Perhaps there was a silver lining on this dark storm cloud after all.

"Normally you would lodge with your students, moving from home to home. But I have a feeling you'll need more privacy than that affords."

"I would prefer it."

Rebekah scrunched her eyebrows together. "I do know of a place. My husband owns property out in Sleepy Hollow. There is a cabin there. It's neglected, but it's a fine, sturdy building."

"Would your husband object to me lodging there?"

She shook her head. "He hasn't visited the place in years. I am sure he won't care. It will need a good washing, and some attending to, but I am confident it will fit your needs."

"That sounds perfect."

"Will Mr. Henry be needing a place to stay?" Rebekah asked.

"Just for tonight," he said. "Mable needs her rest, but we head back tomorrow."

"Mable?" Rebekah asked.

"His horse," Hope said.

"Ah," Rebekah answered. "Well, let's get you fed. And you both can stay with me for the night."

"Missus?" a voice called out from somewhere inside the house.

"Agnes?" Rebekah called back. "I have some folks I would like you to meet."

A white-haired woman with a rounded body and sparkling eyes stepped into the room. She looked to be nearly the same age as Mr. Henry. Her eyes inspected them as she said, "Why, hello. Are you friends of Rebekah?"

Hope stood and took her weathered hand in hers. "I am Hope, and this is Mr. Henry. We are actually friends of Rebekah's cousin."

"This is Agnes," Rebekah said. "My dearest friend."

"Your housemaid, dearie."

"You are so much more than a housemaid."

"And you are so much more charitable than any other employers I have ever had."

Rebekah shook her head. "Agnes's been with me since my mother died when I was five." She turned to Agnes. "Hope will be renting the cabin in Sleepy Hollow. Mr. Henry will be leaving tomorrow."

Mr. Henry took Agnes's hand and lifted it to his lips. "It's a pleasure to meet such a fine woman."

Agnes giggled. Hope could not help but smile at the woman. She may be an old woman, but from the looks of it, she hadn't forgotten what it was like to be a school girl.

"It's a pleasure to meet you too, Mr. Henry," Agnes said. "The meal is nothing fancy," she snuck a quick glance at Mr. Henry, "but, there's plenty for everyone."

"We don't want to inconvenience you," Hope said.

"Nonsense," Agnes said. "It's not an inconvenience at all."

Mr. Henry offered Agnes his arm. "It would be my pleasure to accompany a woman as fine as you to dinner."

Hope held back a laugh. Mr. Henry was sure laying on the charm. If only he could stay. He could use some happiness in his life. He'd been alone for a terribly long time.

*   *   *   *   *

The cabin was tucked between two towering hills lush with trees. It looked like it hadn't been touched in a decade. Limbs were scattered across the rooftop. Leaves and debris had blown inside the open door. Foliage grew all around, including right in front of the door. But Rebekah was right, it was a sturdy home with logs the width of dinner plates. There were no cracks between them, either. Someone had gone to a lot of work to build this cabin properly. Hope wondered why no one lived there now. Cabins of this quality were never forgotten, but somehow this one had been.

"It's not much to look at," Rebekah began.

"It's perfect," Hope said.

Rebekah smiled. "I am glad you like it. I would like to help you clean it out, but my midwife has me doing minimal labor."

"Oh, not to worry," Hope said. "I will be fine on my own. You've already done so much. Though we haven't discussed the price."

"When you find out how much your teacher's salary will be," Rebekah said, "then we can discuss the rent. For now, I will consider it a favor to my cousin."

"Thank you so much," Hope said. "You've been a true angel."

Rebekah shook her head. "It's no trouble, really. And if you can teach half as good as Mr. Henry brags, I will be thanking you for teaching my little one in a few years." She patted her bulging stomach.

"I will look forward to it." Hope smiled, hoping she'd be there that long. But with Eli and the law after her, she could not count on it.

Hope made several trips back and forth from the carriage to the house. She unloaded her belongings, food, a cast-iron cauldron, dishes, and a broom—most of the items supplied by Rebekah.

"I will see you for dinner on Sunday," Rebekah said.

Hope nodded. "Thank you for everything."

"It's my pleasure." Rebekah climbed into the carriage, and a moment later Hope was alone.

She turned back to the cabin and sighed. "Well, you are not going to clean yourself."

With that said, she got to work. Opening the shutters, she was able to properly see to sweep out the dirt and leaves, clean out the cupboards, beat out the bedding, and sift through all the clutter left behind by the last tenant. There wasn't much of use, other than another very large cauldron, dried herbs, and various wooden dishes. Luckily, there was a well brimming with water behind the building and a basin large enough to bathe in nearby. She'd definitely make good use of those.

She got to work on cleaning out the dishes. She'd need to get dinner started soon if she wanted to eat before nightfall. She had to get a full night's sleep. Tomorrow she was meeting with the mayor to apply for the job. Rebekah said it was a blessing for the town that she'd shown up at just the right time, but Hope had learned not to take anything for granted. There were many that did not think much of female teachers.

Several hours later, she lay down in her bed. Her heart fluttered in her chest. She hated starting over. She'd done it years before, but at that time she was escaping a wicked husband. This time she was escaping a death sentence.

She'd nearly forgotten!

Slipping out of bed, she dropped to her knees and offered a prayer. She needed God now more than ever.

Climbing back into bed, her heart took a leap when she heard a moan. Was there someone about? She sat up. The embers cast a red glow about the room, which was obviously empty. She got out of bed and padded over to the door. Pressing her ear against the wood, she listened closely. The wind howled outside, the rustling of the leaves in the trees hissed, and the shutters shook against their latches, but she could not catch the sound of a moan again. Perhaps it was the wind.

Her heart calmed. It had to be.

She climbed back into bed and closed her eyes. The pitter-patter of rain began, and she worried for a moment that the roof might leak. No, there were no signs of water damage. The door was latched, as were all the shutters. She should be safe from the storm.

The rain continued to knock against the roof, lulling her to sleep.

*   *   *   *   *

Hope's eyes shot open, trying to pierce the complete darkness in the room. Something had awoken her and had her heart pounding.

"Hello?" said a deep voice from somewhere inside.

55

Her hands slapped over her mouth as she muffed a cry. The pounding of her chest drowned out the sounds of the rain. Should she answer the voice? Perhaps she—

"Is someone there?" he spoke again.

The tone did not sound threatening. It seemed to be inside the room, but that was impossible. The occasional flash of lightning lit up the room enough to know she was alone. Was the voice coming from outside? Perhaps someone was lost in the storm and seeking shelter.

She stepped over to the door and unlatched it. It flung inward, and she had to push against it. Wind rushed through the opening, bringing a splattering of rain through the doorway. Peering around the door, she searched for a visitor.

In the light of another lightning flash, she could see the tangle of brush growing outside, but there did not seem to be anyone about. She wrestled the door closed again and put down the latch.

"Now I know I heard someone," the voice said, anger lacing his words.

Hope's heart took off in a sprint. She wandered the room in search of the man behind the voice. Finally, she decided to answer him.

"I am Hope," she said, her voice quaking. "I live here now."

"Well, Hope. May I welcome you to my hell on earth."

Her heart pounded once again. "Are you Satan?" she breathed in horror.

"I have no idea who that is, but if you don't release me soon, I am going to make it my life's mission to make your life a living hell."

"How can you know what hell is and not know who Satan is?"

"Are you going to release me or continue to ask pointless questions?"

"For someone who needs help, you are not very solicitous."

"I have been trapped under the floorboards of this accursed cabin for—many years. I don't have the patience to be kind, or polite. I want to get out so I can strip the flesh from the bones of the witch that put me here."

"You say a witch put you there? You've been under the floorboards for years? But how did you eat and drink? How have you stayed alive under there for years? Or, *are* you still alive? Am I talking to a ghost?"

"You are full of questions, are you not?" he said, the words ringing with familiarity. Had she met him before?

"No," he continued, "I am not a ghost. Open up the trapdoor and you'll see who I am."

"Trapdoor?"

"Under the bed."

Hope stepped over to the dining table and snatched a candle. She went to the fireplace and pressed the wick against the still-glowing ember. In a few seconds, the room lit up with its flickering flame. Setting it down on the bedside table, she then dragged the bed away from the wall and searched for the door he was talking about.

And there it was. She hadn't noticed it before. It blended into the floor. Hope shook her head. It was such a small door, about a foot square. How could a full-grown man fit into that? Perhaps he was one of those small men she'd seen in the medical journals. But no, the books said they had the same width as a typical man, but diminished height.

"Are you sure you are not dead?" Hope asked, her heart pounding. She really did not want to open that trap door. She had a feeling when she did, her fears would be realized, and she would find the bones of the man she was talking to.

"I am sure, now get me out of here!"

"No need to shout at me."

She wedged her fingers in between the boards and lifted. She could not make out what was down the dark hole. Reaching for the candle, she moved it over the opening. The eyes of a man squinted at the light as a spider scurried across his face.

"Oh, my dear Maker," she exclaimed, leaning back. Her breaths came out in gasps as her heart pounded out of her chest. She leaned forward and confirmed the fact she hadn't been seeing things. There really was a man lying reposed in a hole in the floor. "How do I get you out of there?"

"You lift me out."

"But . . ." she hesitated. Perhaps the man was daft. Lying trapped there had to wreak havoc on a man's sanity.

"Just do it," he said in clipped tones. "But, don't drop me."

"I cannot lift a full-grown man."

"I am much lighter than I used to be."

"You don't seem to understand. The only part of you that would fit through this hole is your head."

58

"I am well aware of that, and I am afraid that is all there is of me."

"What?" she said, her voice strained. And then a thought occurred to her, and she blew out a quick breath. "I am dreaming!" She went over to her bed and sat down, shaking her head. "Of course, I am dreaming." She smiled. "All of this is so impossible, I am surprised I did not think of it before."

"Hope," he said. "You are not dreaming."

She turned to him in surprise. "You know my name?" She shrugged. "Of course, you do. I know my name, and you are a product of my imagination."

"I know because you just told me. Besides, we've met before."

"We have?" She got up and sat down next to the hole.

"Years ago, I saved you from the man with an evil mind and wicked intentions."

"It's you," she breathed. "I have dreamed of you before."

"You have?"

"Yes, but you were never just a head before. And most of the dreams were shameful."

"Shameful? How so?"

Hope shook her head. "I will not talk about it."

"Oh, come now. This is only a dream, isn't it? Who will know?"

She pressed her lips together and sighed. "We were . . ." she hesitated.

"Yes?"

"Kissing."

"That is all? Nothing more?"

59

"With open mouths," Hope whispered. She glanced around as if fearful someone might hear her confession. Her face heated in embarrassment.

"That is the best way to kiss."

"Calm your wicked thoughts, Mr. Jones."

"Who is Mr. Jones?" he said, surprised.

"Why, you are. At least that is what you've always called yourself."

"In your dreams, right," he snickered. "But we've never gone beyond kissing?"

"Of course not. What kind of woman do you take me for?"

"Not the kind I would usually seduce. Your looks are appealing enough, but you are missing the most pleasurable act of all."

"Oh now, just you stop right there. I know where your thoughts are going. That is something that should only be done between husband and wife to procreate children."

"So, you think that couples should only have sex when they want to make babies?"

"Yes."

"I am guessing you are a virgin."

"You guessed properly."

"Oh, the things I could teach you."

"Well, you are just a head, are you not? From what I have studied in medical journals, you'll need more of your body parts to accomplish your lessons."

His countenance darkened. "I intend to get my body back from that witch. And you will help me."

"I will?"

"Yes."

Hope shook her head. "You'll be gone when I wake from this dream."

"Don't I wish," he mumbled and then spoke louder. "Until then, can you please get me out of here?"

"Oh, all right. Just hold your horses." Hope leaned forward. She cringed as she wrapped her fingers around the back of his head, her fingers weaving into his matted hair as she lifted. His head felt heavier than it looked, but it came out of the hole easily.

"Now, careful," he said, startling her into almost dropping him.

"Shh!" she hissed. "This is unsettling enough without you talking."

For the first time, she got a good look at his head. It was severed cleanly above the shoulders. She could clearly see the openings of his esophagus and trachea. She could also see his vertebra and muscles—still fresh and pink.

"You know it's rude to stare at one's insides." His voice startled her once again.

"Sorry," she mumbled. She turned her attention to the task of finding a place to put him. She should have prepared something beforehand.

"What are you waiting for?" he asked. "That bed looks plenty comfortable to me."

"You are not sleeping in my bed," she said firmly.

"Where do you suggest?"

She looked him over. His hair was filthy and matted with dirt and cobwebs. She did not want him touching any of her clean linen. "You need a good scrubbing in a bath."

61

Holly Kelly

"Believe me, I am well aware of that."

"I could set you on the front step. The rain would wash away a lot of the filth."

"You would not dare," he hissed.

She chuckled, "No, I would not, but it's a pleasant thought." She carefully sat him down on the floor. His head rolled to the side.

"What in blazes are you doing? This is almost as uncomfortable as the hole in the floor."

"I just need to set you down so I can prepare a bed for you."

She located a wooden box, folded an extra blanket, and tucked it inside. "There. This should be comfortable enough."

She retrieved his head and gently sat him in the box.

"Ah." He closed his eyes and sighed happily. "You don't know how good this feels. I have had a rock pressed into my skull for ages."

"I am glad I could ease your discomfort," she said. "Now, would you please not make another sound? I must speak to the mayor tomorrow about a teaching position. I need my sleep."

She realized the absurdity of her words after she spoke them. After all, she was already asleep.

Chapter 8

Hope awoke to the sounds of birds chirping outside her windows. She stretched out the kinks as she yawned. Padding over to the nearest window, she unlatched and pushed the shutters open. The rain had abated, and the glow of the sun brightened the sky. It looked to be about seven o'clock.

She had plenty of time before she needed to leave. Stepping over to her chest, she retrieved her terry towel and a bar of soap and then stepped out the door. She pulled eleven buckets of water from the well—one to clean out the basin and ten to fill it. Stripping out of her clothes, she climbed in the water and sat down. The water took her breath away and started her teeth chattering. She got to work quickly, building up a lather and scrubbing her body. When she was done, she dried, wrapped the towel around her, tipped the basin over, and gathered her dirty clothes.

She hummed a tune as she stepped back into the cabin. This place was so much better than the one room she'd lived in at the inn. With people constantly coming and going, there was little privacy and no good place to take a bath. She had to travel to a nearby river and wash in the sometimes-murky water. At this cabin, the water was crystal clear, she had an entire cabin to herself, and the woods surrounding her were so lovely.

Stepping over to her travel bag, she retrieved clean underclothes and her lavender gown. She had just begun to remove her towel when someone said, "Now that is a sight I could wake to every day."

Hope gasped and pulled the towel tight across her body. Her wide eyes followed the voice and landed on two eyes straining to peer sideways at her from a wooden crate. At that sight, she did what any sane woman would do.

She screamed.

When she was done shrieking, she screeched, "You are a dream!"

The severed head smirked at her. "I have been told that before."

She shook her head. "No, this cannot be happening." She paced the floor. "I cannot lose my sanity now. I am supposed to teach children. I am to be a role model. How can I be a role model and be completely out of my mind?"

"Hey," the voice said. She kept her eyes averted and continued to pace.

"You are not supposed to be seen outside my dreams," she continued. "I have truly lost it. I have most definitely, absolutely, gone mad!"

"Hey," he shouted, his voice ringing her ears.

Hope froze but still refused to look at the head.

"I think there are some things we need to discuss," he said. "Like how are you going to find my body and replace my head."

Hope turned slowly to him and gave a hesitant nod. Then she strode out the front door and closed it behind her.

"How did this happen?" she asked herself. "I never knew insanity ran in my family. My father did not tell me a thing. I thought I was pragmatic, level-headed, and a pillar of mental strength." Hope continued to talk to herself. Why shouldn't she? She was already crazy, and this was what crazy people did, right?

"I am going to have to be committed," she said. "Is there even an asylum nearby? And if there is, should I just show up and tell them I am insane? I will tell them what I have seen, and I am sure they will lock me up. But then, how would I hide from Eli?

"I know, I could use a new alias. He would never think to find me in an asylum."

"Hope," the voice shouted from inside the house. "Where in blazes did you go? Would you get your beautiful, nude self back here? We have important things to discuss."

At his words, she looked down. Oh, dear heavens, she was still naked! She could not possibly show up at an asylum dressed only in a towel. But that would mean . . . She could feel the blood drain from her face. ...she would *have* to go back into the cabin.

"Oh, no, no, no. I cannot go back in there. Please, let there be some other way."

"Hope," he roared. "Come . . . back . . . inside! If you even so much as think of leaving me here, when I get my body back, I will whip you from now until Sunday."

At those words, something in her snapped. The image of Eli assaulting her, driving her into hiding—there was no way under heaven or earth she would allow another man to intimidate her again! If she were well and good crazed, she might as well do as she wished. With nothing else to lose, she stormed over to the door and threw it open, her fear turned to righteous anger. "No one lays a hand on me. Ever!"

"Brave words for a woman speaking to someone completely helpless," he sneered. "But I warn you, with my body, I am a warrior the likes you've not seen. I have never been bested in battle, and I will darn well whip any woman I put my mind to whipping!"

"Whipping a woman is never a brave act," Hope said. "A man who strikes a woman is a coward and a snake."

"You use my own words against me," he said. It looked like he remembered the day they met. He probably had a lot of time to think about it over the years. "I used those words for a man who would rape a woman. Whipping a woman who deserves it is a whole other affair. Sometimes a woman needs to be taught her place."

"Taught her place?" Hope fairly screamed. "Did you say, 'Taught her place?'"

"I did not stutter. You know exactly what I said."

Hope stormed over to the box, took a fistful of hair, picked him up, and stomped over to the old chamber pot. Too bad it hadn't been used lately. "I will teach you your place." Without care, she chucked him inside. His roar and subsequent slew of profanity reverberated off the cabin walls. Hope ignored the vile man, draped an old cloth over the pot, and proceeded to get dressed. She could still hear him bellowing as she made her way down the path toward town.

*   *   *   *   *

Hope's mind raced as she followed the meandering path. What she'd seen was impossible. She knew enough about anatomy to know that a live, talking, severed head was just not within the realm of possibilities. But then, witches and the power they wielded was not supported by science either. And they existed. Didn't they?

Mr. Jones did say a witch was the cause of his unique situation. She had removed his head and left it in an abandoned cabin. How long had he truly been there?

They had met over eight years ago. Could he have been there that long? No. He would have been reduced to a blithering idiot with that much seclusion. It had to have been recent. Still, being trapped beneath the floor with no one to talk to must have been torture.

Perhaps she'd gone too far when she threw him into the chamber pot. Guilt gnawed at her. What she'd done was not very Christian-like. Why did she let her anger get the best of her? She'd never in her life had trouble controlling her temper before. But Mr. Jones *was* exceptionally insufferable—threatening to whip her. The only other time she'd had a hand raised to her was when Eli struck her on their wedding night. Her father had never even raised a hand to her backside. Perhaps, the incident with Eli affected her more than she cared to admit.

There was simply something so wrong about a man who vowed to love and honor and then turned around and beat his wife. She'd seen enough of it to be sickened by it. And everyone turned a blind eye. According to the law, it was a man's right to beat his wife. He was unquestioned in his methods of discipline. Why should a wife need discipline? She was not a child. And from what Hope observed, it was more often the husband in need of correction than the wife.

The path widened into a road. She was nearly to town. Several carriages passed her by, but no one offered her a ride. This town did not seem as friendly as her previous one. Looking at the faces of the people, their expressions seemed strained, their eyes suspicious.

The town hall came into view on the right, and Hope straightened her shoulders. Should she even be doing this? She still wasn't sure of her sanity. In all likelihood, she had lost her mind. But she prided herself in giving people the benefit of the doubt. She herself deserved the same courtesy.

She approached a door with a large glass window. Colorful images flashed across the wavy glass. Looked like this town started early. She hadn't planned to come until nine o'clock, but the situation back at the cabin changed her plans for her.

I really should get him out of that chamber pot.

A man with salt and pepper hair and a rounded belly looked her way. His eyes widened. "May I help you, Ma'am?"

"Um, yes. Rebekah Smith told me you were looking for a teacher."

A frown darkened his face. "But you are a woman. This town has the funds to pay for a man with qualifications. We don't have to scrape the bottom of the barrel when it comes to the education of our children."

"I have ample qualifications, despite my gender."

"Oh, really?" he smirked, doubt written on his face. He turned to two men speaking to each other across the foyer. "Dr. Porter?"

"Yes, Mayor Jansen?" a well-dressed man who appeared to be in his early thirties looked at him and then eyed Hope curiously.

"This woman claims to be well educated. She's here for the teaching position."

"Is she now?" He sauntered over, keeping his eyes on her. "Then I suppose she would not be opposed to answering some questions to gauge her level of knowledge."

"Absolutely not," Hope answered, her voice steady, her nervousness properly masked.

"Why don't you join me in the mayor's office," he said, and he turned to the mayor. "If you don't mind."

"Of course, not."

Hope waited for Dr. Porter to sit behind the desk before she took her seat. "May I ask," she said, her curiosity piqued, "what you are a doctor of?"

"I have two doctorates—medicine and philosophy."

"Impressive," Hope said.

"Might I ask what your husband thinks about you wanting to work outside the home?"

"Mr. Jones is no longer with me," she said, alarmed at the blunder she'd just made. She should have picked a different name. She did not want to give Eli anymore to go on in his search for her.

"I am sorry," he said and then cleared his throat. "Now let's see how impressive you are. Arithmetic skills are important. I would like you to solve a problem without the use of script."

Hope nodded, her stomach tying into a knot.

"What two numbers multiplied by each other will equal three hundred forty-nine?"

Hope felt a measure of relief. She knew this one. "There are no two numbers that will equal three hundred forty-nine when multiplied. That number is prime."

He cracked a smile. "So, it is. Alright. Name the thirteen colonies and their capitals."

"Maine's capital is Augusta, New Hampshire's is Concord, New York's is Albany, Massachusetts' is Boston, Maryland's is Baltimore, Delaware's is Dover, Connecticut's is Hartford, Pennsylvania's is Harrisburg, New Jersey's is Trenton, Virginia's is Richmond, North Carolina's is Raleigh, South Carolina's is Charleston, and Georgia's is Atlanta."

Dr. Porter shook his head.

"Did I forget one?"

"No. I am beginning to be impressed.

He continued to grill her with question after question. Hope's confidence soared. She was sure she'd answered each one correctly.

"Now if you can answer this last question," Dr. Porter said, "you've got the job."

Butterflies erupted in Hope's stomach. *Please let him ask me a question I know.*

"Discuss the path food takes through the anatomy of the body."

Hope's eyes widened. This question was far beyond what a normal teacher of children would ever need to know. Even highly educated, seasoned teachers did not teach anatomy—unless that teacher was instructing a medical school class. She was being sabotaged.

Hope held back a smile. This doctor could not know the study of anatomy was somewhat of an obsession for her.

"First," she began, "food is macerated by the teeth with the help of the tongue. Saliva aids with the breakdown. Then it travels down one's esophagus—passing by the lower esophageal sphincter—on its way to the stomach. There, acids break down the food to a liquid state. Then, the pyloric sphincter opens up and the food continues on to the small intestines. There it moves through about twenty feet of intestines until it transfers into the large intestines. Liquids are absorbed by the intestinal walls, and what's left is solid waste. That is then expelled through the rectum to the outside of the body. The whole process takes about five to eight hours."

Dr. Porter's jaw hung down. He snapped it back together and shook his head. "I am officially impressed, Mrs. Jones." He stood and put out his hand to shake hers. "I would like to welcome Tarrytown's newest teacher."

Chapter 9

As Hope and Dr. Porter stepped back into the foyer, they met the smug look of the mayor. His smile faded when Dr. Porter turned to her and said, "I will meet you at the school Monday morning. Eight o'clock."

Hope smiled brightly. "I look forward to it."

As she turned to leave, she heard the mayor whisper harshly, "You hired her? Are you insane?"

"She's the most brilliant woman I have ever met," Dr. Porter said. "If she were a man, I would be writing a letter of recommendation for her to get into medical school."

"But, she's a woman!"

Hope frowned at the conversation. She would prove to the mayor that she was an asset to the town.

Still, acceptance or not, she had a job. Hope wished she could stop by Rebekah's to celebrate, but she needed to get back. She could not abide the thought of Mr. Jones sitting in that chamber pot any longer than need be.

Perhaps he would be gone, proving she had imagined him. Then maybe she would not have to apologize to the revolting man.

*   *   *   *   *

Conall closed his eyes and tried not to think about the brown crusted streaks pressing into his nose. The smell, though, he could not ignore. That woman was insufferable! He had no idea what he'd found appealing about her before. And to think he'd wasted years dreaming about seeing her again. All the sweet imaginations and lucid dreams could not erase his current predicament. The woman was a menace!

"Mr. Jones?" the familiar sound of her voice floated into the room as the door creaked open.

Speak of the devil.

She lifted the cloth from off his head. He still could not see her, as his face was flattened into the side of the pot.

"Oh," she breathed, disappointment in her tone. "You are still here."

"Where else would I be? And the name's Conall."

"Is it?" she said, sounding surprised.

He did not bother answering her.

"Well, Mr. Conall, I feel the need to apologize. I am afraid I overreacted."

"Can you apologize after getting me out of this damn pot?"

"May I please ask you not to swear in my presence?"

"Get me the hell out of this pot," he roared, the pot amplifying his voice.

"Alright, all right." Her hands came around his head, one of her fingers jabbing into his eye socket.

"Ouch," he hollered.

"Sorry," she mumbled. "I just . . . it's hard to get a good grip from this angle."

The room spun around, and finally it stopped with her face inches from his.

"Now, I will admit," she said, "your treatment of women does leave something to be desired, but your opinion is shared by most men. I was just raised differently. My father always treated me with respect and never raised a hand to me. When I think of the terrible treatment some women have to endure, I go a bit nuts. But the treatment you received by the hands of that witch pales in comparison, and I should have been more understanding of your fear and showed you more compassion."

"I am not afraid of anything."

"Everyone is afraid of something," she said.

He frowned at her.

"This morning I was terrified I had lost my mind. But then I came to accept that because I know witches exist, it's only logical that there may be witches at work in your situation. And although I understand— "

"Do you always talk this much?" he interrupted.

"I . . . well, no, not usually. I am alone a lot."

"Yeah, and you still talk."

"That is a rude thing to say," she said.

"As rude as throwing someone into a chamber pot?"

Hope pressed her lips together. "I apologized for that."

"That doesn't erase what you did."

"No, but a Christian man would forgive."

"I am not Christian."

"Hmm, well, no one is perfect. Speaking of imperfect, you could really use a bath, Mr. Conall."

"It's just Conall. There's no mister."

"Oh, okay, then I guess you can call me Hope."

"I already call you Hope."

Her eyes widened as red blossomed in her cheeks. "So, you do."

He could not help noticing how appealing she looked. He nearly smiled, and then a scowl settled over his face. He almost forgot how furious he was with this woman.

"I think it best," she said, "that we begin with the river. You are quite filthy. Once we have you mostly cleaned up, you can bathe properly in the basin."

"Just don't drop me."

"I would not drop you," she said, sounding offended. She carried him outside the cabin, the trees floating past his vision.

"You nearly dropped me last night."

"I was startled. A bath in the river should offer no surprises. It's not like I will be seeing your manly parts."

"Have you ever seen manly parts?"

"That is not something a proper woman would discuss. But if you must know, of course I have."

His eyes widened in surprise. "Really?"

She shrugged. "I was a nurse. Now shush! I refuse to talk further about it." Kneeling, she lowered him toward the water. He could hear it rushing below him. "It would be best if you could hold your breath. By the way." She paused, curiosity burning in her eyes. "How do you breathe with no lungs?"

"The witch may have cut my head from my body, but her magic keeps us connected. I breathe, it breathes."

"And will the water flood from the openings where you . . . you know. Where she cut you?"

"Her magic sealed it."

"Interesting. Alright, here we go."

Cold water saturated the back of his head, and he took a deep breath. Hope plunged him completely under the surface and massaged his matted hair in the current. His face broke the surface, and she gave him time to take another breath before plunging him down again, this time face down. She tugged and pulled at his hair.

75

It was very long, and it seemed she was having difficulty untangling it.

She brought him to the surface again. "Perhaps," she said, "we should cut your hair."

"No," he said firmly.

"But—"

"Absolutely not. I like my hair the way it is."

"Tangled into a matted mess?"

"You know what I mean."

"If I could just—" Her words ceased abruptly as her eyes widened. It looked as if she was staring at his ear. Oh, right. Human ears were rounded.

"What . . . are you?" she stammered, and then he tipped.

She cried out as her fingers swiped at his head. The surface of the water flew toward him. He barely had time to take a big breath when he tumbled into the river. He could hear her muted scream as he rolled and bobbed away with the current.

She'd dropped him!

Why was he not surprised? He would have been better off left under the floorboards.

* * * * *

Hope shrieked when the current carried Conall away. Splashing into the water, the current swirled around her, sweeping her off her feet. Hope screamed and then the icy water engulfed her face. Stroking toward the surface, her face broke through. She gasped in deep breaths of air as she fought to keep her head above water. Her heavy gown made it difficult, but at least she had arms and legs to accomplish it.

Where was Conall?

76

There he was! She could see the white strands of his hair in front of her. Stroking toward them, they were obscured by the water again. At least they were moving in the same direction.

This time she saw his head bob to the surface, his frantic face showing as it rolled along. She needed to get to him before he drowned! Could he drown? Her speed picked up as several boulders passed her by. The water splashed over Hope's face as the current pulled her down. Her foot encountered something solid, and she pushed off. Her head broke the surface once again, and she took a breath and swam more vigorously.

They needed to get out of this river! But she wasn't about to leave Conall. If she died trying to save him, that would be her just desserts.

Hope searched for him again. This time she spotted him close by. His blond hair was nearly touching her. She swiped at it and got a grip on it.

She got him!

Now to make it to shore. She remembered what her father told her about this situation. He instructed her to not swim directly for the side. Swim diagonally toward it.

Hope looked to the direction of the river and heaved a sigh. As they came around the bend, it opened up into much calmer waters. She swam hard and fast along the shore with shallow waters in sight—Conall's hair clasped tight in her hand. The current slowed, and she finally felt solid ground beneath her.

She pulled at Conall's hair, his head not far behind. His eyes were closed. He looked . . . dead. *Please don't let him be!*

Staggering up the shore, Hope coughed the river water from her lungs. Conall should be coughing too.

77

"Conall!" she shouted between coughing jags as she lifted him to face her. She sank down on the dry shore, exhausted. "Conall, oh please don't be dead!"

He blinked and then glared at her. "It would serve you right if I did die."

"Why are not you c-coughing?"

"Do I look like I have lungs to cough?"

"No, but you don't have lungs to t-talk either."

He raised an eyebrow and scowled at her. "How far did we travel?"

Hope looked up. A breeze raised goosebumps over her whole body, and she shook from the cold. "N-not too terribly far. About a m-mile, I think."

"You are hard to understand when your teeth are chattering so. The sooner we get back to the cabin, the sooner you can build a fire and warm up."

"S-so you are concerned for m-me? Even after—"

"If you die of exposure, who will find my body and bring it to me?"

"So, it's all selfish concern?"

"Absolutely."

Hope rose to her feet. Her legs shook beneath her, and her wet dress was terribly heavy, not to mention the fact it was doing nothing to warm her. Despite the difficulty, Hope set off along the shore to get back to the cabin.

"So, what are you, truly?" Hope asked.

He paused for a moment before speaking. "I am Elven."

"Elves do not exist."

He laughed. "You're kidding, right?"

"They're from faery tales." Hope frowned. Her practical world was crumbling around her.

"Faery tales often have threads of truth in them."

"Is that why you are still alive, despite the fact all that is left of you is your head? Is it because you are an elf?"

"The witch said this would not work on a human, only an elf or faery."

"Faeries are real too?"

"Yes."

"So, do giants, ogres, and trolls exist too?"

"Well . . . yes, they do. In my world, at least."

"Where is your world?"

"It's very far, but not far at all."

"You are making no sense. Did that tumble through the river addle your brain?"

"Hmm," he said. "How do I explain this so that you will understand?"

"Right, because I am a stupid woman, incapable of grasping simple concepts."

"Where did that come from? I never said you were stupid."

"You implied."

"You have an inferiority complex, woman."

"I do not," she said firmly. "I am just tired of people assuming I am unintelligent simply because of my gender."

"Well," he said, "I am not one of them. Being a woman has nothing to do with it. Now being human . . . humans are not the most intelligent of creatures."

"What?" She stopped walking. "If you thought to placate me with that statement, then you are the one who's an idiot!"

"I was not trying to placate you. I was simply stating fact."

"Oh, really." Hope turned his head so that he faced the ground. "Well, you can just shut up for the rest of the way. I am done talking to you."

It wasn't long before the cabin came into view. Hope breathed a sigh of relief. "I cannot wait to get out of this wet dress."

"Yeah, me too."

Hope glare down at him. "You. If you don't clean up your words and thoughts, I will put you outside to sleep."

Conall did not answer her. As soon as she stepped into the cabin, she placed him in his cushioned box and draped a light blanket over his face. She proceeded to peel her wet clothes off her body and hung them on coat hooks to dry. Then she dried herself with a terry cloth and got dressed. Putting on clean, dry clothes never felt so good. She was finally warm.

"The blanket under my head is quite wet now," Conall's muffled voice said.

Hope looked over to the box and sighed. Stepping over, she sat on the bed and draped a new terry cloth over her lap. She lifted him from the blanket and looked at him. His eyes reflected the humiliation he felt having to ask her for help. Her heart ached for him. He may be rude, arrogant, and ill-informed, but this situation would be hard for anyone to endure.

Gently, she dried his face and hair. Plucking the brush from her side table, she worked at the tangles in his hair. He looked at her with a curious, surprised expression.

It took a painfully long time to work the tangles out, but the parts she'd finished looked sleek and bright. He really had lovely hair for a man. His eyes were now closed, and she took advantage of that to examine his face. He was handsome, with a strong chin, long, slender nose, and those eyes. . ... She could never forget how they looked. They were the most striking feature of all, like blue ice. He might be the most handsome man she'd ever met.

That was, if he had his body. She remembered it clearly. One did not forget a body like his—broad shoulders, bulging muscles, long narrow waist. Just thinking about it made her feel—

Hope shook her head and turned her eyes away. She needed to tame her thoughts. She was entertaining unclean thoughts for a man who was now a severed head.

Still, he needed to be cared for. It was the Christian thing to do. She'd finished brushing his hair. But before she put his head in the box, she replaced the blanket with a dry one and carefully laid him in it.

"Thank you." His deep voice rumbled softly.

She avoided his gaze, afraid he might see through her to the unladylike thoughts she'd been having. But still, she answered, "You're welcome."

Chapter 10

"Today is the perfect day to begin the search." Conall's voice rang with frustration.

"It's Sunday," Hope said, propping Conall's box against the wall so he had a view of more than just the ceiling. "The Bible says it's a day of rest. Hiking along the highway and trudging through the woods is not rest. Besides, I need to attend church. This is my first Sabbath here. I don't want people to think I am not a church-goer."

"And you intend to leave me here," he said.

Hope avoided looking at him; she could feel his scowl. "I don't understand your aversion to being alone."

"Yeah?" His voice rose. "Well, you weren't trapped in a dark hole for decades."

"Ah, now don't exaggerate," she said. "It could not have been that long. We met eight years ago."

"It was a long time to remain alone." He paused, driving sadness into her heart. That would have been torture. And then he continued. "For both of us."

She turned to him, surprised. "I haven't been alone."

"How old are you?" he asked.

"That is a rude question."

"Only if you are ashamed of your age."

Hope pressed her brows together in a scowl. "If you must know, I am twenty-eight."

"Twenty-eight and not married."

"Not exactly."

"How can you not exactly be married? You told me yourself you are a virgin."

"I did not," she said in a gasp.

"Yes, you did."

Hope frowned at him. "I was sort of married."

"You are making no sense. You are either married or you are not."

Hope explained to him exactly what happened, including her escape.

Conall's bellowing laughter rang out.

"I don't see the humor in this," she snapped.

"Then you are not looking very hard. You, my dear, are an amazing woman. What I don't understand is why you've kept yourself unwed for this long. Well, that is not exactly true. I can understand anyone not getting married, but I would prefer to be hacked into a thousand pieces than live a life of celibacy."

"Would you also rather be hacked into a thousand pieces than get married?"

Conall shrugged. "It would be a tossup."

Hope shook her head. "You are insufferable. I remained unmarried because it's the only way I could keep my virtue."

"But you are not married," he said. "You did not say 'I do,' so you did not do it."

"The law thinks I am married. Well, it thought I was. I just found out Eli has gotten our marriage annulled."

"Well, then, there you go. You are free to marry."

"I am too old now."

Conall barked a laugh. "That is the most ludicrous thing I have ever heard. First of all, twenty-eight is not old. Second of all, you are a beautiful woman. I am sure you have men lined up who would only be too happy to bed you. Excuse me, wed you."

Hope shook her head at Conall's obviously intentional word blunder. He raised an eyebrow. "I would want to bed you myself—if I had my body back, and if you weren't so saintly."

"This conversation has become obscene." Hope lifted her Sunday bonnet out of a box and tied it on her head. "I think it's time I leave for church."

"And leave me alone. At least I have this conversation to think on. That should give me a few lingering chuckles."

"You have wicked thoughts, Mr. Jones." Hope shook her head.

"Wicked thoughts are the best ones," he said with a wink.

She suppressed a smile, shook her head and stepped out the door.

*   *   *   *   *

Hope approached a gray flagstone church with a white bell tower. The building was surrounded by tombstones. The last congregation's stragglers were herded inside by a tall, thin woman with a stern expression.

Hope had spent too much time arguing with Conall. That man was uncouth as could be with his mind constantly in the gutter.

She slipped in just before the door was shut and took a seat on the edge of the nearest pew. She noticed Dr. Porter watching from the far side of the chapel. He smiled and gave a little wave. Hope smiled back and mouthed, *"Hi."*

Hope's attention was turned when a man with a strong jaw and narrowed eyes stepped up to the pulpit and grasped the edges of it as if he thought it might try to escape him. "Evil is afoot in our little town," his voice bellowed. "Satan has great hold upon his people. And how can we know if we are in the clutches of the devil? Evil attracts evil. If you have witnessed witchcraft, or specters haunting the night, you can know you are in the gall of bitterness and must speedily repent before Satan has you forever in his grasp."

A hum of whispered voices rose inside the church as Hope shifted uncomfortably in her chair. According to this minister, just the fact she had a bewitched head in her cabin meant she herself was wicked. How could that be true? She'd only ever behaved saintly. Oh sure, she had her momentary slips, but her heart was pure. And Conall? Sure, he was uncouth, and had unclean thoughts, but she remembered clearly the day he protected her from an evil man. And would this minister say that as a victim of witchcraft, Conall himself was wicked?

Hope much preferred the minister of her previous town. He was a kind-hearted man who would give a person the food off his table and go hungry himself rather than see someone in need. He personified faith, hope, and charity.

Hope endured the entire service, but it left her with a sick feeling in her stomach. If Conall was found in her possession, she had no doubt this congregation would judge *her* guilty of witchcraft and execute her. There very well may be a witch in the vicinity, but it was most definitely not her!

Hope needed to find the witch and Conall's body and resolve this issue before she got burned at the stake. She searched the faces of the people around her. How would she even recognize a witch if she saw one?

If there was one thing Hope was good at, it was reasoning. This sermon would give any god-fearing Christian a good dose of worry, but a witch? A witch feared nothing. Hope searched each expression for a tale-tell sign of confidence.

As Hope's eyes went from face to face, she saw only fear. And then she saw the preacher's wife. She was a stern woman with not a hint of fear. No, it could not possibly be her.

The woman seemed to feel Hope's gaze. A jolt went through Hope when the preacher's wife glared at her. Could she. . .? No, not the preacher's wife. Of course, Hope had met one other so-called religious man with a heart filled with wickedness. She knew all too well that the people who professed righteousness could have the blackest of hearts.

By the end of the sermon, the congregation was missing only two things—torches and pitchforks. The preacher worked them up into such a frenzy that Hope wondered how they could all leave peaceably. She slipped out at the end, not speaking a word to anyone, and made her way back to the cabin.

*   *   *   *   *

Conall examined Hope's clothing lying about. Normally, she cleaned up before leaving, but he'd put her into a tizzy before she left. He relished the memory of it. Now he was once again left with silence, though Hope's voice seemed to echo in the cabin. Her presence had a powerful effect on the environment around her. She'd had a powerful effect on him too, if he were being completely honest with himself.

Hope threw open the door to the cabin. "The people of this town are crazy! I thought the days of witch trials were over, but apparently Salem taught us nothing." She slammed the door,

86

pulled off her hat, and replaced it in the box. "These people are practically salivating to catch themselves a witch. And do you know who is likely their first victim?" Hope turned her anxious eyes on Conall. "Me!"

"Why would they think someone like you could be evil?" Conall scoffed.

"Oh, I don't know. How about the fact I am talking to a severed head?"

"You've never behaved in any way other than kind and compassionate—except for the time you threw me into a chamber pot."

"That is exactly what I was thinking!"

"If they capture you, what will they likely do to you?"

"Gaging by the frenzy the congregation was worked into, I'd say there are several options. They could drown me, burn me at the stake, or hang me. None of these are good outcomes. I should have stayed in Albany. At least I would have had a quick death."

"Whoa," Conall said. "What do you mean you would have had a quick death?"

"Um," Hope stammered. "Well, you remember Eli?"

"The snake who annulled your marriage?"

"Yeah. He came looking for me. Apparently, he has witnesses who say they saw me murder my father."

Conall breathed out a curse. "You did not kill your father."

"You don't think I know that?"

"In my eight hundred years of life, I have never seen a woman with more atrocious luck."

"Wait." Hope gasped. "You are eight hundred years old?"

"Give or take. I don't much keep track anymore. Now back to the matter at hand. I think it best if you keep me with you at all times."

"Oh yeah," Hope said, "because I would be much safer carrying around the thing that would get me killed if I am caught with it."

"No," Conall said. "You would simply be much safer with me around."

"But you're just a head."

"I may not have as much power as I do with my body intact, but I do have some."

Hope's curiosity rose. Her memory flashed back to when Conall made Eli disappear and then disappeared himself. "What can you do?"

"Look in the mirror," he said.

Hope walked over to the table at her bedside and lifted the mirror. Her eyes were wide, her face pale. She appeared like she'd had a fright. Well, she had! And then she was gone.

Hope gasped as her hand slapped against her cheeks. She was still there. She could feel her flesh under her palms, but she could no longer see her own face. "How did you do that?"

And then she was back, her wide eyes blinking.

"It's an illusion," Conall said, sounding breathless.

Hope looked over to him. There was a sheen of sweat on his brow. "You look like you've run a great distance."

"Using my power is not as easy when there is so much less of me. But it's enough to afford you some protection."

"I did not think you cared."

"I don't," he said. "You are my best bet at getting my body back. If you are executed, that won't happen."

"Right," Hope said with a hint of a smile, and then she shook her head. "Nope, that is not it. You really care whether I live or die."

Conall scowled.

Hope knelt beside him. He took a quick glance at her face before looking away. Hope leaned forward and pressed her soft lips against his forehead. When she pulled away, she said, "You smell like pine and honeysuckle."

"Yeah, I know."

A warm glow filled her soul. For some reason, knowing he cared made her feel safe, comforted. "Thank you," she said softly.

"For what?"

Hope shook her head. "Just, thank you."

Chapter 11

Hope walked along the road toward the schoolhouse. Nervousness fluttered in her chest. "Come on, Hope," she mumbled to herself as she walked. "You've taught school thousands of times. There's nothing to be afraid of."

"You talk to yourself a lot," Conall said, making her jump.

How could I forget he's there? She looked down at the heavy burlap bag. Conall's head bulged from inside— sandwiched between her books and her lunch of bread and dried venison. It obviously wasn't a very comfortable way to travel, but she could not very well give him his own bag and raise questions.

"Shh," she whispered. "You agreed not to talk."

"I said I would not talk when you were around others. Now, unless you want people to think you are mad, I am taking a wild guess that we are alone."

"I shouldn't have brought you." She frowned. "I am only teaching school. I would be safer by myself."

"We agreed you are safer with me. Besides, I cannot abide the thought of being alone for the entire day. The last years in seclusion was a fate worse than death. Even you are not cruel enough to do that to me again."

"I would not leave you for years at a time. It would only be a few hours. And what do you mean, 'Even I am not cruel enough'?"

"Well, you did leave me in a chamber pot."

"For only a little while. Besides, you deserved it."

"So, you are only cruel when someone deserves it?"

"You are twisting my words. I am not cruel at all."

"You, my dear—"

"Shh," she whispered. "We are almost there, and there are people about."

Thankfully, his voice fell silent, though she was truly curious about what he was about to say.

Up ahead, a dozen children milled under a birch tree in the school yard. She frowned at the strange sight. The children she'd taught before had boundless energy—laughing and playing hard until she rang the school bell. These children looked as if someone had told them their favorite pet died.

Doctor Porter stood in the doorway of a small log building and lifted his hand when he saw her. He pulled out his pocket watch and glanced at it.

When she got near enough to speak to him, she smiled and said, "Good morning, Dr. Porter."

"Good morning, Mrs. Jones. You are right on time."

She nodded. "I pride myself in punctuality."

He took her hand and placed it in the crook of his arm. The warm smile he gave her left her feeling uneasy.

"Let me show you around," he said.

There wasn't much she could not see when she entered. There was just enough room for eighteen students and herself. Three rows of wooden benches spanned the breadth of the room, and a pulpit sat at the front. Beside the pulpit sat a wide slate board. The board surprised her—most schools did not have that luxury. This community really did value their education.

Dr. Porter led her to a small rickety bookshelf with a mere three books on the shelves. *They should have used the money they'd spend on the chalkboard on books instead.*

"These are the books chosen for you to glean your instruction from," Dr. Porter said.

"But there's only three," she said, and regretted her words immediately. It was too early in her employment to criticize.

Dr. Porter simply chuckled. "That is exactly what I told the mayor. I will see if I can talk him into bringing in a few more to add variety to the lessons."

"I would appreciate it," Hope said. "I also have some books that can help. Still, they are treasures to me, and I am not fond of the possibilities of what might happen to my books in the hands of children."

"I completely understand," Dr. Porter said, holding her gaze for a bit longer than she was comfortable with.

Oh, please. I really don't want another eager suitor.

"I would be only so happy to petition the mayor for more books," he said. "Then you can keep yours at home where they can be safe.

"Thank you."

"By the way," he said, "where do you live? You do know it's customary for teachers to board with their students."

She shook her head. "That is not necessary. I am currently staying in a cabin in Sleepy Hollow. It's owned by Mr. Smith. His wife has graciously offered it to me."

Dr. Porter paled. "You are living in Sleepy Hollow?"

"Yes," she answered, lifting her chin. The man made it sound as if she were living in the gutters. "It's a fine, sturdy building and more than adequate."

"Most of our residents would be afraid to reside in Sleepy Hollow. There are strange happenings there. Are you sure you would not rather lodge with the students' families?"

"I am certain," she answered.

"Well," he said, shaking his head and then sighing. "If you are committed. I would feel better accompanying you home."

"That is really not necessary."

"I insist. I will be there after school today to walk you home."

"I really appreciate the offer, but—"

"I cannot have anything happen to our new teacher. Now, the children are not expecting a full day of learning, seeing as it's your first day and you haven't had time to go over your lessons."

"That is not a problem," she said. "I am always prepared with lessons to give."

He nodded. "Alright, then you are welcome to give them. I do have to warn you: the mayor may stop by to observe what you are teaching these children. In fact, I would expect him to. I am afraid he is of the mind that you exaggerated your abilities."

"But I did not—"

"I know," he interrupted. "I have the utmost confidence in you. I just wanted to warn you."

"Thank you," she said. She had her work cut out for her with the mayor.

A moment later, Dr. Porter left, and she was alone in the schoolhouse. She lifted the flap off her bag and looked down at Conall's face.

"I will be calling the children inside in a moment," she said. "I just want to go over the rules once again."

"You call yourself Mrs. Jones?" he asked.

Oh shoot! She forgot about that.

"It's just a name. An alias, if you must know."

"But you call *me* Mr. Jones. Should I be reading something into that?"

"No," she whispered harshly. "You absolutely should not." She chanced a glance at him. He was smirking at her. With a huff, she threw the flap back over his face. "I need to start class."

Placing the bag inside the hollow of the podium, she went to call the children.

They wandered in, one by one. Only a few smiled at her. Something was seriously amiss.

"Hello, children," she greeted from the front of the class. "My name is Mrs. Jones. I will be your teacher for the rest of the school year."

The children eyed her curiously. She was happy to see students with a variety of backgrounds. These were not just children born of rich parents; several wearing simple attire sat alongside those with more expensive clothing. Even better, there were nearly as many girls as there were boys. Still, their countenances were sad.

Hope explained a little bit of her background—her role as a nurse in the War for Independence, her teaching experience, and her love of needlework. The children seemed only mildly interested. She then asked them to state their names and two things about themselves. They gave simple answers, but none of them smiled.

Hope stopped talking and paused. When all the children's eyes were all on her, she asked, "I have to say, I have never seen a group of youngsters who seemed so melancholy. Would someone like to fill me in on what happened?"

Eyes widened, but no one spoke. Finally, the small hand of a young girl in a baby-blue dress rose in the air.

"Yes, Martha," Hope said.

"Mr. Crane was murdered."

Hope's heart went out to them. "That is simply terrible. Did you all know Mr. Crane?"

"He was our last teacher," an older boy snapped, as if her not knowing was an offense.

Hope suppressed her shock. Why hadn't anyone told her? "I am sorry, William, but Dr. Porter and the mayor did not tell me, and I am afraid I'm not from around here. Have they caught the perpetrator?"

A small boy with sandy hair raised his hand and asked, "What's a perpetrator?"

"It's the person who committed the crime,"

"They'll never catch him," an older boy said.

"I don't think you have enough faith in the sheriff," Hope said.

"You don't understand," the boy continued. "He was murdered by a ghost."

"It was the headless horseman," a girl with red hair and freckles said.

Hope's heart pounded in a mixture of excitement and fear. "The headless horseman?" she breathed. "Are you saying there is a man riding a horse without his head?"

"A ghost," the older boy supplied, eyeing her curiously. "He was a Hessian soldier who had his head blown off by a cannon during the war. Every night he rides the road in Sleepy Hollow, searching for his head. At daybreak, he returns to the churchyard, where his body is buried. If you are unlucky enough to be on the road at night, he will cut off your head."

"That is what happened to Mr. Crane," the redhead girl supplied.

A deep, "Hmph," came from under the pulpit.

Hope gave Conall a kick. He grunted at the impact. She searched the faces of the children. No one seemed to notice, thank heavens. This was her first day of teaching, and she was determined to do an excellent job. Besides, she could do nothing about the headless horseman during the day. From what the children were saying, he only rode at night.

"I am very sorry about what happened to your former teacher," she said. "But do you think he would want you to neglect your studies?"

The students mumbled and shook their heads.

"Then in his honor, I think it would be best to show him what wonderful students he had and how much you have learned from him. So, I want you to tell me what you've learned so far this year. And please, no more speaking out of turn. I expect you each to raise your hand and be called on before speaking, is that clear?"

The students nodded as one little boy raised his hand.

"Yes, Abraham?"

"Yes."

"Yes, what, sweetie?"

"Yes, it's clear."

Hope smiled and held back a laugh. "Excellent."

An hour into the day, the door opened, and the mayor walked in. She smiled at him, and he sneered at her. How did such an unpleasant man get to be the mayor?

She returned her attention to the students. "Mr. Crane has certainly set your feet on the proper path of learning. Now before I explain where we will go from here, I want to hear what you would like to learn this year."

An eager hand shot up.

"Yes, is it Lizzy?"

"Yes, Mrs. Jones. I want to learn about the natives. They seem so savage, but they are part of God's creations, so they cannot be all bad, right?"

"I suppose you are right. Do any of you know any of the natives in this area?"

"There are no more natives here," the mayor said.

Hope turned to the mayor. She hadn't expected him to participate in her class.

"Oh, they've moved on?" Hope asked.

"You could say that."

"What's that supposed to mean?" Hope said, and immediately regretted her words. She was trying to get on the mayor's good side.

They're dead. And good riddance to them all."

Hope's stomach soured. She wanted to ask how they died, but she knew the sad stories of the demise of many native tribes. She did not want the mayor to give these children details that would give them nightmares—or even worse, harden their hearts.

"Does anyone else have something they want to learn?"

Several more children gave suggestions, and Hope assured them they would cover those subjects. When class was over, the mayor lingered as the last of the students wandered out. And then he lumbered over to her.

"Well, you've lived up to my expectation of you."

"I see," Hope said, gathering her things. She pulled her bag against her chest and squeezed her fingers into the fabric, trying to hide the fact that her hands were trembling.

"You asked the children what they wanted to learn? You are the teacher, are you not? You dictate what will be taught. Not the students."

"That is true to a point, but there is always room to cover the things that interest them."

"You don't understand. Then again, you are a woman, and thus have a weaker mind."

Hope's anger rose at the unfairness of his words.

"You are not just teaching facts, Mrs. Jones, you are shaping future citizens. They need to learn obedience and conformity. They must learn not to question authority. If you continue with your teaching methods, chaos will result in our little community."

"Obedience and conformity?" Hope said. "That is not what this nation is built on, Mayor. If the founders of this nation had been obedient and conforming, we would even now be under British rule. Our nation is what it is because we were open to new ideas, to the idea of liberty and the courage and sacrifice it took to get there. The kind of teaching you are proposing for me is un-American, Mayor, and I will not bend in my methods, and not you or anyone else will ever convince me otherwise. Now if you'll excuse me, I have more important things to attend to."

"Well, I never. . .," he said as Hope strode past him.

Her heart was pounding when she stepped out the door and nearly ran Dr. Porter over.

"Mrs. Jones!" Dr. Porter exclaimed as he rushed to keep up with her. "Is something the matter?"

"Dr. Porter," the mayor shouted at his back. "I need a word with you."

"Oh um," Dr. Porter stammered as he looked back and forth between them, "if you could just wait a moment, Mrs. Jones. I would like to see you home."

"That is not necessary."

"Dr. Porter," the mayor shouted once again.

"I am coming," he said, and rushed to the irate man.

Minutes later, her pounding heart slowed and her spirits sank. "Well, that job did not last long."

"Don't discount it so quickly," Conall said from inside the bag. "That man was a bully, and you put him in his place. I know his kind. He may grumble, but you've gained his respect."

"I highly doubt that. Besides, earning the respect of a man like that is the last thing I want to do."

"All right," Conall said, "then how about earning *my* gratitude? We've found my body, and I need you to retrieve it for me."

"That, Mr. Jones, is a fine idea."

Chapter 12

Hope put her needle and thread into her purse, along with a carved wooden cross. *What do you take to protect you from a witch and her headless henchman?*

"I don't like this," Conall said.

"What?" Hope turned her eyes on his worried face. "You are the one who has been hounding me about going after your body."

"That was before I had a chance to think about things. The witch has added murder to her long list of offenses. I just don't want you to be her next victim."

Hope shook her head. "I am not going to be. Do you know how many times I have had someone out to get me?"

"Twice."

"N—Well, yes, you are right. And I survived both those times. I will survive this time too."

"Do you have any thyme?"

"I have got all the time in the world."

"No, *thyme*, as in the herb."

"Oh," Hope said. "Yes, I do."

"I need you to make a tea from it and drink it."

"Why should I do such a thing?"

"It allows you to see past glamour and magical illusions."

"Really?"

"Yes."

Hope went to the cupboard and pulled out a jar of thyme and sprinkled a tablespoon in a small pouch. "You know, once you get your body back, we'd make an excellent team for hunting down witches."

"Not all witches are evil," Conall said. "In fact, most are not."

Hope shook her head. "That cannot be right. All witches are inherently wicked."

"That is a narrow-minded way of looking at things. Doesn't your Bible say that all who do good are of God?"

Hope frowned at him. "I thought you did not believe in the Bible."

"I don't," he answered, "but I cannot help but hear. Not only do you talk out loud, you read out loud, too."

Hope poured hot water over the thyme in her mug and let it steep. "You are speaking of Third John verse eleven. The scriptures also say that we should seek God for guidance, and not the guidance of mediums, fortune tellers, or witchcraft."

"And by that reasoning," Conall said, "it's better to consult a physician when you are sick, but it doesn't mean your mother who might also attempt to treat your illness is inherently evil and should be stoned for it. Does that sound right?"

"Hmm," Hope said, not wanting Conall to know he had her stumped. Was there something to what he was saying? Hope sipped the hot tea, and it warmed her. The taste was appealing too—a rich, earthy tea with mint undertones. She turned to Conall, intent on telling him how good the tea tasted when she took in a quick, astonished breath and coughed.

"You can see it, can you not?" he said.

Hope looked at him again and nodded. Lights danced and sparkled around him as his head glowed. At the base of his neck, the air around him shimmered—brimming with magical energy. And his ears . . . they were most definitely pointed.

"I told you the thyme would work."

"If you are to come with me—"

"I *am* coming with you," he said firmly. "As desperate as I am to have my body returned, I don't like that you have to confront it. There's no way I will let you go alone."

"Alright, but you'll need to stay in the bag."

"No," he said.

"No?"

"I think we should go with the assumption that the boy in school is right. My body is in search of me. Let's let him find me."

"But what about the witch?"

"She may not even be around. Why would she let him ride about Sleepy Hollow every night? It doesn't make sense. It looks like she may not have total control over him. Besides, my magical glow can light your way."

"I do have lanterns for that."

"You don't want to use them. Someone might see you. It's highly unlikely that any other traveler has consumed thyme tea this evening. No one else will see the glow of the witch's magical energy—which gives you the advantage. But still, you should wear your cloak, the dark one, and keep your hood up. So even if someone *were* to see you, they'd be less likely to identify you."

"I don't like this plan," she said.

"I am not thrilled about it either. If I could, I would leave you here where you are safe and go after my body myself. But I cannot, can I?"

"No."

Hope stepped out of the cabin and searched the wooded area around her. The moon was but a sliver and did little to help her. "I can barely see where I am going," she whispered to Conall, tucked under her cloak.

"That is good," he answered. "Others will have a hard time seeing you too."

"How soon before I can uncover you?"

"I would wait until we are far away from the cabin. So even if they do see you walking on the road, they won't figure out who you are and where you live."

"Right," Hope said and then stumbled over a branch, nearly falling down before finding her footing.

"Be careful!" Conall said.

"I *am* being careful. You try to make your way through the woods in complete darkness."

"I am never in complete darkness."

"Well, some of us don't have elven eyes to guide us. Us lowly humans simply have to deal with darkness."

"Stop complaining and tell me when you reach the road."

"What happens then?"

"You are going to walk along the road and wait for the headless horseman to show up. When he does, I want you to lift me up for him to see."

"Wait," Hope said. "How is he going to see you? He has no eyes."

Conall sighed. "He's guided by magic, Hope. Otherwise, he'd be driving his horse into trees, homes, and other obstacles, right?"

"Oh, right."

Hope kept the North Star in her sights as she moved. Without it to guide her, she could easily get lost out here.

After stumbling through the woods for a long time, her feet finally found the compacted surface of the dirt road. "Alright, I found it," she whispered.

"Just remember our plan," Conall said.

Hope nodded and then realized he could not see her. Oh, well. He knew she heard him.

She wandered up and down the road for what seemed an eternity. The darkness was oppressive, and she could imagine all sorts of creatures inhabiting its depths. Hope concentrated on breathing while her father's favorite hymn played in her mind.

> *I sing the wisdom that ordained*
> *the sun to rule the day;*
> *The moon shines full at God's command,*
> *and all the stars obey.*
> *There's not a plant or flower below,*
> *but makes Thy glories known,*
> *And clouds arise, and tempests blow,*
> *by order from Thy throne;*
> *While all that borrows life from Thee*
> *is ever in Thy care;*
> *And everywhere that man can be,*
> *Thou, God art present there.*

The darkness deepened and the shadows stretched across the road as the hymn faded from her thoughts. What was she doing out here? Why would anyone in her right mind wander a road that was said to be haunted? Hope brushed away the thoughts and continued to walk. Her left foot throbbed. She'd probably have a good-sized blister on her heel when this was all over.

A warm breeze blew against her back as the scent of old musty mildew washed over her. The hair on the back of her neck stood on end. Hope froze. She could feel something standing at her back. With her eyes wide, she slowly turned around. Her breath stole away, and she stumbled back.

The flaring nostrils of a monstrous horse with glowing red eyes blew her hood off her head as a scream gathered in her throat. She really did not want to look. Why did she feel compelled to look?

Her eyes rose to its rider. His shoulders were as broad as the side of a barn, and he clutched an axe in his gloved hand. But his head . . .

She knew what she'd been looking for but seeing it in the flesh—a monstrous figure on horseback with no head—there was no way to contain her reaction.

Her scream pierced the night air and sent the birds to flight. She screamed long and loud until she had no air left. And then her scream turned to whimpered sobs. She could hear Conall in the background, shouting at her. But she could not possibly listen to what he had to say while the headless horseman had his axe raised above her head.

To her relief, the monster did not swing immediately. He sat, his chest heaving as he regarded her. Seconds later, he dismounted. Hope stumbled back. Even without his head, he seemed larger than life. He moved quickly, grabbing her by the cloak. Hope struggled in his grip. The clasp of her cape broke free, and she turned and ran. A heartbeat later, he snagged her around the waist and turned her around. He drove forward and pressed her against the trunk of a tree.

Now she was too terrified to scream. He moved in closer, and she squeezed her eyes shut. She could feel him leaning over her. The familiar scent of pine and honeysuckle filled her nostrils.

Conall! He smelled just like Conall. Her heart calmed as her mind told her Conall would never hurt her. But this wasn't truly Conall. Conall was just a head, and he was . . .

Where was he? Had she dropped him?

Her thoughts were derailed when she felt the horseman's hands caress the sides of her head. *He's not a monster, this is Conall. This is Conall . . . this is Conall . . .*

Both hands traced her face and then brushed over her hair, lingering on her curls as he gently tugged them. She continued to try her best to convince herself that this hulking figure was Conall. The scent coming off him was the most compelling evidence. And she could feel his powerful presence. He *felt* like Conall. His hands continued their downward journey over her body.

All Hope could do was focus on Conall's scent. She kept Conall's face in her mind as his hands continued their inspection of her. Hope had once met a blind man, and he had used similar techniques to "see" her face. Only Conall's hands did not seem to know what was appropriate for him to touch and what wasn't. It seemed he wanted to "see" all of her. It was only mildly comforting that he did not linger on her breasts, but only brushed over them briefly. Still, her heart jumped at his touch. She was almost sorry when he broke the contact and stepped back.

106

Hope was appalled when she realized she had actually begun to enjoy his touch. What was she thinking? She had felt something akin to lust. No. She could not possibly have! Good, Christian women didn't lust—especially not after a headless monster who had murdered who knew how many people!

But to her eternal shame, she *had* enjoyed the contact—even if it were for a moment.

The only explanation she could come up with was that since he smelled like Conall, she had imagined it was Conall touching her. She'd simply had a momentary lapse in judgment. It had to be her mind's way of coping with something horrific by putting her into a less threatening place.

But lust? Why lust? Shame built up in her at the appalling emotion she'd felt. There would be hours spent repenting of this. Not to mention, she should confess this to the priest. But then, if she did that, he undoubtedly would have her burned at the stake.

Hope could hear the horseman moving away from her. She finally ventured a peek at him. The headless horseman leaned down and took the axe he'd dropped. He mounted his horse. It turned its glowing red eyes at her, as if regarding her curiously. She breathed a sigh of relief when it turned back to the road, took off in a gallop, and disappeared with its rider around the bend.

Why had he left her? It was said he was searching for a head.

He was searching for a man's head! His rude inspection of her was his way of confirming that she was a woman. And when he'd received the confirmation that she indeed was female, he'd left her alone.

107

But she wasn't alone. Her heart took off in a sprint. Where was Conall?

"Conall," Hope whispered harshly. "Conall! Where are you?"

He did not answer her. Oh, please let him be all right. Her heart rate spiked when the thought occurred to her that he might have been trampled by the horse's hooves. She'd failed him. How could she live with herself if something happened to him?

Hope stumbled over something lying on the ground. It felt like fabric. It was her cloak! It lay where she'd lost it. She lifted it up, and there he was. His eyes were closed. He wasn't moving. Not even a twitch, and there was only a hint of a glow. He looked . . . dead.

Hope brushed his hair away from his eyes and her fingers came away wet.

Her heart stopped. It was blood. He *had* been injured.

Chapter 13

"Conall. Oh please, speak to me."

He did not respond. She could not even tell if he was breathing. She lay him on her bed and felt at his neck to see if she could feel his pulse. There was something. Very faint, though. Hope choked back a sob when she realized she could not be sure she'd felt it.

She stoked the fire and lit the cabin with a warm glow. Hope could see Conall clearly. He looked deathly pale. She found the wound he'd sustained. There was a three-inch gash on the side of his head, and she could see a depression. His skull was fractured. "Oh, Conall. I am so sorry! How could I have . . ." She could not finish her words. They were too disgraceful. She had been enjoying the horseman's touch as he lay bleeding, injured, and possibly dying on the ground. The horseman wasn't the real monster. She was.

Hope boiled some water and let it cool enough to use it to wash his wound. Then she applied witch hazel and stitched it closed. She looked him over as tears filled her eyes. That was all she could do.

When she reached to pick him up and held him against her chest, she felt how truly cold he was. She sobbed. "Oh, what have I done?" Hope cried as she rocked him gently. Her heart was literally breaking. When had her feelings for him grown so strong?

He was rude, he was crude, and he drove her to the point of madness, but she cared for him regardless. And she was the reason he may not survive the night. That thought and the accompanying guilt was a crushing weight on her heart. She lay in her bed and covered them both in her blanket. She kept him cradled in her arms all night long. She slept very little and cried very much. When morning came, she wrapped him in her softest blanket and took him to school with her. Forgetting her fears, she put him in his own bag so that her books and lunch would not disturb him. She wished she could continue to hold him, but that would be a disaster. Someone would insist on seeing what she was holding. If he were found, there was no telling what would happen to him. So instead, she placed him carefully in the hollow of the podium below her.

She worried so much throughout the day that it made her sick. It felt as if someone had blown a hole in her chest with a cannon, and her stomach could not abide the thought of food. After three days of this, she had grown so weak, she had to sit while she taught. Even then, she felt as if she might pass out.

Conall remained as still as death. She hoped beyond hope that he was still alive. He'd saved her. She owed him her life. And she would gladly trade it if it would save him.

A plan formed in her mind. If Conall did not return to her, she would commit every waking moment to finding the witch and bringing her to the authorities—even if it meant her own death. It was the least she could do to make restitution. Hope lay down in bed with Conall cradled against her chest and, for the fourth night in a row, once again cried until the wee hours of the morning.

*   *   *   *   *

Conall awoke with a pounding in his head and something soft and warm pressed into his face. He blinked his eyes open and found himself under the cover of a blanket with his face pressed into two lush breasts—a thin nightgown was the only thing separating them from him. The smell of Hope's lavender soap, mixed with her own unique scent, surrounded him. He'd think himself in heaven if he weren't in so much pain.

"Hope?" he mumbled against her soft skin.

"Conall?" she cried out as the blanket was ripped away. Hope's tear-streaked face came into view. Her eyes were red and swollen. It looked like she'd been crying—and not just a few tears. And then she broke into sobs, confirming his assessment of her condition. "I thought I had lost you."

She pulled him tight under her chin and then she loosened her arms. "Oh, I am sorry. I need to be gentler."

"What happened?" he asked. The last thing he remembered was Hope's scream. It had been horrifying, hearing her shriek like that and not being able to do a thing to help her. He'd used his power to shield her from view, but it did not seem to work on the horseman—probably because he did not have eyes to begin with. And then what happened?

Oh, right, she'd dropped him.

"It was the horseman's steed," she said. "He trampled you. He left a gash in your head and broke your skull. I wasn't sure if you had survived. I could not tell if you were breathing, and your pulse was so weak, I thought you would likely . . . die."

"Still, you took care of me?"

Hope nodded. "Of course, I did. I could not give up on you that easily."

"And what happened between you and the horseman?"

Conall's eyes narrowed when a crimson color gathered in Hope's pale cheeks. She turned away from him.

"Did he do anything inappropriate to you?" he asked. "So, help me, if he did, I . . . ." His words dropped off when he realized he couldn't do a thing. He'd rip apart anyone who put a hand on Hope, but in this case, he'd be destroying his own body. Besides, he had no way to retaliate.

"No," Hope said. "It's not that. I... well, it's my burden to bear."

"What's that supposed to mean?" Conall said.

Hope shook her head. "I don't want to talk about it. Besides, I am in need of a bath."

"I don't think you should be alone," Conall said, pressing his brows together. "I could use a bath myself. We should take one together." He smirked, attempting to liven up the mood. Hope's reaction caught him off-guard.

"What kind of woman do you take me for?" she snapped without a hint of humor. "I don't go lusting after every man I see."

"Where did that come from?" he said, appalled. "I said nothing about lust. I was simply teasing you, Hope. I knew you would not really take me up on the offer."

"Oh, I..." she began, as tears once again filled her eyes. "I am sorry." Her voice broke on the word "sorry." "I am really not usually this emotional. It's just . . . it's just been hard."

Something was seriously wrong with her. If only he could read this woman's mind. She could be so confusing sometimes. She gathered her clothes and stumbled out the door. He was left alone to puzzle about her behavior.

Minutes later she returned, completely clothed and her hair up tight in a bun. With her hair pulled away from her face, he could see dark circles under her eyes. Her cheeks were sunken in, and it looked like she hadn't eaten or slept in days. Perhaps she hadn't. That would explain her erratic behavior.

"We need to leave in just a few minutes," she said. "I cannot be late for class."

"You are not seriously going to teach school in your condition, are you?"

"Of course, I am," she said. "I cannot afford to lose this job. Food doesn't grow on trees, you know." She gathered some cheese and bread from the cupboards and stuffed them into her bag.

"Um," Conall said. "Yes, it does." He would have laughed at her blunder if he wasn't so worried about her.

Hope waved him away. "You know what I mean."

"No," he said. "I don't, actually."

She turned on him. "If I lose this job, I will starve and be rendered homeless."

"Do you really think Rebekah would evict you and let you starve to death?"

"How do you know about Rebekah?"

"You've talked about her."

"I have never told you about her," Hope said.

"You've mentioned Rebekah on several occasions, when you were talking to yourself."

"You are exaggerating."

"If I am, then how did I know her name?"

Hope shook her head. "Stop trying to confuse me." She picked him up and stuffed him into a bag with soft blankets to cushion his head. This was much better than traveling with his head pressed into the spine of a book.

"You are giving me my own bag?" he asked.

"You are injured."

"But—"

"Would you *please* stop arguing with me?" she shouted.

Conall snapped his mouth shut. There was no reasoning with her in this state. Still, there was one thing he had to know. "I have to ask, how many days will I have to endure before you get a proper night's sleep?"

"Today's Friday," she answered, "and I intend to retire early and sleep the day away tomorrow, if you really must know."

"That is the first reasonable thing you've said this morning."

Chapter 14

Hope awoke with a start. Her heart pounded when a voice mumbled from under the covers.

"Are you going to answer that?"

It was Conall. She must have fallen asleep with him in her arms again.

"Answer what?" she asked. *Knock, knock, knock.*

"Oh, my heavens," she gasped. "Who could that be?"

"Hope?" Rebekah's voice called out.

"It's Rebekah!" Hope whispered harshly. She sat up with Conall wrapped in her arms and pressed against her chest.

"Might I suggest you hide me in a box before she begins to worry and comes in?" Conall said.

"Oh, right," Hope said. She placed Conall in his box. She paused a moment to look him over and sighed in relief at the color he'd gained. He actually looked quite well. *Knock, knock, knock.*

She quickly draped Conall with cloth and pushed the box next to the wall. She put on her robe as she rushed to the door and opened it.

Rebekah's eyes went wide when she saw Hope. "Were you still sleeping? It's well past noon."

Hope nodded. "I have had a very trying week."

"Oh, really? What happened?"

Why did she have to ask?

Hope opened the door wide and stepped back, allowing Rebekah to enter. "I don't want to burden you with my troubles."

"Oh, nonsense," Rebekah took off her bonnet and sat down at Hope's meager table. "Is it the mayor? I heard he was giving

115

you a hard time. So, help me, I have about had my fill of the man! I may just have to remind him who built the city hall building."

"Did your husband build it?"

Rebekah shook her head. "My father did. I got the deed when my parents died."

"I am guessing your husband now holds it."

Rebekah had a twinkle in her eye when she said, "Yes, he does. When my husband and I wed, he gained titles to half the town's holdings—not that he needed them. His own wealth dwarfed my own. But the loving soul he is, he let me choose where we live."

"And you chose Tarrytown?"

Rebekah shrugged. "I grew up here."

"If you don't mind me asking, how old were you when you married?" Hope asked.

"I had just turned thirty."

Hope held back a gasp. "Did you worry you would never wed?"

"I was too busy caring for my parents' holdings to give it much thought. Victor was the first man who actually made me stop and think what it would be like to *have* a husband. He pursued me for over a year before I gave him my heart and married him. And I haven't regretted a moment of it since."

Rebekah stretched and pressed on her rounded stomach.

"How much longer before your baby comes?" Hope asked.

"She's due in two weeks' time, but I would not be surprised if she came early."

"She?"

"I am just giving my husband a chance to get used to the idea. He has his heart set on a son, but I know he'd love a daughter just as much. Though he claims he would not have any idea what to do with a girl. I told him girls are easy. They simply require hugs, kisses, and pretty clothes."

Hope smiled. "You are so right."

"Now." Rebekah straightened her shoulders. "I came here to invite you to dinner tonight. My husband's sister and her spouse are coming also."

Hope wanted to refuse, but Rebekah had already been so generous to her, she could not possibly. "I would be happy to come. What would you like me to bring? And what time should I be there?"

"Just bring yourself, and we will be eating at six."

"I will be there. Thank you for inviting me."

Minutes later, Rebekah left, and Hope's fretting began.

*   *   *   *   *

Hope approached Rebekah's house, and her heart leapt into her chest. Glancing down at the bag hanging by a strap slung over her shoulder, she whispered. "The minister and his wife are there. Maybe I shouldn't have brought you."

"It's too late to turn back now," Conall said. "Just keep me close enough to hear you."

"Alright."

"They won't think anything of it. Who would search through a bag of fabric and needlework?"

"Right," Hope said. He was absolutely correct. Still, her heart pounded as fear crept into it.

117

"Now don't say another word to me," Conall said, "or they'll think you're crazy."

Hope kept her mouth shut until Rebekah raised her eyes to greet her and said, "Hope! I'm so glad you could make it."

"Hello, Rebekah," Hope answered.

Rebekah looked at Hope's bag. "Are you planning on staying? The horseman hasn't been giving you trouble, has he?"

Hope shook her head as she attempted to hold back her shock. "No, I was just working on some needlework down by the river and then came straight here."

"The horseman?" The minister's curt voice cut in, and he glared at her. "Why should a proper churchgoer be worried about the horseman?"

"Oh, shush," Rebekah said. "I am just joking. Everyone with half a brain knows the horseman is not real. It's an old wives-tale that has been perpetuated by unfortunate happenings. A man with no head riding about Sleepy Hollow at night? It's ludicrous."

Two weeks ago, Hope would have agreed wholeheartedly. She could not fault Rebekah's reasoning.

"It's Satan's work," the minister said.

"And what does Satan have to gain from such a thing?" Rebekah said. "A story like that puts the fear of God in people. It seems to me that is counterproductive to Satan's work."

"But if the devil is gathering souls . . ." the minister's wife said.

"Then he should be gathering the souls of the wicked," Hope could not help but interject. "From what I have heard about Mr. Crane, he was a good man who cared very much for the children he taught."

"I am sorry," Rebekah said. "Where are my manners? Hope, this is Pastor Goodman and his wife—Mrs. Goodman, my husband's sister."

"Yes, I came to their service on Sunday," Hope said. "It's nice to meet you, Pastor Goodman, Mrs. Goodman." She put out her hand and shook the hand of both the minister and his wife. What luck. The two people most likely to accuse her of witchcraft were Rebekah's relatives.

Hope held the bag tight as she kneaded the fabric in her grip. Looking up, she was surprised to see Dr. Porter walking up the pathway.

"Oh," Rebekah whispered, "I forgot to tell you Dr. Porter is coming to dinner, too. I thought you might want to get to know him better."

Hope chuckled. "Are you playing matchmaker?"

"I admit nothing." Rebekah smiled with a glint in her eye.

"Hello, ladies," Dr. Porter said. His eyes lingered on Hope. "Hello, Mrs. Jones."

"We are not in school, Dr. Porter, call me Hope."

"All right, Hope. But then you can show me the same courtesy and call me Alden."

Hope nodded and smiled. "Alright, Alden."

When his eyes lingered on hers, she felt heat rise in her cheeks. He appeared interested in her. She might have considered the possibility of him courting her if her life wasn't completely consumed by the elf in her bag and the danger surrounding him.

A handsome man with strong features approached.

"Hope," Rebekah said, "this is my husband, Victor."

Hope nodded to him. "It's nice to meet you, sir. And I would like to thank you for allowing me to rent your cabin in Sleepy Hollow."

"You are living in Sleepy Hollow?" the minister fairly shouted the question as he shot a look at her. He walked forward and stopped just a few feet from her with a sour look on his face.

Oh, great! She'd probably just been branded a wicked woman.

"At *my* suggestion," Rebekah said. "If you are going to call anyone evil for her place of residence, it'll have to be me." She shot a pointed look at the minister.

"You are skating on thin ice, Rebekah. Lucifer would only be too happy to get you in his clutches."

"He'd have to go through me," Victor snapped as he glared at the minister.

Pastor Goodman shook his head. "You are both in danger of hell fire."

"And you are in danger of being thrown off my property," Victor bellowed and then he turned to his sibling. "I am sorry, sister, but I cannot allow anyone to defame my wife's character."

"And I must stand with my husband," she said as she narrowed her eyes. "Do not test my loyalties, brother. You should not have allowed your wife to rent out the cabin in Sleepy Hollow. As I have said before, the place has the mark of the devil." Her eyes darted to Hope.

Hope felt a jolt at her glare. There was something sinister in her eyes. No, she had to be mistaken. This was a minister's wife. Still, this was the second time she felt uneasy under her gaze.

"Now if we can put aside our differences," Rebekah said. "Agnes made a lovely meal. I would hate to see it go to waste."

At those words, Agnes's laughter filtered in, and she stepped into sight. Hope gasped when she saw who was with her.

"Mr. Henry?"

His smiling eyes raised to meet hers. "In the flesh."

"I thought you had returned to Williamsburg?"

"I did. Long enough to sell my lands and holdings and return here."

Holdings? Hope had not guessed that a man such as Mr. Henry would have investments. How much money did the old man have? Even as the thought crossed her mind, she had a twinge of guilt. She'd prided herself on not judging others, but here she had judged Mr. Henry.

"But how could you leave?" Hope said. "You've lived there for forty years."

"And I would say that was plenty long. I much prefer the scenery in Tarrytown." He locked his eyes with Agnes's as he spoke.

Agnes blushed. Hope had never seen a woman of that age blush before.

Rebekah took Hope by the arm and said, "I have been looking forward to this all day."

Hope smiled and walked them through the dining room door. The smell of roasted turkey greeted their entry and caused Hope to salivate. It was too bad Conall could not eat. It would be horrible to not be able to taste a morsel of food in eight years! Hope's heart ached for him. Sometimes she forgot how awful his state really was. She'd find a way to break his curse if it was the last thing she'd do.

Hope placed Conall's bag carefully out of the way beside the arched entryway to the dining room, and they all sat down. Dr. Porter took the seat to her right. When Hope looked up to his face, she was surprised to see him watching her. Hope turned her eyes down to examine the flower pattern on her plate.

"Pastor Goodman," Rebekah said. "Would you mind saying grace?"

"I am always happy to speak to my Lord," he said, and reached out to take the hands of Victor and his wife.

Hope took Rebekah's hand and then Dr. Porter's. When they were all holding hands, Pastor Goodman's prayer began. It was not like any prayer she'd ever heard said at a table. He spoke a good ten minutes—giving a short thanks for the food, and then a long list of needed protection from Satan and his minions, and then an even longer list of thankfulness for him and his wife being more righteous than all those around them. And then even more asking for all others to see the errors of their ways and repent before Lucifer dragged them down to hell. He seriously thought he and his wife were the only righteous people in town? By the close of the minister's prayer, Hope had lost her appetite. Still, she forced herself to eat. It wasn't Rebekah's fault her brother-in-law was such a pompous, self-righteous man.

They ate in silence for the next few minutes. It seemed the minister's words had rendered them all speechless. Hope felt sorry for Rebekah. She had worked hard to put together this event. Hope lifted the bite of turkey to her mouth and moaned at the moist, flavor-filled morsel. "This is really good, Agnes."

"Don't thank me," Agnes said. "I may have made all the fixings, but Victor's the one who smoked the turkey. He's simply brilliant at smoking meat."

Having broken the ice for conversation, the discomfort eased, and they made small talk. The minister and his wife spoke very little—which was a good thing, in Hope's opinion.

"How are you liking your job?" Dr. Porter asked.

"I love it. But then, I have always loved teaching."

"I am glad you like it," he said. "I do have to apologize for the mayor's behavior, though I must say you handled him very well."

Hope shook her head. "I am afraid my emotions got the better of me."

"Regardless, the mayor is going to think twice about trying to fire you. The repercussions could be dire for him. You make a compelling argument for your methods. Have you always given the children a choice in what they'd like to learn?"

"Of course. It helps the learning all around if they feel they have a say. And it gives them something to be excited about every time they come to school."

"That makes sense. By the way, I never did hear where exactly you taught before."

"Oh, um," Hope considered her words. If she lied and got caught in the lie, not only would she be sinning, she just might lose her job. Besides, what harm could it do to tell the truth?

What harm, indeed. Being hanged definitely falls under the category of harm.

But what were the chances that Dr. Porter would cross paths with Eli? Dr. Porter raised an eyebrow.

"Williamsburg," she said hastily.

"Oh," he said. "I have never been to Williamsburg. Do you have family there?"

Hope shook her head. "I was an only child when my mother passed away, and my father died in the war for independence. I have no other close family."

"I am sorry."

"It's fine. I have got good friends."

Dr. Porter looked at Rebekah. "Yes, you do."

As the night drew to a close, Hope worried about her travel back home. It was about two miles to the cabin. She would be alone on the road, and it was now well past dark.

Rebekah appeased her fears when she said, "Victor would like to give Hope a ride home. A lone woman should not be walking the roads of Tarrytown at night."

The minister's wife spoke up. "He doesn't need to put himself out, Rebekah. We'll take her home."

Hope was horrified over the suggestion. "I can walk. It's not an overly far journey."

"Oh, nonsense," Rebekah said.

"I would be happy to take her," Mr. Henry said. "The minister and his wife don't need to trouble themselves. Besides, I have some things I need to discuss with her."

"I would be grateful for your assistance, Mr. Henry."

"Then it's settled," Rebekah said.

Dr. Porter followed her as she got her bag. "I wish I would have brought my carriage. I would be happy to take you home myself. It would give me an excuse to continue our conversation."

"Yes, well. I appreciate your willingness."

"That looks heavy for a sewing bag," Mrs. Goodman said, causing Hope's heart to pound.

"I am also an avid reader," Hope said, "and books are rather heavy." That was a clever thing to say, and it wasn't exactly a lie.

"So they are," she said, frowning.

Minutes later, she and Mr. Henry were on their way.

"I am so glad you decided to stay," Hope said. "Agnes did not have anything to do with that decision, did she?"

"Of course not," Mr. Henry said. "I don't discuss my financial affairs with women."

"That is not what I mean, and you know it."

"She is a handsome woman, don't you think?" he asked.

"Yes, she is."

"You don't think I am too old for courting, do you?"

Hope held back a smile. "Of course not! You are a fine man yourself. She'd be lucky to snatch up a man like you."

"Oh, now, don't be overdoing it, lassie. I am a crotchety old man."

"I don't think that is how Agnes sees you. She seems quite taken with you."

"You think her affections are genuine? I thought perhaps she was too kind-hearted to break an old man's heart."

"No. She's over the moon for you."

A warm smile broke out over Mr. Henry's face as his eyes lit up. He shook his head and cleared his throat. "Enough about me, how are you doing, lass? I must say I have been hearing tales that concern me about your wellbeing. Are you sure you are safe living where you are?"

"I am fine. Really, I am."

"So, you haven't seen anything strange there?"

Hope did not know how to answer. She did not want to worry Mr. Henry, but it would be an outright lie to say she hadn't seen anything strange. Instead, she settled on saying, "I am fine, Mr. Henry. The cabin is sturdy, and I feel perfectly safe there."

Mr. Henry frowned but nodded his head. "I see what you mean."

Hope looked up. The light of the carriage lantern fell on her cabin as it came into view.

"Even in the darkness," Mr. Henry said, "I can see the craftsmanship that went into it. But," he turned to her, "if you have any trouble, any trouble at all, you let me know."

Hope nodded her head. "I will, but truly, there is nothing to worry about."

"I certainly hope there isn't."

Hope climbed out of the wagon, and Mr. Henry handed her the bag.

"Them books are heavy," he said, and Hope felt her face heat. Hopefully it was too dark for Mr. Henry to see and suspect something was amiss.

"Yes, they are," Hope responded. "Thank you for the ride. You really are a dear."

"Don't mention it, missy. You just take care of yourself."

"I will."

Mr. Henry waited until she was inside before he pulled away.

Hope latched the door, lay the bag on the bed, and sank down beside it, exhausted. Thank heavens the night was over.

"Hope," Conall's voice shouted from inside the sack. She lifted the flap. "We have a problem."

Chapter 15

"The pastor's wife is your witch?" Hope's heart pounded in her chest.

"She's not my witch," he sneered. "But yes, she's the wicked, black-hearted, whore of the devil that cut off my head. I'd recognize her voice anywhere. And she's probably on her way, if she's not already here. Now I need you to do exactly what I say and do it quickly."

Hope nodded. "What should I do?"

"You need to put a line of salt at the doors and windows. Make sure it's a continuous, unbroken line."

"Salt's expensive," she said, wondering why he would have her do such a thing.

"It also repels witches."

"Oh, all right. Really?" She sat him down on the bed and retrieved the salt. Thank heavens she had bought enough to get her through the season. She put an unbroken line at the door and across each window sill.

She came back to him. "I did what you said. Is there anything else I can do?"

"Do you have any rosemary?"

"There's a rosemary bush outside."

"That is no good."

"But I can be out and in in just a moment."

"No. Absolutely not."

"But if it means protecting you—"

"If you think this is all about protecting me, you are wrong. I am not a good man. I deserve what I got. You, Hope, are nothing like me. Hell, you are the most selfless, saintly woman I have ever met. And now you are the target of a witch's wrath. If something were to happen to you because of me . . ." His expression pained her. "I have been selfish and self-serving. You shouldn't be risking your safety for the likes of me."

"If I don't protect you," Hope said, her chest constricting, "who will?"

"It doesn't matter."

"Of course, it does!"

"You don't understand," Conall said. "When I met Lavinia, I behaved terribly. I was cruel to her, heartless. That is who I am. I have always only looked out for myself. What happened after was nothing less than what I deserved for all the terrible things I have done in my long life. My own brother banished me here, and now I have put *you* in danger, even risked your life. Time and time again, you've risked everything for me. And I have let you."

He sat silent for several long moments. "But no more. Your life is worth more than the life of someone like me. And I will not put you in danger again."

"That is quite the confession," Hope said. "You almost sound repentant."

"Stop. Just stop right there. I am not going to convert and become a Christian. I am a wicked man, and that is all there is to it. Nothing can change that. But for once in his life, this wicked man has decided to do the right thing. And you are going to do everything I say and do it exactly as I say it."

"Oh, really? And what do you expect me to do?"

"You'll need to leave."

"Leave the cabin?"

129

"No. Leave Tarrytown. But not tonight. It's not safe."

"And what are *you* going to do?"

"The same thing I did before you came. I am going to await my fate."

"Well, that plan is all well and good, but you are forgetting one thing."

"And what is that?"

"You, my pompous, overbearing elf, cannot tell me what to do. I would never leave you at the mercy of a wicked witch, and I am afraid you are just going to have to accept the fact that you cannot stop me from—"

A thunderous crash came from the front door, causing Hope's heart to take off in a sprint. She grabbed Conall from out of the bag and rushed to find a place to hide. Looking around the cabin, she found nothing. It was one room, with a small table and chair, one bed, and kitchen cupboards too small for her to climb into. The best she could do would be to crawl under the covers— like that would not be obvious. Instead, she sat down on her bed with Conall pressed against her chest.

The silence that followed was almost as frightening. "Was that Lavinia?" Hope whispered.

"Yes."

"But the salt will keep her out, right?"

"It should."

"What do you mean, 'should'?"

"Lavinia's a powerful witch."

At those words, there was another booming crash, but this time against one of the shuttered windows. Hope was shocked it did not break. Again and again, each of the windows rattled as if an angry bull rammed them.

"You cannot stay in there forever, Hope," Lavinia's voice screeched like an owl on the wind. "And I'm sure you know by now who and what I am. I could kill you, make you suffer a long and horrific death. But I am willing to give you a chance. Give me the elf's head, and I will let you leave town and live your simple, pathetic life in peace."

"Ask her to swear an oath in the name of Morrigan," Conall said.

"I am not going to ask her that," Hope said. "And I am not going to turn you over to her. I am sorry, Conall, but you are stuck with me."

"You don't understand, Hope. This woman is dangerous. She already killed Ichabod Crane and who knows how many others since she imprisoned me here."

"I am not afraid to die," Hope said.

"If she swears an oath and you turn me over, you won't have to die."

"Yes, but then I *would* be afraid to die. I could not possibly meet my Maker with that kind of sin on my conscience."

"Do it and then repent later," he said.

"That is not how it works," Hope said.

"Dammit, Hope," he bellowed. "I cannot watch her kill you."

"You won't have to."

"How can you know that?"

"I *don't* know. I have faith."

"Well, I don't have faith."

"No one is perfect."

"Have you made your decision?" Lavinia shouted.

Hope took a deep breath, walked to the door, and shouted, "You cannot have him. You are an evil woman, and I will not be a part of any of your wicked designs."

Lavinia laughed. "We'll see how long before you change your mind. /there are a lot of uses for the crushed bones of a saintly woman. Of course, I had better kill you quickly. If Conall corrupts you, I will have no use for you."

"And what happens if I convince Conall of the error of his ways?" Hope shouted.

Lavinia's laughter bellowed. "Now that would be a miracle. Though if you can accomplish it, your bones would be priceless. There's a big difference between a saintly woman and a true saint. Of course, it would also break the curse I have on him. Though the benefits would definitely make it worth it."

Ah ha! I know now how to break the curse! The beginnings of a plan formed in her mind.

"Hand Conall over to me, and I will let you live. Don't give him up, and I will slice you from sternum to pubic bone and make you both watch as I remove your organs one by one until you die. You have three days."

Silence followed. It seemed Lavinia had gone.

Hope felt a bit sick as Lavinia's words played in her mind. But still, there was hope.

"Don't even think about it," Conall finally said, his voice low.

"What are you talking about?" Hope asked.

"I can tell what's going on in that mind of yours. Lavinia's right. There's no way I am changing—especially not after eight hundred years. And you gambling your life on me—"

"But you've already begun to change," Hope interrupted. "I am sure with my gentle prodding, you could become a proper Christian in no time."

"You, my dear, are delusional. You might think Lavinia is bluffing, but I know her well enough to know she's not. She will kill you in the most heinous way and not lose a moment of sleep over it."

"I think we should start tomorrow."

"You are not going to listen to a word I say, are you?" Conall asked.

"I hear you," Hope said. "But I have my own mind, thank you very much."

"Unfortunately," he said.

Hope sighed. "It seems she has gone. It's getting late. We have a big day tomorrow. We'll both need a proper night's sleep. It's a good thing I won't be going to church services. I refuse to go to a church where the minister is wicked, and his wife is one of Satan's harlots. So, tomorrow is the perfect day to start your lessons."

"You shouldn't be leaving the house any—Wait a minute, what kind of lessons are you talking about?"

"Well, we will have Bible study, and then I have some lessons I used in school that teach about honesty, charity, faith, and other topics like that. I am sure I can adapt them to you."

"Is there any convincing you to turn me over to Lavinia?"

Holly Kelly

Hope was surprised at his expression. Conall looked like he'd sucked on a lemon. "You would rather go back to that witch than endure a few Sunday school lessons?"

"I don't think you want me to answer that question honestly."

"Honesty will be a key component in your rehabilitation."

"Can I offer another suggestion?"

"Absolutely."

"Just shoot me now. At least then my misery will be over quickly."

"Now's not the time to joke."

"I am serious."

"Now be quiet while I change. I am truly feeling dead on my feet." Hope lay him on the bed and covered his face so she could get ready for bed.

"I have a feeling," Conall said from under the blankets, "that no amount of sleep will prepare me for tomorrow."

Once Hope was dressed in her sleeping gown, she retrieved Conall, blew out the candles, and lay down with him.

"Um," Conall said. "How is letting me sleep with you teaching me to be a good Christian?"

"We are not sleeping together. Well, technically we are. But we are not. This is completely platonic."

"With my cheek pressed into your breast? I am sorry, but my thoughts are not platonic in this situation."

"You are just trying to bait me. You are not thinking anything of the sort."

"Believe me, I am, and without my body, it's beyond frustrating."

"Fine," she huffed. "You can sleep in your box."

"I don't want to sleep in a box. If you would just turn me so my face isn't pressed into your bosoms, I would be able to control my thoughts more easily."

Hope sighed. "Fine." She turned him away so that the back of his head was pressed against her. "Is that better?"

"That is a hard question to answer. My thoughts are more chaste in this position, but I would not say it's better."

"Oh, just hush yourself, or I *will* put you in the box."

He did not say a word after that. It seemed he really did not want to sleep in the crate. Well, truth be told, Hope did not want him to either. She'd become rather fond of snuggling up with him. She settled in place and sleep soon overtook her.

Chapter 16

"That makes absolutely no sense!" Conall scowled at Hope as she tried to garner more patience. "If anyone were to beat me with a lash, spit on me, and then deliver me up for crucifixion, I would feel nothing but pure hatred towards that person."

"That is because you are human."

"I am not."

"You know what I mean. You are not perfect. None of us are."

"I will tell you what I would do. I would gather my brother's army and lay waste to Jerusalem."

"But . . . that is not the point."

"Are you trying to tell me those murderers wouldn't deserve it?" Conall asked.

"They probably would, but—"

"No buts, that is exactly what I would do."

"And what of the children? What of those who were not at his trial and did not shout for him to be crucified? Would you kill them too?"

"Of course not."

"How would you know who is guilty and who is innocent? Wouldn't it be better to give them the benefit of the doubt and let God judge them?"

Conall seemed to consider her words. "Alright, if I can trust He would exact justice against the guilty parties, I might consider it. But how am I to know He would?"

Hope sighed. "It's called faith."

"And you lost me again. A person who claims to have faith is a fool."

"Gawh!" Hope exclaimed as she stood and paced the floor. "I was the fool to think I could convert you to Christianity."

"I tried to tell you."

"Yes, I know," she said as she continued to pace. And then she stopped and looked him in the eye. "But you are a good man. I have seen glimpses of it."

"Just because I am not pure evil does not make me a good man. Now you, Hope, are definitely one of a kind—honest, gentle, selfless, virtuous. . ... If anyone deserves mercy, it's you. If your God is so all-knowing and all-powerful, why did he allow a troll sucker like André to drive you from your home and threaten to take your life?"

Hope's chest tightened as she blinked back a tear. She had never allowed herself to articulate those accusations against God— even in her thoughts. She simply could not go there. Her faith was everything to her. She would not—no, she simply could not lose it! "God's ways are not our ways. I trust that someday I will understand. But for now, I must continue to exercise faith in Him." She stood, unwilling to discuss this further. "I think you've had enough lessons for today. Now I have a few things I need *you* to teach me."

"Like what?" he asked.

"Why did salt keep a witch out of my home?"

"Salt is a pure substance," Conall said. "Purity repels evil."

"Is there something I can wear to keep her away from me?"

"Sure," he said. "Sprigs of rosemary, the foot of a rabbit—"

"Ew." She scrunched her nose. "You want me to sever the foot of a rabbit and wear it like a trinket?"

"You asked. You also want to make sure you don't make direct eye contact with a witch. They have a way of seeing into your soul. Don't give her that advantage."

"But I have already looked her in the eye."

"Don't do it again."

"How do you know so much about witches?"

"Witches are supernatural creatures. Some have been known to travel between your world and mine. They've wreaked havoc in both our realms."

"What is your realm like?"

Conall sighed as a sadness settled like a shadow across his countenance. "It's beautiful. Where you have winter, spring, summer, and fall, in Faery it is always spring. Flowers bloom year-round, everything is filled with life. In the forest surrounding my home, the trees are tall enough to reach the clouds, and colorful pixies flit about like shooting stars beneath the canopy."

"Pixies?"

"Yes, little creatures that look like humans, the size of a small bird with wings not unlike dragonfly wings, and they glow in various colors of the rainbow."

"If you catch one, will it grant you a wish?"

"Hardly. It would most likely bite you."

"I wish I could see one. Do you think I could visit your world?"

Conall's expression darkened. "That is out of the question." His tone was sharp and completely unexpected.

"Why?"

Conall pressed his lips into a fine line. He scowled as if he were livid. And then he looked her in the eye. A jolt caused her heart to pound.

He was afraid.

"What is it? What would happen to me?"

Conall frowned, and silence stretched out behind him. Finally, he spoke. "The humans in our realm are treated little better than play things. Used only as passing entertainment. And when they no longer prove entertaining, they are discarded."

"Discarded?"

Conall sighed. "Killed."

"That is awful! But what kind of entertainment do we humans provide?"

"Hope, my dear, you are so innocent."

Confusion clouded her mind for a moment until she realized what he was talking about. "Do you mean they would take advantage of me," she said, disbelief thick in her voice. "But," she began, her mind going back to the time when Conall saved her from Eli, "You are not like that."

"No. I am not."

"There have to be those in your world that think like you. Ones that would not harm an innocent man or woman."

Conall raised an eyebrow. "If there are, there are not many."

"What about your brother, the king? Couldn't he do something?"

"My brother hates humans. He doesn't even bat an eye to a human being gutted like an animal and then roasted and eaten at a troll's feast."

Hope's eyes widened in horror as her stomach sickened. "Do they really do that?" His silence was his answer. "Have you ever. . .? She could not bring herself to finish her question. She wasn't even sure exactly what she was asking. Still, Conall seemed to understand.

"Humans are too intelligent and look far too much like Elves for me to take part in that."

"Did you ever attempt to intervene? Save an innocent life, like you did for me?"

Guilt clouded Conall's features. He hesitated for a moment before saying, "I think you have garnered enough information to protect you from witches. This conversation has grown tiresome. You need to gather your supplies while you can. Church services will be over soon, and then Lavinia will be free to return."

"She gave me three days," Hope said.

"And you think she's not above lying to get what she wants?"

Hope shook her head. She could not help asking one more question. "Why have you been so protective of me? A lowly human?"

Conall blew out a quick breath and paused. "I truly don't know. But just the thought of anything marring one as innocent and sweet as you. . .." He seemed to struggle to find the words. "It's simply unacceptable."

Hope's heart ached for the pain she heard in his voice. She was taken aback at what that meant. He cared for her.

*   *   *   *   *

Conall was an insufferable ogre.

"I will not leave," she said for the hundredth time as she stitched the hem of his trousers. She was nearly done sewing him a set of clothing. He'd need them when he was reunited with his head. The clothes the horseman was wearing were worn and tattered.

"I agreed to let you bring me with you. What more do you want, woman?" Conall growled.

"I won't rest until you are whole again. My father did not raise me to be a coward."

"He also did not raise you to be murdered and hacked to pieces."

"There's no call for being so gruesome."

"I am just telling you the truth!" Somewhere along the way Conall's tone changed from angry to desperate.

Hope put down her sewing and sank into a chair in front of him. She placed her hands on either side of his head, weaving her fingers in his hair as she brushed over the points of his ears—a physical reminder of how different they were.

"I get that you are afraid for me," she said.

"Damn right I am," he growled, avoiding eye contact.

"Conall," she said. "Conall, look at me."

Reluctantly, he did. His eyes widened as she leaned down, pressing her forehead to his. She closed her eyes.

She could not guess whether her intrusion was welcome or not. But her heart was telling her he welcomed the contact. "Conall," she said. "I know that this whole situation is crazy."

"You don't know how desperately I want my body back," he said.

"I am sorry. I cannot even imagine how broken you must feel."

"That is not the reason why. It kills me to know that I cannot protect you," he said, his voice defeated.

"Maybe you are the one who needs protection," she suggested gently. "I know that must be hard to accept. But you don't really have a choice. I wish you did. But I feel compelled to tell you. I care for you. Very much. I have never felt this way about any other man. And I will do all I can to see that you have a future."

"Hope." Conall breathed her name with such reverence, her heart pounded harder in her chest. "You need to know. There can be no future for us. If you think you'll save me and I will carry you off to some happily ever after, you need to know it won't happen."

Hope nodded, her head still pressed against his. She could hear the pain in his words. He did care for her. But there was nothing he could do about it. Fate would always be their cruel warden.

"If, by some miracle," he said, "my body is returned to me, eventually I will have to go back to Faery. Your best hope at a happy life is to leave me behind and forget me."

"And if I agree?" She asked with no intention of leaving him. She was simply curious as to where his mind was going.

"I will be able to accept my fate," he said, "happy in the knowledge that you are safe."

As if I would leave him to die. But perhaps she was going about this in the wrong way. Maybe she needed to let him know what he had to live for. That he did not have to play the martyr. At that moment, a plan hatched.

"I would ask one thing of you," she said. "I know I shouldn't. But I also know I cannot abide another minute without this one request."

"Anything," he said.

"Kiss me."

He closed his eyes, his expression stricken almost as if she'd asked him to cut out his own heart.

Her heart sank. He did not feel the same way she did. In fact, he seemed repulsed by the idea. Why did she not think this through? She was no siren; he would not be making life and death decisions based on his attraction to her. Or lack of. "I am sorry. I shouldn't have asked. I mean, if you don't—"

"Hope," he said softly, his eyes now on her. She blinked back tears, desperate for them not to fall.

Hope nodded and closed her eyes. "Yes?"

"You'll have to kiss me," he said.

Hope's heart took off in a sprint as her eyes flew open. "What? But I thought you didn't want to. I mean, there's no need to feel obligated."

"You think I don't want to kiss you?" His brows pressed together.

"You weren't exactly jumping for joy at my request."

"I have never wanted anything more. Truly. But it pains me that you have to make the first move."

Hope found herself once again unsure of herself. "I . . . I must confess. I don't know how. I have never kissed a man before."

He chuckled, raising her ire. Her expression must have shown her disapproval, because he said, "Don't be mad, my dear,

143

innocent Hope. Give me your lips and close your eyes, and I will show you how to kiss."

Reluctantly, she pressed her lips to his and closed her eyes. Warmth lit inside her, starting as a pinprick in her belly and growing to a roaring flame as he worked his magic. His mouth, coaxing and caressing hers, caused desire to rise in her. She opened herself to him and found herself leading, demanding. Exactly what she was demanding, she did not know, she only knew she wanted more. She felt his arms come around her and gasped.

His lips pulled away only to trail down her neck as he mumbled against her skin, "Keep your eyes closed. Don't break the spell."

"How are you doing this?" She squeezed her eyes shut as she felt him lift her up and wrap his hard body around her in an embrace so overwhelming, she'd swear it was real.

"Don't think," he whispered. "Just feel."

Once again, his lips found hers and she did just what he said, caught up in his heat as he made love to her with his mouth. The experience was overwhelming—his taste, his scent, the feeling of being encompassed by him. He felt powerful, with a strength like no other. Yet with her he was gentle, caressing her like he was a faithful follower and she his beloved goddess. It seemed an impossible feat, to feel so small, yet so powerful in his arms.

Far too soon, the warmth of his body faded. She shook her head, knowing the magic was fading. "No. Please, don't leave me."

"I am sorry, love," he said, breathless. "I have used too much power as it is."

His lips left hers. Tears trailed down her cheeks as cool air washed over her, turning the heat to ice. A sob shook her chest as she found herself alone. Opening her eyes, she stifled a gasp. Conall's face was ashen, his eyes dull.

"I shouldn't have used so much power," his voice rasped as his eyes drooped. "Now I cannot protect you."

Hope shook her head. "You don't have to. You told me what to do. I can protect us both."

"I . . . shouldn't have," his eyes closed as he breathed, "kissed . . . you."

"But you did not," Hope said. "I kissed you."

He did not respond. It was like before. He appeared dead, though she knew he wasn't. Hope found herself alone—a dangerous place to be with a witch bent on destroying her. Regardless, she could not bring herself to regret that kiss.

Chapter 17

Lavinia rushed through her chores as she fought back the nausea. That stupid schoolteacher could cost her everything—her husband, her status, even her life! If she had to, Lavinia would destroy the perky little woman and use her entrails to cast a binding spell. And Conall? If she were truly wicked, she'd crush his skull like a melon and burn his corpse. But she wouldn't. She'd simply hide his head in a more secure place. Besides, one never knew when one would need a henchman. If her husband ever discovered what she was, she'd definitely need one.

Rushing out to the well, she drew a bucket of water. Once the floors were mopped, she'd be done and free to pursue her art. If only Matthew wasn't so pious, she could open up to him about who and what she really was. But Lavinia knew her husband well enough to know, wife or not, he'd have her burned at the stake. He thought he was so righteous, but Lavinia knew better. He had more than his share of darkness inside his heart. It's what drew him to her in the beginning. And being the wife of the pastor, she was the last person anyone would suspect to be the cause of the town's supernatural troubles.

"Wife!" Matthew's voice boomed.

Lavinia's heart took off in a sprint. What was he doing home at this time?

He came bursting into the kitchen. His eyes immediately searched the room, his countenance lightening when he saw she was busy with her chores.

"What's the matter?" Lavinia asked.

"That school teacher is up to no good. Did you know she came to school with a sprig of rosemary in her pocket? I know you don't understand the significance of that, but I do. Rosemary is what the heathens use to ward off an enemy."

"So, what are you going to do with her?" Lavinia leaned her mop against the wall and stepped to her husband's side.

"There isn't anything I can do . . . yet. When asked about the herb, she simply said she'd gathered it to use in her stew. That lying witch! I know she's up to no good. I could tell there was evil in her the moment I laid eyes on her."

"Do you intend to accuse her?"

Matthew shook his head. "Not yet. I want the full support of the town."

"You have their full support."

Matthew shook his head. "I can't simply throw an accusation out there with only a sprig of rosemary for my reason. I need more to go on." He turned to her in earnest. "You can get it. You're a woman. Pay her a friendly visit and search for the evidence I need. I can tell you what to look for."

Lavinia smiled. "I will, husband. I'll do it for you, but I want you to do something for me." She stepped close and toyed with the button at his chest as she raised her pleading eyes to him.

His eyes took on a predatory glint. "But it's in the middle of the day. If I didn't know better, I'd say you have a bit of the devil in you, too."

Lavinia shook her head. "Just a desire to provide you with a child, my love."

"As long as your motives are pure and not filled with lust. The act between a husband and wife is for procreation only. Any pleasure gained is for the husband only."

"I understand."

Matthew left twenty-five minutes later to return to his ministrations.

Lavinia felt a twinge of pain in her lower back. She worried for a moment about her baby. Perhaps she shouldn't have seduced her husband in the kitchen. She shook her head. A few herbs would nourish the child.

She should probably tell Matthew she was pregnant, but she knew full well what would come next—months of celibacy. No, she wasn't ready for that. She'd keep her pregnancy hidden as long as she could.

She sipped a cup of raspberry leaf tea and gathered her supplies. She would see the schoolteacher just as her husband asked, but she doubted she'd let her in to chat. And Lavinia had no intention of finding evidence to lead to the woman's arrest. That would be much too dangerous. They couldn't have any inkling that Lavinia might be involved with the headless horseman. And the woman would undoubtedly talk.

No, there were only two ways out for Hope. She must leave Tarrytown or die. The latter scenario being the safest.

Chapter 18

Hope's heart pounded as her feet hit the road. She hastened her steps, anxious to get home. Not only did she worry the witch would intercept her on the road—the sprig of rosemary did little to add to her comfort—but she also hated that she'd had to leave Conall at the cabin. With everything going on, it was likely the safest place for him. *Please don't let him wake while I am gone!*

After all, it had now been four days. The time has passed for her decision to be made. She was living on borrowed time. But she could not leave, not yet. She had to figure out how to break the spell. Converting Conall to Christianity had not worked, and she was desperate to see him whole again.

Perhaps then we could share many more kisses.

The thought came unbidden to her mind. The feel of his mouth on hers—the way it worked magic with her senses. His arms lifted her up, pressing her against him. The warmth and hardness of his strong body under her hands . . .

"No, I will think of it no longer," she said, determined to follow through on her promise even as her heart sank at the prospect of living without the type of passion she'd felt in Conall's arms. "Hope, when did you become so shameless?"

"Shameless?"

Hope spun around and came face to face with Lavinia.

"I certainly hope you are not serious." Lavinia lifted a carving knife so that her eyes peered over the blade.

Hope's eyes widened as panic seized her heart. She turned and sprinted toward her cabin. If she could only get past the salt, Lavinia would—

Pain flared in her scalp as she pitched backward. Hope slammed against the ground and found herself lying on the road.

Lavinia's sneering face came into view. "You think you can outrun a witch?"

Hope struggled to catch her breath. "What are you going to do with me?"

"Which part? Come on, Hope, be more specific. If you mean, what am I going to do with your liver, I'm going to use it to predict the sex of my first child. Or perhaps you meant what am I going to do with your heart? I have reserved that to determine if my husband is faithful to me. or maybe you wanted to know what I'm going to do with your lungs? Those—"

"You are an evil woman with a heart as black as pitch," Hope said.

"I assure you," Lavinia said, "it's as pink and healthy as yours. Now, what was I saying? Oh, yes, your lungs will show me my future self. And your blood, it is the most important of all. Your blood I will use it to steal away the years of your life and reserve them for myself. That is, if you are as sickeningly virtuous as you seem to be."

"So," Hope said, doing her best not to panic, "you are not only a witch, you are a murderer."

"I am willing to do what it takes to be the most powerful witch in the New World. And I *am* the most powerful." Lavinia lifted a chain from around her neck. A large ruby in the shape of a teardrop dangled from the silver chain. "Do you know what this is?"

Hope shook her head.

"This is a talisman of my own creation. It is the link between Conall's two halves. Without this, he would be dead. If I destroy it, he will die in minutes. It also gives me control over his body. I tried to take control of his mind, too, but he was too strong-willed for that. So, to complete my designs, I must break him. Weaken him. Only then can I seize his free-will. But then you came along and messed up my plans."

"What are your plans?"

Lavinia laughed. "Power. It's always been about power. Do you have any idea how much magical energy Faery contains?"

Hope shook her head.

"I could literally rule the world with that much power. And Conall is the key. Can you even guess how angry I am at you for messing that up? For giving Conall hope?" She raised an eyebrow. "Quite literally, it seems."

"And what of your soul?" Hope said. "Eventually you will have to meet your Maker."

"I don't plan on ever dying, but if, on the off chance I do, I expect to exist happily in the bosom of Morgana," Lavinia said.

"Somehow," Hope said, "I think the devil might have something to say about where you reside. Hellfire and damnation are what awaits a person such as you."

Lavinia laughed. "I don't think so." The knife rose above Hope. "And now you will see what happens to those who cross me.

The piercing sound of musket fire rang out as the knife flew from Lavinia's hand.

Lavinia's eyes snapped up, wide and searching.

"Ha." Lavinia smiled when her eyes landed on something. Hope reached out to push Lavinia away from her, but Lavinia grabbed her around the wrist and wrapped a magical cord around it. Hope's heart pounded in fear, but then the cord snapped easily, and Hope scrambled away.

"I think it best you step away from Mrs. Jones," a familiar voice said.

Hope looked up and saw Mr. Henry, a smoking musket in his hand.

"Or what?" Lavinia chuckled. "You already fired off your musket, old man."

"You may be right," he said, strolling up close to the witch, "but that don't mean I am unarmed." He slid a nine-inch jeweled saber out from under his shirt.

Lavinia paled as she stumbled to her feet and stepped back. "Where did you get that knife?"

Mr. Henry raised an eyebrow.

"You would not harm a defenseless woman," she said.

"No," he sneered. "But you ain't no defenseless woman. You are a wicked witch."

He lifted his knife to strike her down when she raised her hand and shouted, "I am pregnant!"

His knife hovered as doubt clouded his face. "You are lying."

"No," she said, her hand raised. "I swear."

"Swear to Morgana."

"I swear I am pregnant," Lavinia said. "If I am lying, may Morgana strike me down."

Mr. Henry frowned. "You are comin' with me. We'll see what your sainted husband thinks about his wife bein' a witch."

"He'll never believe you."

"He'd believe me enough to have you searched. And if I know witches, they will always be found with their herbs and tools. Between my word, Hope's word, and the evidence they find . . ."

Lavinia reached in her pouch, uttered a few words, and threw something at the ground. Hope was blinded by a flash of light for a moment. When her eyes adjusted to the sudden dimness again, Lavinia was gone—a smoky haze, the only evidence she'd been there in the first place.

"Well, don't that beat all," Mr. Henry said, looking around. His eyes fell on Hope.

"Thank heavens you passed by this way, Mr. Henry."

"Providence is smiling on you, Hope. Now I think it best we get you home."

Hope nodded. "That is the safest place for us both. Lavinia cannot enter my home. It is protected."

"Now how did you learn to protect yourself from a witch?"

Hope pressed her lips together. Should she tell him? Show him Conall? What would he do? She wasn't as worried for herself, but she did not want him harming Conall. More than ever, she was determined to save him. She just hadn't figured out how.

But Mr. Henry was the kindest, dearest man she'd ever met. And if she hoped to restore Conall, she would need help.

Hope swallowed her fear and took a leap of faith. "I have someone I want you to meet."

Mr. Henry looked suspicious. "Someone who knows a thing or two about the supernatural?"

"You could say that," she answered.

"Let's get you home," he said. "You can introduce me to your friend later."

"My friend is in my home."

"If she knows so much—"

"It's not a she; it's a he."

"There's a strange man in your home? Do you two—has he taken advantage of your good nature?"

"What?" Hope gasped, heat filling her cheeks. "No. It's not like that."

"I certainly hope it isn't. I am not opposed to reloading my musket and forcing him to do right by you. Though it may take time to bring in a proper reverend."

"I am not going to marry him, Mr. Henry. Even if I wanted to, I could not." Her voice broke as emotion squeezed her chest. Her cabin came into view and her heart took off in a sprint. Conall was near. She always felt tremendous relief having him close by.

Mr. Henry frowned. "It sounds like you are already in love with the man."

"I do love him, but I am not . . ." She was about to say she wasn't *in* love with him, but she could not say the words. The truth was, she might be in love with him. She truly did not know what she felt. She was a jumbled of emotions—affection, exasperation, attraction, frustration . . .

Still, it did not matter what she felt. She could never have him. They lived in two different worlds. They were not meant to be.

"Does he love you?" Mr. Henry asked.

"No. Maybe. I don't know. It doesn't matter. He cannot stay in the colonies anyway."

"And you cannot leave? It's not like there's anything significant keeping you here, dearie."

Hope shook her head as she put her hand to the door handle. "It's complicated." She paused before opening it. "Now, I want you to keep an open mind, all right."

"You would be surprised how open my mind can be."

They stepped into the room. Hope eyes were on the bed. Conall's head bulged from underneath a light blanket.

"Looks like your friend isn't here," Mr. Henry said.

"He's here, all right," she answered as she moved to sit down next to Conall. Her heart pounded as she took the edge of the blanket and pulled it back.

He was still sleeping.

"Hope Jones," Mr. Henry said, "why do you have the head of an elf on your bed?"

She turned to him in disbelief. "You know what he is?"

Mr. Henry did not look nearly as shocked as she thought he would. In fact, he did not look shocked at all, simply suspicious with a hint of disapproval.

"Are you the one who killed him?" he asked.

"What?" Hope asked as panic filled her. She turned back to look at Conall. "He isn't dead. He cannot be." Tears welled in her eyes. Did Lavinia break her necklace in retribution?

Conall's eyes fluttered for a moment and then they opened. Hope felt weak with relief.

"I am not dead yet," Conall said. "But when I do die, I would not put it past Hope to be the cause of it."

Mr. Henry gasped out a curse as he stumbled back. Thankfully the table was behind him to keep him from falling. When he finally regained his wits, he said, "It's alive."

"He's alive," Hope corrected. "Mr. Henry, I would like you to meet Conall."

Chapter 19

Hope wrung her hands as Mr. Henry sat her down at the table. It appeared he had a lecture in store for her.

"Your life is worth more than that of any elf," Mr. Henry said.

"This one's a prince," Hope said.

"I don't care if he's king of the Elven court."

"That is his brother," Hope said.

Mr. Henry shook his head. "Like I said— "

"I completely agree," Conall said from the other side of the room. "Maybe now you'll see reason."

Mr. Henry's eyes darted over to him in surprise and then returned quickly back to her. "Do you have any idea what elves think of humans? We are varmints to them. Killin' us is akin to squashing a spider to the likes of him."

Hope shook his head. "He's not like them. And how do you know so much about this?"

Mr. Henry pursed his lips and sighed. "Well, I guess there's no point hiding the truth any longer. Not after all you've seen. I am what you call a tracker—retired, mind you. I used to work for something called The Order. It was my job to track down unsavory supernatural folks and . . ." he hesitated. "Kill 'em. I had a knack for sniffin' 'em out. Though I must be losing my touch. You say Conall's been here the entire time?"

Hope nodded. "I found him under the floorboards."

"I knew there t'were evil afoot in this town, what with the people so terrified of the Headless Horseman. And then Agnes, bein' a witch, she filled me in on everythin'."

Hope felt faint. "No," she gasped.

"Oh now, don't look like that. She's one of the good ones."

"I never even knew there were good witches— "

"I told you there were," Conall interrupted.

Hope looked toward him and said, "Like I was saying. I never knew there were good witches until Conall told me. And there are good elves too."

"I know that," Mr. Henry said. "We had an elf on our team that was a healer. She was as kind as they come. I am just saying there ain't many of them."

"So, wait a minute. Did you stay because of the trouble here?"

"'Course I did. You think I would leave a woman as sweet as you when there's so much evil afoot? I have to do one last job. To make sure you were safe. Though I haven't had much luck so far."

"And what job is that?"

"Kill the Headless creature, of course."

"But . . . you cannot! Conall needs his body."

"That abomination killed the other members of Agnes's coven. She's the last of 'em. The horseman got all the rest. Agnes knew why they were being targeted, but Mr. Crane was a surprise. She had no idea why he had to die. He was a simple school teacher. I tell you, I've had a heap of trouble keepin' my eye on the two of you."

"But how do you know they're all dead? Mr. Crane could still be alive. Couldn't he have just run off? Perhaps this *is* just a witch's matter."

"They found Mr. Crane's body downstream. His head missin'."

"Really? When?"

"Night before last."

"Why did it take so long for him to turn up?"

"I could explain, but a delicate woman like yourself shouldn't have to hear such things."

"But I—" Hope began.

"Mr. Henry," Conall said from across the room. "May I speak to you alone?"

Mr. Henry frowned as his eyes darted to Conall. "Excuse me, Missy. I think the elf and I are overdue for a talk."

"But, but," Hope stuttered. "Why can I not hear?" She looked over at Conall. "You are not planning something stupid, are you, Conall?"

"No, Hope, I am not."

Mr. Henry strode over to Conall, picked him up, and strolled out the door.

Did they seriously just leave me? Hope knew exactly what they were going to talk about. That idiot Conall had been trying the play the martyr since her run-in with the witch. Well, they were not going to get away with it. And she was absolutely not going to let Mr. Henry kill Conall.

If only she could get a hold of that necklace. She'd rip the chain right off Lavinia's neck.

A thought struck Hope. A realization. Excitement flooded her heart.

Hope looked out the window, relieved to see there was still light outside. If she hurried, she could get away before they knew she was gone.

She cracked open the front door and peeked out. Mr. Henry and Conall were nowhere to be seen. Hope grabbed her cloak, a cord of rope, her sewing kit, and slipped out the door.

*   *   *   *   *

Earlier this morning, Conall had awoken with a strange mixture of feelings. He was terrified for Hope's safety. She'd been in danger. And he had been stupid enough to drain his power to satisfy his desire. Even now, he craved Hope's touch. He could not forget the feel of her mouth against his, her body melding against him. Though it hadn't been real, simply a magical illusion, it was seared into his mind. He desperately wanted to be reunited with his body for the express purpose of making love to Hope, teach her what it meant to be worshiped by one such as he.

But his desire was overshadowed by an even stronger emotion, one that surprised even himself—his determination to protect her at all costs.

Now he was about to do something completely out of character. He looked up from the stump he sat on to meet Mr. Henry's eyes.

"I want to help you," Conall said.

"Help me do what?" Mr. Henry said, narrowing his eyes.

"Destroy the witch. By doing that, the Headless Horseman will no longer be a problem, and Hope will be safe on both fronts."

"If I kill Lavinia," Mr. Henry said, "you'll die."

"I am aware of that. But, like you said, Hope's life is worth more than my own."

"She loves you," Mr. Henry said simply. "She may not be ready to admit it, but it's as plain as the nose on her face."

Conall closed his eyes, attempting to push back the pain and regret those words brought.

"And you love her," Mr. Henry said, surprise ringing in his voice.

"There can be no future for us," Conall said. "I cannot stay here. My brother may have banished me here for a time, but he would never let me remain here indefinitely. And you know why I cannot bring Hope home with me."

Mr. Henry nodded, resigned. "What do you want me to do?"

*　*　*　*　*

Hope rushed to get there before the light faded too much for her to see. Hurrying down the beaten path, she worried she wouldn't be able to tell exactly where she'd run into Lavinia. If she could not figure it out, finding the jewel would be an impossible task. If only she'd realized what had happened immediately.

It wasn't a magical cord Lavinia had tried to stop her with. Her hand must have gotten caught in the chain from the necklace—the one that held the key to breaking the tie between Conall and his body. And she simply had to find it.

Hope's eyes landed on a scorch mark on the road. *This is it! This is the place!* She searched the ground around her, kicking up leaves and rocks, attempting to reveal where the ruby had fallen. Minutes later, a glimmer several yards away caught her eye. She rushed over and dropped to her knees.

There it was. Its brilliance sparkled in the fading light.

Hope snatched it up. It felt warm in her palm. She could practically feel the power emanating from it. Dropping it in her pouch, she jogged along the road, hoping beyond hope that the Headless Horseman was predictable. She had to work quickly. Who knew what kind of plans Conall, and Mr. Henry were making?

Hope raced along the road, desperate to arrive on time and terrified of doing so. Her mind raced to come up with a plan. She would face the Headless Horseman and bring him back with her if it were the last thing she did. She pinned her hope on the talisman. It was the key. She was sure of it. Lavinia could control the horseman, and it had to be the talisman that allowed her to do so.

Best case scenario, the horseman would willingly follow Hope back to the cabin. There she would sew Conall's head back to his body—carefully, methodically, perfectly… and then she would smash the stone. Conall—being Elven—would heal and be as good as new.

Worst case scenario, she would tie the horseman up and drag him back. Yeah, she knew he was strong, and if his muscular physique were any indicator, insanely strong. And he was heavy. She just might have to tie him to a mule to complete the task.

Regardless of the situation, she was an intelligent woman. She could figure it out.

Hopefully.

Hope's heart stopped when she saw the horse's red eyes. Oh, right. The monster horse. How could she have forgotten him?

Looking up, the headless form of Conall towered above her. She struggled to take even breaths as she pulled the stone out of the pouch and held it up for the horseman to see. Though, how he would see it without a head, she had no idea. He stopped as soon as the ruby was raised. Perhaps he could.

Attempting to muster some courage, she shouted, "Horseman? I need you to come with me."

He seemed to regard her as he sat still upon the horse's back.

She took her first tentative step back and the horse took a step forward. Another couple of steps, and he mirrored her action.

This was working!

She kept the stone held high as she turned and walked toward home. She felt the breath of the horse on the back of her neck as she made her way. Her heart pounded with each step.

She looked up at a shout in the distance, and her chest clenched. It was Mr. Henry, raising his musket.

"Run, Hope!" he shouted.

She raised her hand and shouted, "Stop!" But her voice was drowned out by the sound of musket fire.

Terrified that he might have injured Conall's body, she spun around to assess his condition when she found herself lifted off her feet. A heartbeat later, her back pressed against him and his arm locked around her waist. The wind whipped her hair back as they galloped into the darkness. She heard Conall roaring in the distance, his voice filled with pain and regret. He must have been there with Henry, and he was terrified for her.

Truth be told, she was a bit frightened herself as they raced down the old country road. But after she gathered her wits about her, she realized something. The Headless Horseman had protected her from a perceived threat. At least, it seemed he did. Why else

163

snatch her up and carry her away? He even threw her onto the horse gently enough not to jar her.

At that realization, her heart slowed from a sprint to a run. Conall's arm was locked around her—as tight as an iron bar, but he wasn't hurting her. Pressed up tight against him, she felt every movement, every rise and fall of his chest. She ventured a peek over her shoulder, and her eyes followed the line of his thick arm to his shoulder at eye level with her, reminding her how massive he was. Thankfully, Conall's scent surrounded her, bringing her a measure of comfort at a time she might be inclined to panic.

When the horse slowed further, she turned to see the silhouette of the old church against the starry sky. The horse entered the graveyard and meandered between tombstones. A heavy silence surrounded them. There were no sounds of crickets, owls, or other creatures that tended to venture out at night—only the ghostly howling of the wind.

He passed by the church without pause and continued to the far end of the cemetery, toward the thicket. There did not seem to be a break in the foliage until they were nearly upon it. A gaping abyss opened up before them, and Hope's heart slammed into her chest. This was not what she wanted. The horseman was supposed to follow *her* home, not the other way around. The ground sloped downward into a hidden ravine. The darkness deepened as the last of the moonlight was choked out by a rocky tunnel. The only light that remained was the light coming from the glowing eyes of the steed.

The horse stopped. The horseman swung his leg over the horse's rump as he dismounted and pulled her down to stand beside her.

Hope stood, stunned, wondering what the headless horseman had in store for her. He stood before her as if regarding her. His hands lifted to her head and traced down her shoulders and to the front.

"Oh, no, you don't," she said, and pushed his groping hands away. He did not resist her as his hands dropped away. "You really need to learn what is appropriate and what is not. I don't need another week of penitent pleading for forgiveness. I happen to be a proper lady."

The horse snorted as if he'd heard her and voiced his disagreement.

Hope looked back to the headless man in front of her. "Do you understand anything I say?"

He bent forward, just slightly, as if bowing to her.

Hope pursed her lips as she regarded him. "Raise your hand."

At once his hand raised above his head.

Hope's eyes widened, and she gasped. "Merciful heavens!" Stupefied, she paused for a moment. "Stand on one foot." Without hesitation, he did as she said. Hope shook her head in disbelief. "So, you are to obey and protect me?"

He wobbled a bit as he tried to bow, still on one foot and with his hand lingering in the air.

"Oh, put your foot and hand down."

He did as she asked.

"You won't let anything hurt me?"

Again, he bowed.

"The bow must mean yes."

Another bow.

"What if I try to hurt myself?"

He did not bow but took a step toward her.

Hope's brows pressed together in confusion. As an experiment, she picked up a rock off the dirt floor and swung it toward her head. If she was wrong, she'd have a bump to show for it.

His hand darted out faster than she could see and clamped down over her wrist.

Perhaps there is a bit of Conall...

Hope shook her head. No, it was the jewel that had him protecting her.

Faint shouting came from the mouth of the cave. Distant but unmistakable. She attempted to run to the voices, but Conall's hand stayed clamped down on her wrist, preventing her from moving.

She turned to the horseman and whispered, "What if that is Conall and Mr. Henry? You need to let me go." She expected him to obey her and let her go, but he did not. He stood with her locked in his grip. Then, to her surprise, he turned and strode toward the back of the cavern, dragging her along behind him.

"What are you doing? You cannot just kidnap me and haul me off to your hidden cave! You are supposed to follow my commands!" She tried to break free of his grip as she said, "Let go!"

Not only did he not obey her, he continued to walk for what seemed like a great distance. She stumbled once and found herself swept up in his arms, pressed against him. The familiar planes of his chest and tantalizing scent brought back memories of the kiss she and Conall had shared. As soon as she realized where her mind was going, she shouted, "No, no, no, you will let me go at once. Unhand me and put me down."

And then she was falling. What had she done? It was going to hurt when she hit the ground.

Instead, softness cushioned her fall. She did not even get a chance to get her bearings before the horseman pushed her over and climbed down beside her.

What was she lying in?

She chanced a glance around, trying to see from under the hair that hung over her eyes. The little that she saw revealed a bed, hidden in the cave.

The horseman's arm clamped around her waist as he pulled her up against him, draped a knee over her leg, and settled down. Her sewing bag pressed against her back uncomfortably. At least she hadn't lost it.

But Conall was not close by. She had no clue as to how she would get him close to this headless behemoth plastered up against her.

"Seriously? You I . . . we are not sleeping in the same bed!"

She could feel every part of him that was pressed against her. She tried to slip out of his grip only to find it tighten. This was completely unacceptable!

His hand brushed over her hair, removing it from her face. How did he know it was bothering her? He did not stop there. His fingers brushed over the planes of her face, studying her features. Then they moved down to the nape of her neck.

She clamped down on his hand. "Stop touching me." The hard edge of her voice left no room for argument.

His hand pulled away and settled down over her waist. His breathing deepened, and she sensed he'd gone to sleep. She waited for what seemed an eternity before she attempted to extract herself from his arms, only to have him tighten around her again.

A good while later, she tried again, and once again he thwarted her attempts to escape.

Exasperated, she huffed, "Well, I am good and well stuck here. I hope you are happy. Conall will be furious with you, I will have you know. You remember him, don't you? He's your head, and he has a fondness for me. You don't want to anger him. I am not so happy with you myself."

She continued. If she could not get away while he slept, then why should she care whether he slept at all? If he even could sleep.

Finally, Hope was too tired to continue. Wrapped in strong arms and with a heavy thigh draped over her hip, she fell asleep.

Chapter 20

Lavinia settled into bed beside her husband—close enough to feel his warmth, but not close enough to touch. In the quiet of the night, she was more aware of the sinking feeling in her stomach. If only she'd killed Hope when she got the chance. That stupid old man had the worst timing in the world. And there was something unsettling about how calmly he confronted her—as if he'd dealt with witches before. And then there was the matter of the knife. Where an old man would get a demon's dagger, she had no idea.

She should probably set the Headless Horseman on him and kill him before he could cause her any more trouble.

She wondered briefly where her henchman was tonight. She shook her head. If she'd known how much trouble he'd be to control, she wouldn't have chosen to spell him. No matter what she did, she could not get him to cease his nightly rides in search of his head. In addition to the coven, she'd had him kill, he'd decapitated six men. Lavinia had to clean up the mess each time—not to mention the struggle it took to get the bloody, battered head away from him. It was fortunate that the men from the town knew enough to avoid riding the road through Sleepy Hollow at night. Five of the six men were travelers passing through, and thusly they were not missed by anyone in town. Ichabod Crane was an unfortunate occurrence. And the fact that his body rose from his watery grave to be discovered spoke volumes of the state of his spirit. Lavinia herself had seen his ghostly figure roaming about near the covered bridge.

She should have burned his body like she had the witches. Then there would have been nothing left for the villagers to discover. But she hadn't. And now there was a frenzy. They were calling for blood, for retribution from whomever was responsible.

Lavinia brushed her fingers at the nape of her neck and stiffened. Her heart took off in a sprint.

It was gone!

She stopped herself before she bolted out of bed. That would surely wake Matthew. She had to leave quietly—which she did, minutes later.

The moon lit the way down the road as her mind raced. It had to have been while she wrestled with Hope. She must have lost her necklace then. But where exactly did they fight with one another?

Lavinia searched the area, her eyes narrowing when brittle grass crunched under her feet. She squatted down and smelled burnt grass.

This had to be the place.

She scoured the ground, looking for the gleam of the ruby, but came up with nothing. If only she could search in the daylight, but it was too dangerous. Her husband might start asking questions.

Lavinia shook off the fear that that thought garnered. Why should she be afraid? She was the most powerful witch in the Americas. The problem was, she loved her husband—a man who would burn her at the stake if he knew what she really was.

But he didn't know. And while he remained ignorant, she could keep him by her side. She dreaded the possibility of what she might be forced to do if he found out about her.

She searched for a long while but came up with nothing. Her heart sank at the possibility that Hope had the stone. She became more and more certain of that as time ticked away.

What was that little schemer doing with it? She seemed quite fond of Conall, and she was an idealist—not to mention a bit naive.

"I know exactly where she is!" Lavinia said.

She pulled up her skirts and ran toward the church.

*   *   *   *   *

Hope strolled down a stone path. A canopy of trees surrounded her as wildflowers lined the trail—a few of them even poking their colorful heads through the pavestones at her feet. A pixie the size of a mouse fluttered in front of her, smiled, and then flew away. Hope searched the foliage and found many more pixies glowing like fireflies. The land of Faery was beyond beautiful. Why didn't Conall want her to come live with him here? They could be quite happy.

The ground shook with a low rumble, and her heart raced. She darted behind a tree as the ground quaked again and then again. Were those footsteps?

She peered around the tree and her heart stopped. A ten-foot ogre with a gnarly, wart-ridden face was crossing the path, dragging something behind him. As he continued to move, she heard the wailing of a man. And then his frantic face came into view. The ogre dragged him by the ankle, his head bumping along the ground.

Oh, right. Ogres ate people in Faery. What was she thinking? Of course, she could not live here. Hope's heart went out to the poor man. She should try to help him.

171

"There's nothing you can do." Conall's warm voice spoke in her ear. *"If you try to help him, you'll be added to the menu."*

Hope spun around, threw her arms around his neck, and buried her face in his chest. *"How can I not do anything to help? That wretched man is going to die."*

"I know, love. I am sorry you had to see that."

"How could a place so beautiful have such horrors?" She trembled in his arms.

"No place is safe from the terrors of the flesh. As long as men, or ogres, have darkness in their hearts, the innocent will suffer."

Another familiar voice spoke in earnest. *"Wake up, Hope."*

"Father?" She raised her head and searched for his face.

"Hope, wake up now!" her father's voice bellowed at her.

Hope's eyes flew open as something flashed toward her. She had just enough time to roll to the side as a heavy axe came bearing down on her. A scream caught in her throat as she heard the thud as the axe that was meant to sever her head hit the mattress. Scrambling off the bed, she searched for a route of escape. The horseman swung again, and Hope ducked.

Movement near the entrance caught her attention. Her eyes fell on Lavinia.

"You stole something of mine," Lavinia said, holding the ruby aloft.

"Look who's calling the kettle black." Hope looked back, not daring to take her eyes off the headless horseman for long. "You took Conall's body!"

"He's from Faery. Do you even know what they think of us?" Lavinia raised her hand as the horseman prepared to swing

172

again. He froze mid swing. She took deliberate steps toward Hope. "We are their playthings. They are happy to shower us with flattery, tell us they love and adore us, take from us our virginity, use us for their own pleasure, and then when they tire of us, leave us to the mercy of their world—where we'd most likely perish over a spit at a troll's festival."

"Conall already told me about how it is. But he's not like that."

Lavinia laughed. "Right. And what reason would he have to say any different? He needs you. Without his body, he is helpless." Her voice rose in volume as she spoke. "To them we are a plaything. Now *he* knows what it feels like!"

The anger in Lavinia's voice caught Hope off guard. Then she was taken aback with a realization. "You've been there. To Faery."

Lavinia's chest rose and fell as a tear leaked from her eye. She slapped it away. "Yes, I have." Her expression hardened. "I was banished there by those who were closest to me—my coven. At first, I thought it was a blessing. Faery is beautiful beyond compare. And the faery who found me was so handsome, I could barely breathe when he looked at me." Lavinia hesitated, her face crumbling into sorrow.

Miraculously, Hope felt a spark of pity. "What happened?" she asked gently.

Lavinia's hands trembled. Hope's eyes darted to them, and then Hope said, "You're going to kill me anyway. It might help to get it off your chest."

Lavinia answered in a low voice. "He seduced me. I was easy prey. I thought it was love at first sight. So, I denied him nothing. I gave him my body . . ." she sighed, "and my heart. He kept me around for several months. And then one bright morning, he promised to take me to meet his friends at a festival. I was so excited. I had never met any of his friends or relatives. I reasoned he must be planning to propose and wanted to prepare them. I was young and very naive." Lavinia's eyes took on a far-off expression, and Hope wondered if she even remembered who she spoke with.

"When we got to the festival, his demeanor changed." She shook her head as if still in denial. "Like night and day. He did not look at me, he did not touch me. When I tried to speak to him, he silenced me with a growl. Then he found his friends. He laughed and embraced them, and then. . .."

Lavinia hesitated.

"What happened next, Lavinia?"

Lavinia closed her eyes, releasing tears as she bit down on her lip. Her voice shook when she finally spoke. "He finally got around to introducing me—as the night's entertainment."

"No," Hope gasped, regretting immediately her surprised outburst.

Lavinia nodded. "It was a very long night. I was unconscious when they left the next morning. When I finally awoke, my body was so broken and abused I could not even walk. So, I found the hollow of a thicket and lay in there, hoping to die. But I did not die. I survived, and eventually made it back to the human world."

"I am so sorry," Hope said. "No one should have to endure what you did."

Lavinia glared at her. "I don't deserve your pity."

Hope shook her head and a realization struck her. "You don't think you deserve sympathy?"

"I did not get banished to Faery because I was a saint. I made mistakes, and one of my mistakes cost the life of my brother, an innocent boy. I may not have meant for him to die. But he was dead just the same. I begged and pleaded with my coven to forgive me. But they would not hear of it. And looking back now, I can see that I deserved my fate. What I did, how he suffered. It was unforgivable. But then I realized my coven was not innocent either. They were my guides, my teachers. They were the ones who showed me the spell—the one that would cure my brother's best friend. They neglected to tell me that when saving one life, another must take its place. His friend was saved, but John, my own brother . . . he was beyond saving. He died a horrific and painful death. When I survived Faery, I vowed to make things right. The guilty parties would pay."

"Did Victor know what you did?"

Lavinia shook her head. "He followed the path of my father—one that said witchcraft was of the devil. I never told him about my late-night excursions."

"What about Agnes? Are you going to kill her too?"

Lavinia shook her head. "She alone stood up for me. But she didn't stop the rest of the coven from banishing me."

"Lavinia," Hope said. "There can be forgiveness for you yet. God knows your intentions, and all you intended was to save a child's life. The guilty have been punished. You can choose a better path now."

Lavinia's eyes took on a sheen of unshed tears. "You of all people know how far I have fallen. I would have killed you if I had the chance."

"But you did not. Maybe that was God's way of extending mercy to you. He did allow you to come back, did he not?"

"That was not God," Lavinia said. "That was all me. I am a very resourceful witch."

"'From thy own lips, art thou condemned.'"

A deep voice spoke from behind, and Lavinia visibly paled.

Pastor Goodwin stepped out from the darkness of the tunnel, disgust on his face as he looked at his wife. Several other large men stepped forward, surrounding him. Lavinia backed away in horror.

"Wait. You don't understand."

"What don't I understand?" her husband asked. He gestured to Hope. "Here is the school teacher injured and bleeding, with the headless monstrosity holding his axe above her, and you admitted your crime. What other conclusions can I draw?" Without giving her a chance to answer, he said, "Bind her tight. And prepare for her interrogation."

"Please, don't hurt me," she screeched as they grabbed her and roughly tied her wrists together. "I am pregnant!" She looked at Pastor Goodman. "I carry your child, husband."

"I am not your husband," he growled and spat at her. "A woman can have only one spouse, and you are a witch. Your husband is Lucifer, and the child you carry is his."

"No," she screamed. "This is your child!"

"Lies!" he bellowed. "If it were my child, why is it you haven't told me? You did not want me to know because you carry the devil's child!"

"No, I do not."

"Bind her mouth. I am tired of her lies."

As they stuffed her mouth with rags and tied a strap of fabric over it, Lavinia turned her pleading eyes to Hope.

Hope could do nothing. Still, her heart went out to the woman. Despite the fact she had tried to kill her, Hope found she could not hate a woman who had experienced so much heartache and abuse in her life. And even now she was desperate to protect her child. Hope dared not raise her voice but mouthed the words. *I am sorry.*

Lavinia's eyes widened and turned to the ground. Then they snapped back up to Hope and back to the ground.

Hope's brows furrowed in confusion. But then Lavinia kept her eyes on the ground and nodded her head toward it.

Hope's eyes followed Lavinia's and landed on the gleam of stone peeking out from the dirt below.

The amulet!

Hope knew exactly what she needed to do. She had to restore Lavinia's hope in God and humanity by saving Lavinia and her child. And to do that, she'd need to restore Conall. If there was anything the Bible had taught her, it was that repentance was possible for even the most depraved of souls. And there was good in Lavinia, Hope was sure of it now. She was simply a victim who was fighting back anyway she knew how.

Lavinia struggled in her captors' grasps. Pastor Goodwin slapped her hard across the face.

Hope nearly missed her chance to retrieve the amulet as the shock of his abuse hit her. Thankfully, she recovered quickly, snatched the stone off the ground, and slipped it into her pocket. She looked back at Lavinia, and her heart sank when she saw her limp and unconscious in the arms of her abusers.

When one of the men stepped over and raised his musket at the horseman, Hope barely had time to step in front of the barrel.

"Hell-fire and damnation lass, I about shot you." His gravelly voice matched his gruff and rugged features.

"You cannot kill it that way," Hope said. "You'll have to burn the body. But first thing's first, let's take care of the witch. He'll not move unless he's commanded."

"Yeah." He nodded. "Besides, I don't want to miss any of the interrogatin'."

"Then you better hurry up. You are being left behind."

The men were so focused on Lavinia, they didn't give Hope a second thought, and the next thing she knew, she was left alone with the horseman.

With the amulet tight in her grip, she stepped up to Conall's body and whispered, "If there's another way out of here, show it to me."

He did not hesitate but turned and strode toward a dark corner of the cave and disappeared into a crevice in the wall.

"Wait, wait!" Hope shouted, tripping over stones in the pitch blackness as she attempted to follow. "I will need you to carry me."

She nearly shrieked when he swept her up in his arms. She took a few shaky breaths, trying to calm her heart, and then said, "Alright, get us out of this cave."

Chapter 21

Hope heard the horseman lumbering behind her as her cabin came into view. Leaving him behind, she flung the door open and searched for Conall and Mr. Henry. The room was empty. "Conall! Where in the blazes are you?"

She rushed to the back window to see if they might perhaps be around back. There was no sign of them. Shaking her head, she pulled the drapes. "Of all the times you choose to disappear, it would be when I finally have your body." The horseman stepped inside. She went to the door and slammed it shut behind him and then proceeded to pull all the curtains closed. Sprinting to the table, she cleared it of its dishes and cloth, then she grabbed her medical kit.

"You have to come back sometime, Conall, and when you get here, I will be ready." She turned to the horseman. "Well, what are you waiting for? I need you to lie on the table."

The wood creaked as he lay down. His enormous body sprawled across the surface, his legs hanging over the side. She looked toward the stump on top of his shoulders and frowned. "Now that won't do. I need you to scoot down so your head will have somewhere to rest when I sew it back on."

The horseman obeyed. Now his legs were completely off the side of the table. He looked as if he could easily slide off. It was just not large enough. Searching for a solution, her eyes landed on the bed. "Ah ha, this should do nicely." She scooted the bed next to the table and hefted the horseman's legs up to rest on it. It was just the trick to keep him from sliding onto the floor.

"Now, we just have to wait for your head. I know you've been searching for it for a long time. You must be excited at the prospect of finally being reunited with it. Though, come to think of it, I don't know how you could be. I mean, excitement happens in the brain, and you don't have one, do you? Your whole situation is perplexing. How did Lavinia accomplish the feat of keeping you alive without your head in the first place? Though I think it would be easier to keep a body alive than the head. You have your heart and all your organs. You are simply missing the thinking part of you."

Hope looked around. Darkness blanketed the corners of the room. "This won't do. I will need more light to work with. If I could open the curtains, that would work. But it's too much of a risk." She rushed to the fireplace, and her heart sank. There did not seem to be any remaining embers. "Conall, have you been about all night?" A low rumble had her heart pounding.

"Thunder? That better have been thunder." She shook her head.

Snatching a candle off the table, she retrieved the fireplace poker from against the wall. She poked and stirred the ash, looking for . . .

And there it was—an orange glow.

Pressing the wick against the lone ember, a flame ignited. "Providence is smiling down on me." She smiled and wasted no time lighting all the candles in the room. Then she set about making a fire in the hearth. When it was going strong, she looked up. Conall's body lay on the table, her supplies placed just where she'd need them, the amulet was safely stored in her pocket, and there was ample light. She was ready.

The only thing she was missing—Conall's head.

Light flashed from behind the billowing curtains. A heartbeat later, a thunderous boom made her jump. "Oh, please don't let it storm. There's so much I need to do. Pastor Goodwin's men will not wait for the storm to pass."

Hope paced the room, hoping beyond hope that Conall would return soon. After all, he could not possibly find the Headless Horseman, since he was lying here in her cabin. Conall and Mr. Henry would have to return sooner or later.

*   *   *   *   *

"I just cannot believe it was so easy to convince them," Conall said from inside the burlap sack. His face pressed against Mr. Henry's side. "Especially her husband. I thought he would have given us more trouble."

Light flashed through the fabric, and seconds later, thunder rumbled.

"I don't think that t'wer anythin' I said. I have seen that man's eyes wanderin'. This gives him an excuse to seek greener pastures, if you know what I mean."

"And I thought elves were heartless. How long do you think before they execute her?"

"Oh, that'll be a while. They'll want to torture her first. I would say, let's give it three days. If she's not dead by then, we will help them along." Mr. Henry jerked to a stop. "Tarnations, it looks like every candle in the cabin is lit. Is Hope afraid of a little thunderstorm?"

"Are you kidding me? That woman isn't afraid of anything."

Conall heard the door slam open and looked toward the cabin.

"You are back," Hope exclaimed as she rushed outside. "Thank the heavens! That is Conall, right? Bring him inside. We have to hurry!"

"What are you talking about?" Conall said. "Get me out of this infernal sack."

Her frantic face came into view. "I have your body! It's lying on the table, ready to go."

Conall was rendered speechless. How in the world did this slip-of-a-woman get the headless horseman here and on the table?

"How did you accomplish that?" Mr. Henry asked, echoing Conall's thoughts.

"I have got the talisman controlling him. Now, hurry up. We don't have much time. We have to save Lavinia and her baby!"

"Lavinia's what?" Conall asked, confused.

"Lavinia has been arrested and they think she's pregnant with the devil's baby—which of course is completely absurd. I mean, the devil doesn't go around impregnating women."

"Hope," Conall growled, gaining her attention. "What were you saying about my body?"

"Oh," she said, looking toward the house. "He's in there." She took Mr. Henry's hand and dragged him toward the door.

"Stop," he snapped. "Mr. Henry, you go in before and make sure it's safe."

"Don't be ridiculous. I have been waiting in there with him for hours. It's perfectly s—" Hope came up short as the horseman's figure filled the doorway.

"What are you doing off the table?" Hope said as if speaking to an errant child.

Mr. Henry pushed Hope behind him, and the horseman took a menacing step toward them.

"Don't," Hope said. "If he perceives you are a threat to me, he'll try to protect me."

"Protect you?" Conall said, not daring to take his eyes off his body.

"Yes." Hope stepped out from behind Mr. Henry and took the horseman's hand. "Now, everyone will follow me inside. I need to sew your head back on."

"Do you think he'll let you?" Mr. Henry asked.

"Oh, yes. He's been searching for Conall for a long time."

Moments later, the horseman lay down again on the table. Hope took Conall gently from Mr. Henry's grasp and turned him to face her. Conall was shocked to see a glimmer of a tear in her eye.

"If this doesn't work..." She could not continue.

"It'll work," Conall said. "If I were human, it would be impossible. But I am not. I have a tremendous ability to heal, remember?" He sure hoped he was right. If he wasn't—He did not want to even consider the possibility.

Hope nodded. "I am going to sew everything together before I break the amulet. I'm not going to take any chances."

"Alright." Conall felt Hope's hands tremble as she placed him on the table above his body. It felt strange having his neck pressed against the horseman's body. He thought when they were reunited, everything would just come together naturally. But the body below him felt foreign. Separate.

And then, pain hit him like nothing he'd ever felt before.

Hope screamed, and he knew at that moment, they were too late. He was a dead man.

* * * * *

Blood squirted from the horseman's neck, drenching the table in seconds. Conall's mouth gaped open over and over like a fish out of water. He was trying to breathe!

"Oh, please God, no!" Whatever spell Lavinia had cast keeping Conall alive was gone. Hope knew the clock was ticking. If she wasn't quick, he would die. Blood poured from his neck as he thrashed around.

"Mr. Henry," she shouted, "hold him down."

He threw himself on top of Conall's body and pinned down his arms.

Hope looked at the openings of his esophagus and the bones from the spine and carefully lined them up before pressing them together. If she was off, even by a bit, it would not work. Truth be told, it would be a miracle to work at all. Her heart pounded.

"Oh, please don't die, Conall," she said as she pressed the two sides together.

Conall gasped in a mighty breath of air, and his body stopped thrashing.

"You better work fast," he rasped. "I am not feeling so well."

Hope removed one of her hands to retrieve the thread from the table, and the two halves gapped apart. She gave a surprised shriek and moved to press them together again. "I need to hold you in place." She pressed her stomach against the top of his head to

184

keep it wedged together. He gasped for air again. "I don't have it lined up right."

Conall's body went limp, and his eyes closed. He'd passed out.

Or died.

No! She would not even consider that possibility. He had to be alive!

"Oh, dear heavens," Hope gasped as she pulled him apart again, her hands shaking.

Conall's eyes stayed closed, even when she pressed him back together. She was sure it was right. Well, she was mostly sure. But Conall did not have time for her to keep adjusting him. If she pulled him apart again, he would surely die.

At once, she stitched quickly—long, tight stitches—as she held him in place. She could not afford to skimp on the job. These stitches had to hold about ten pounds of weight.

It took a painfully long time to accomplish the task, and Mr. Henry had to turn him onto his side in the process—which was extremely difficult to do while Hope kept him in place. Finally, she'd stitched completely around his neck. She did not know if his veins, arteries, and spinal cord would bind together on their own. If he were human, this would definitely not work.

But Conall wasn't human. He'd healed from wounds that would kill any other human she'd known. Who else could recover from having their skull bashed in? But still, that wasn't nearly as devastating an injury as having his head cut off.

No, he *would* recover. He had to.

Once again, she could not tell if he were breathing, but when she pressed her fingers into his neck, she felt the hint of a pulse. She truly hoped she wasn't imagining the gentle throbbing of the artery.

Hope covered Conall in a blanket and sank into a nearby chair. A warm, withered hand patted her on the shoulder.

"You did good, lass."

"If it isn't enough . . ." her voice cracked as tears leaked out of her eyes.

"It's enough," Mr. Henry said. "I did not think it possible, but he's alive. He just needs to heal."

Hope took a shaky breath. "I'm assuming since the spell wore off, Lavinia is dead."

"Most likely," he answered. "Are you sad about that?"

She nodded as exhaustion overtook her. "She really wasn't as bad as we thought, and her babe was innocent," she mumbled. She lay her head down on Conall's arm, took his hand, and fell asleep almost immediately.

Chapter 22

Hope awoke to a pounding on the door. Her eyes flew open as she shot up in her chair. Looking down, Conall was still completely out and covered in blood. She ran her hands over him to reassure herself that he was just sleeping and hadn't slipped away during the night.

He felt warm to the touch, and his chest gently rose and fell.

She breathed a sigh of relief. He was still alive. In fact, his coloring did not look half bad.

"Hope," a frantic voice called out, "it's Rebekah, please open up!"

"Oh, dear heavens," Hope gasped. She searched around for a way to hide Conall. Desperate, she pulled the blanket over his head. But, now his feet were showing. "That'll never do." Rushing to her trunk, she grabbed another blanket and quickly covered the rest of him.

She nearly jumped out of her skin when the door flew open. Like a frightened child, Rebekah rushed in. "Hope. I am sorry to—" her voice dropped off as her eyes widened. "What happened to you?" She took Hope by the shoulders. "Are you hurt? Should I call on the doctor?"

"No," Hope shook her head and looked down to see her dress covered in blood. "I am fine. It's not my blood."

"Then whose blood is it?"

"That is a difficult question to answer."

Rebekah's brows scrunched as she caught sight of the table. Hope turned to look at it and cringed. Why did she ever think a couple blankets would hide Conall?

"Who is that?" Rebekah asked. She turned an accusing eye on Hope. "Is that. . .?" Fear washed the color from Rebekah's face.

She thinks I murdered someone!

"It's not what you think," Hope rushed to assure her.

"Then you tell me what I am seeing."

Hope hesitantly stepped over to Conall and pulled down the blanket. Rebekah gasped. Hope studied what Rebekah saw— Conall, lying down, pale with harsh splashes of red blood on his skin, black stitches sewn all around his neck holding together newly healed pink flesh.

And then there were his ears.

"Is he alive?"

Hope nodded. "He almost did not make it." The corner of a piece of paper peaked from under the blanket. Hope pulled it out.

Miss Hope,
I have gone to garner some help for you and Conall. I expect I will be back sometime tomorrow.
Your favorite crotchety old man,
Mr. Henry

Rebekah looked over Hope's shoulder. "Conall? Is that his name?"

"Yes."

"And Mr. Henry knows about him?"

"Yes."

"What is he? Where did he come from?"

"He's Elven. He comes from Faery."

"Like the land of the Fae? But that is only a faery tale."

Hope shook her head. "It's real."

Rebekah's eyes widened. "He's the Headless Horseman, isn't he?"

"Yes," Hope answered. "Lavinia cursed him and took his head."

"Lavinia," Rebekah gasped as her worry increased. "She's who I came to tell you about. I need your help. Matthew has accused her of being a witch." She gave a harsh laugh. "Well, I guess that one is true. The evidence is lying in front of me. But still, she's pregnant. Most women who are pregnant are spared until after they deliver. But her husband has convinced everyone that her baby is a devil's child. They're trying to kill it. They've given her herbs to rid her of her baby. So far, they haven't worked, but they're bound to eventually."

"Lavinia is still alive?"

"She was when I left."

"What can we do?" Hope asked.

Rebekah shook her head. "We have to convince them. Victor is there now, but perhaps we can help."

Hope rushed to grab her cloak.

"Um, I think it best if you wash and change," Rebekah said.

"Oh, right," Hope said, looking at her hand caked with dried blood.

It only took ten minutes for Hope to wash and dress in clean clothes. After all, she was on a mission to save a mother and her child. She took one regretful glance at Conall and then tucked

189

the blanket around him. She truly hated to leave him, but she simply had to. As they neared the place of interrogation, an oppressive darkness descended over them. It was so thick Hope could almost touch it. They kept to the trees, not wanting to reveal themselves until they knew what they were walking into.

Just beyond the break of the trees stood a mound of firewood, and then to the right, they could see the backside of a man locked in the stocks. Blood smeared the wood planks where his wrists and head were locked. He'd obviously been struggling. There was something familiar about him.

When Rebekah stepped around Hope to get a better look, she gasped and slapped her hand over her mouth.

Hope looked at Rebekah and mouthed, *"Victor?"*

Rebekah nodded. They had a lot of nerve, locking him in there. He owned half the town.

Hope gestured for Rebekah to stay put and crept forward. When the stock was close, she grabbed hold of the side and peered around to get a good look at Victor. His face was swollen, and purple bruising blossomed on his cheek. His eyes were closed—he appeared to be sleeping, though she didn't know how he possibly could be.

"Victor," she whispered.

His eyes flew open. "What are you doing here?" he whispered back. "Is Rebekah with you?"

Hope nodded.

"Both of you need to leave now."

"I have to free you first," Hope said. "Do you know where the keys are?"

"No. Leave me. I will be all right. There's nothing they can do to me."

"It looks like they have already beaten you."

"And you think I want my wife to be beaten too, especially when she's carrying my child?"

"They won't beat us."

"That is what I thought walking into this. But you see how far I got. All I did was argue with them. They've lost their reason. They're completely ruled by fear."

Hope examined the stocks and found a weakness. The nails holding the hinge were starting to work their way out. She looked around and found an old horseshoe lying on the ground. She immediately snatched it up and started tapping away at the nails, attempting to loosen them.

"They're going to catch you trying to free me. You need to leave."

"I will not leave you here to suffer at the hands of those men," Hope said.

The first nail loosened up easily, and she was able to pull it from the wood with her fingers. The second one took more time, but she finally worked it free. She used the hinge itself to pry the other two free.

Finally, all the nails were out. Hope lifted the plank and freed Victor.

"That wasn't so hard," she said.

"That is not the hard part, but I thank you for setting me free."

"And now we need to save your sister."

Shouts and cheers arose from somewhere across the camp. Someone shouted, "The creature is dead!"

Victor led Hope into the safety of the foliage. As soon as they neared, Rebekah threw her arms around Victor and sobbed.

"I cannot believe they did that to you!" she cried. "You are not a witch!"

"I lost it when they would not see reason. It's unfathomable that they would kill my sister's baby. They say it's of the devil, but it's not true." He shook his head. "I just cannot believe that Pastor Goodwin would kill his own child."

"He's an evil man with a black heart," Rebekah said. "And you did nothing wrong."

"I am the witch's brother. I guess that earned me some pain and humiliation. I kind of see their point. I did not see what was so obvious. I ignored the signs in Lavinia that something was seriously wrong with her. She was never the same after little Johnathan died. And then she disappeared, and when she came back, she was a different person. If only she had confided in me, perhaps I could have helped her."

"Blaming yourself will not help her baby," Hope said.

"I am afraid we may be too late. If the cheers are any indication, I fear they've already killed her child."

"What do they have planned for Lavinia?" Hope asked.

Victor swallowed hard and blinked back tears. "They say every freckle, every mole, every blemish on her body, is a mark of the devil. They plan to rid her of them by flaying her skin from her."

Rebekah gasped. "No."

"We have to save her," Hope whispered harshly.

"She is guilty," Victor said. "She admitted it to me herself. She's responsible for the headless horseman. She's responsible for many deaths. And despite her regret, there is a price to be paid for what she's done."

"Yes," Hope said, "but what they have planned for her . . . it's too much. Why won't they just hang her? Why do they have to torture her so?"

"It's Pastor Goodwin," Victor said. "To him, the fact this whole time she was right under his nose, sleeping in his bed, and he did not know what she was—It's an embarrassment to him. He's making her pay for his humiliation."

"But she's his wife," Hope said.

"That just makes for an even greater betrayal," Victor said.

"So," Rebekah said. "What do we do now?"

"You and Hope need to go back to the house," Victor said. "I have unfinished business here."

"No," Rebekah whispered harshly. "Absolutely not. You are not sending me away so you can die and leave me a widow!"

"Rebekah," Hope said. "Listen to reason. We came to save Lavinia's baby. We cannot risk you losing yours. I will stay and help Victor in any way I can."

At first Hope thought Rebekah would continue to argue, but she sighed, looking defeated as she rubbed her swollen belly. "All right. I will go. But please, both of you. Don't do anything stupid. If either of you die, I will be extremely upset."

"We'll be just fine," Hope said.

Rebekah gave her a quick hug. "You had better be." She turned to her husband, threw her arms around him, and pulled him in for a kiss. Hope turned away. Then she heard Rebekah say, "If you die, I will never forgive you. Do you understand?"

"I will be fine."

Once Rebekah had left, Hope asked, "Do you have a plan?"

"First," Victor said, "I'm going to attempt to draw the men out," he said. "Once it's safe, you free Lavinia and take her to your cabin. I will meet up with you there. Don't let anyone see you. You don't want these men to come after you when this is all over."

"It would not be the first time," she said.

"What?"

"Oh, nothing. All right, where are they holding Lavinia?"

He pointed through a thicket. "On the other side of those trees."

Hope nodded, and Victor turned to leave.

"Wait," she whispered harshly. "What are you going to do?"

He smiled mischievously. "I may have been caught off guard when they put me in the stocks, but I came prepared." And then he was off running into the trees.

Hope turned and made her way around the thicket. She stifled a gasp when she saw Lavinia. She sat stone-faced on the ground, stripped bare—broken, bruised, blood oozing from red stripes crisscrossing her skin. Her hands sat limp in her lap, tied at the wrists. A dozen men circled her.

"You are not so powerful now, are you?" A man with black hair and trimmed beard taunted and then spit at her, wetting her cheek with saliva. Lavinia did not respond, did not even blink.

Another man approached from behind with a whip in his hands. "You think you can bring evil to this town without retribution?" He raised the whip and struck her across her back, creating yet another stripe across her skin. "Believe me, you will feel the wrath of God before you are thrust down to the fiery pits of hell."

Hope shoved her fist in her mouth to keep from crying out. *Please, Victor. Hurry!*

Again, Lavinia did not react. Didn't cry out. Didn't move at all. Her face held a look of complete indifference.

A thunderous explosion shook the ground, and shouts erupted. Smoke filled the air, billowing from the south. Men yelled and stood, not knowing what to do. Hope waited for them to leave, but they did not.

Minutes later there was another explosion, this time coming farther to the west.

"We are under attack," someone shouted, and then chaos ensued. The last lone man in the clearing was Pastor Goodman. He looked more angry than fearful.

Striding over to a large tree trunk, he grabbed an axe and turned to his wife, fury in his eyes. He stalked toward her. "You brought this upon yourself, wife. You lied to me. You deceived me." His voice rose until he was shouting in anger. "You made a fool of me! There will be no retribution great enough for what you've done. Even killing our son wasn't enough. Torturing you will likely not gain me any more satisfaction than that did." He leaned down and roared, "Look at me!" His spittle hit her face as he bellowed, yet Lavinia continued to sit, unmoving.

Another explosion came from the north, but Pastor Goodman did not take his eyes off his wife. Instead, he raised the axe, preparing to bring it down on her head. "I am done with you."

Hope did not think beforehand what she was doing. She only knew she simply had to stop what was about to happen. So, she ran between Lavinia and her husband and raised her hands as the axe came down.

Chapter 23

Conall awoke feeling as if he'd been pummeled in the neck with the club of a mountain troll. He attempted to swallow but had difficulty accomplishing the feat. What happened last night? He couldn't seem to recall. Conall raised his hand to his neck and pressed down on the tender flesh and felt something odd—thread.

His eyes flew open.

He looked down to see his body stretched out below his neck. Raising his other hand, he inspected it as if seeing it for the first time. It was a bit battered and bloody, but it was his.

"By the forest gods, she did it," he rasped through his swollen windpipe.

He searched the room, surprised when he did not see Hope. Where had she gone to? His eyes fell on a note. He picked it up and read. Mr. Henry is going for help? For what?

He needed to find Hope. But first, he'd better clean up.

He could not help but smile when he stripped the bloody clothes off and washed his body in the river. Frigid water never felt so good. When he was clean, he strode back into the cabin and opened the chest that held the clothes Hope had sewn for him. Surprisingly, they fit. Hope had a good eye.

Now where in the human world was that woman?

A booming explosion caught him off guard and set his heart pounding. Something serious was afoot, and he knew Hope well enough to guess she'd be in the thick of things.

Rushing out the door, he looked to the skies and saw billowing smoke. And then there was a flash of light, accompanied by another booming explosion. Using his power, he cast a glamour

197

over himself to blend in with the humans and then transported near the commotion. He took a step back when a woman ran headlong into him. Reaching out to steady her, he mumbled, "Excuse me."

The young woman looked up and gasped, "Oh, dear sir, you don't want to be traveling that direction. There's a witch spreading dark magic and killing innocent people."

"I need to find my wife." He spoke the lie easily. "Do you happen to know where she is?"

"Who is your wife?"

"Hope Jones, the school teacher. I am her husband, Conall."

"Oh, I thought she was a widow. Um, I haven't seen her." She did not stay but raced off away from the commotion. Conall rushed into it.

Fire raged around him, burning the town hall, an adjacent home, and the jail.

"Mrs. Young," a familiar voice shouted. "This way."

Victor? If anyone knew what was going on, this man did.

Conall raced over to the voice and found a man nearly as tall as himself herding townspeople away from the flames. "Victor?"

Victor turned to him. "Do I know you?"

"I am Hope's husband."

"I thought you were dead," Victor said.

"Stories of my demise were greatly exaggerated. I am looking for Hope. Have you seen her?"

Victor frowned at him and paused. "I know where she is. Follow me."

Conall's heart clenched as a feeling of foreboding descended on him. As they neared a grove of trees, he heard an angry voice. Conall did not hesitate as he raced toward the voice. When he finally reached the clearing, his heart stopped at the sight—Hope with her hands raised as an axe descended down on her. Without a second thought, he reached out his hand and froze the scene in place.

Victor scrambled up behind him and hissed out a curse. "What did you do to them?"

"He manipulated time," Lavinia said, sitting on the ground, naked and bloody. "His kind are masters of manipulation."

Conall looked at his former captor and opened his mouth to make a snide comment.

"Don't . . . just don't say it," she growled.

Conall obeyed. There was something off about Lavinia. She looked broken. A shell of her former self, but through the cracks in that shell, he sensed a fury the likes of which he'd never seen before.

Lifting herself off the ground, she reached toward Hope, slipped her hand in her pocket, and pulled out her amulet.

Alarmed, Conall took a step forward.

"Don't worry," Lavinia said. "I am not going to hurt her, or you, for that matter. I think that is the least I can do to repay her for her willingness to give her life for mine. I give no such promise of protection to my once dear husband."

Lavinia brushed her fingers over Hope's hand and Hope broke free from the spell. She squeaked out a cry, still expecting the blow of the axe to fall on her. Conall rushed forward and scooped her up in his arms. "It's all right, love. I am here," he whispered in her ear.

"But Lavinia—"

"Lavinia is safe now." He looked back at her. Lavinia kept her eye on her husband as she strode by him like a predator circling its prey. He stood frozen with the axe in his hands until she caressed his face. The axe fell, striking the ground. He looked around, confused.

"What? What kind of magic is this?"

"And now you want to know about my magic? I could have taught you. I would have opened up to you everything I know. I could have given you the world, husband. Instead, you had me stripped, beaten, lashed, and even killed the child, our child, I carried in my womb."

Pastor Goodman roared as he slapped his hands against his head and dropped to his knees. His hands dropped away, and he gasped for breath, then raised his hands as if they could protect him from Lavinia's power.

"Lavinia, love," he sobbed. "I am sorry. I made a mistake."

"A mistake?" she shouted. "You call what you did a simple mistake?"

He shook his head. "I am sorry. I really am, but we can have another child. We can have a dozen, if you wish. Just let me live."

Lavinia glared at him. Hatred burned like fire in her eyes.

Pastor Goodwin looked around him, obviously searching for help. His eyes landed on Victor. "Please, brother-in-law. Tell your sister to spare me. Tell her to not do anything she will later regret."

Victor shook his head. "If I were to promise her anything, it would be that I would kill you myself."

"My brother has nothing to do with this," Lavinia snarled. "But I will make a promise to *you,* husband. I promise to make you suffer as I have suffered, only a thousand times over. And though I doubt you care, I will destroy every hand that was laid on me in my trials."

"Lavinia," Hope said.

Conall put his hand on her shoulders and pulled her up against him. He would be ready if the witch decided to attack her.

"Please, don't do this. You have a chance to make a better choice. I will help you. We all will help you move on from here and find a better life. Redemption is still possible for you."

Lavinia shook her head, a hint of amusement lighting her crazed eyes. "I appreciate the offer, Hope. But I am not looking for redemption; I am looking for vengeance. Conall?"

"Yes," he answered.

"You really don't want her seeing what I am about to do here."

He nodded. "It's time to go, Hope."

Hope shook her head. "No, Lavinia, please."

Conall did not wait for Hope's consent. In that moment, he transported the three of them to Victor's home.

* * * * *

Conall held Hope to his chest and kissed her head as she cried. "I could have saved her," she said. "If only I had more time."

Conall shook his head. "You cannot save someone who doesn't want to be saved." He looked up. Victor had his arm around his wife, his eyes filled with love as he looked down on her.

"I am so sorry, Victor," Hope said. "I know how you love your sister."

"There's no reason for you to be sorry," Victor said. "You did everything you could to help her."

"I cannot help but feel I could have done more."

Victor shook his head. "Lavinia is not a child. She was raised learning right from wrong. She did not sin in ignorance. Her choices are her own to make."

Hope nodded against Conall's chest.

Victor looked up at Conall. "I have been thinking of something Lavinia said. She said your kind are master manipulators. And I saw you manipulated time. What are you?"

"Manipulate time?" Rebekah's eyes widened.

Conall glanced at Rebekah and then turned his gaze back to Victor and shrugged. "After all you've seen, I might as well show you what I am." Conall dropped the glamour. They could now see everything—his ears, the black stitching around his neck, even the glow he emanated.

Victor gaped at him in shock.

"I am Elven. I come from a place called Faery. My brother sent me to earth as punishment years ago. Lavinia found me and removed my head. She kept me alive and forced my headless body to do her bidding. Then she locked me—my head—in your cabin." He looked at Hope. "Until Hope found me."

"And he's been with her all the time she's lived at the cabin," Rebekah said.

"Yes, he has," Hope said. "Well, at least his head has."

"But now that you are whole again," Rebekah said, "will you be staying with us, or will you have to go back?"

"He has to go back," Hope said.

"No." Conall rubbed his new, somewhat tender skin. The stitches hurt like pinpricks. "I cannot leave. I desperately need something from Hope."

Her brows pressed together in confusion. "What is it?"

"Marry me."

"What? But I thought . . ."

"I don't care what my brother says. I will not leave you. I love you, Hope."

Hope shook her head, in confusion. She stood. "Conall?"

"Yes, love?"

"Would you accompany me on a walk?"

"A walk?"

She nodded, resolute.

Minutes later, they were next to a small stream.

"You still haven't answered me," he said.

"Technically what you said was more of a statement than a question. Besides, you told me there could be no future for us."

"I am not going to keep waiting around for my brother. Time passes differently in Faery; days there translate to weeks here. He may not even show up in your lifetime. Besides, there is no future for me without you."

"I thought I was alone in my affection," she said. Her voice broke, revealing her tender feelings.

He stepped toward her and wrapped his arms around her. "After the kiss we shared, how could you doubt how I felt about you?"

"You said yourself that you have no qualms about seducing women," she said. "I thought myself a fool for imagining there might be more than lust in that kiss."

"I feel plenty of lust for you, but there's something else no other woman has ever elicited from me."

"And what would that be?" she asked, breathless.

"I would lay down my life for a simple smile from you, woman."

Her eyes brightened. "Really?"

He leaned forward and brushed her cheek with his fingertips. "Without a doubt."

She tilted her head back, licked her lips, and then closed her eyes. He chuckled as she obviously expected him to kiss her. He did not disappoint her as he captured her mouth with his and lifted her off the ground.

She wrapped her arms around his neck, causing a dull ache in his still-healing flesh. He only gave the discomfort a passing thought as he concentrated on everything about her—her taste, the feel of her body, the fresh smell of her. When he finally forced himself to pull away, she sighed and dropped her head against his chest.

"We should probably get married sooner than later," she said. "I have discovered I have a terrible weakness."

"You? You have a weakness?" He chuckled.

"It's not funny. It's rather embarrassing."

"I am sorry I laughed. What weakness do you have?"

"I don't even want to say it."

"Nothing you could say will change how I feel about you."

She stood for a moment, chewing on her bottom lip. Finally, she said, "I am feeling . . . lust. There, I said it. I am sure you are appalled."

He did his best not to laugh again. "I am the opposite of appalled—unless you are wanting someone other than me. Then I am afraid I would have to kill the man."

"Of course not. And murder is a mortal sin."

"It's a good thing I am not mortal. And as for your weakness, I could not be happier."

"You don't understand. Proper women do not lust."

"Thank the gods, you're not a proper woman."

"That is not a nice— "

He interrupted her with another kiss, which after a stunned moment, she returned with fervor.

Chapter 24

Conall held Hope's hand in his as they made their way back to the house. Fall leaves crunched under his boots, and the lingering smell of smoke mingled with the earthy smell of decaying vegetation, ripe apples, and baked goods. Strangely enough, it was a pleasant smell. In fact, everything around him was appealing—especially the woman at his side.

How he ever thought he could leave her behind, he had no idea. She was a breath of fresh air. With the innocence of a child and the strength and power of a dragon, Hope was a force to be reckoned with. And he had fallen under her spell.

Conall's heart skipped a beat when he caught another scent—musky like the scent of a wild animal. And then were other scents—charred, white oak, and honeysuckle. He pushed Hope back. "Stay behind me," he hissed.

"What is it?"

"Unexpected visitors."

The front door of Rebekah's home burst open, and Mr. Henry stepped out. "Now don't be shy! I have friends that need introducin'."

"This must be the help that Mr. Henry promised to bring," Hope said.

Right. The letter.

Conall kept Hope close to him, not trusting Mr. Henry's so-called "help."

Inside, next to Mr. Henry stood two men and a woman. The woman was Elven, with big green eyes and jet-black hair. She wasn't the worry; the man on Mr. Henry's left was a vampire, and the other next to him was a werewolf. *Strange mixed company.*

"Conall, Miss Hope," Mr. Henry said, "these are my friends in the Order. Rose is a healer, and Vladmir is the director, and Richard's a tracker like I once was."

"Why did you bring them here?" Conall asked.

"Thought we might need help. After all, it's not every day you come against a witch as powerful as Lavinia. And now that she's caught . . ."

"She's free," Conall said.

"How'd she get free?" the werewolf snapped.

"I helped her escape," Hope said. "You don't know the terrible things they were doing to her, what they planned to do to her."

"You stupid woman—" the werewolf began, and he then slapped his hands against his throat. His eyes bulged, and his face turned a blotchy crimson color.

"Are you all right?" Hope asked.

"Conall," Mr. Henry chided. "Let him go."

Conall hesitated, giving the shifter a chance to reconsider how he should treat Hope in the future. Finally, he released him. The werewolf took in a gasping breath. Rose shook her head. "I told you not to provoke him, Richard."

He coughed. "I did not even look at him."

"Yes," Rose said, her eyes sparkling, "well, he's obviously taken a liking to the human girl." The elf approached Conall hesitantly. "Your majesty, I don't know if you remember me, but we met at a festival near the Chiffland village years ago."

207

Conall examined her, waiting for recognition to hit him. But he got nothing. "Sorry, I don't remember you."

She shook her head. "No, it's all right. I did not really expect you to remember. I am the daughter of a farmer. No one you would take notice of."

He nodded. "How did you end up here?"

She shrugged. "I spurned the affections of a spell spinner and he banished me."

"He did not have the right to do that," Conall said, wondering who had the audacity to banish her to another realm.

"There's not much I could do about it from this side."

"If you could go back, would you?" Hope asked.

Rose turned to her. "If you had asked me that ten years ago, I would have said, 'Yes, absolutely.' But I am happy here. I have a husband, a daughter."

"Speaking of marriage," Rebekah said, turning to Hope, "have you answered Conall?"

Red blossomed in Hope's cheeks. "I have."

"Well?" Rebekah asked. "What did you tell him?"

"I told him yes."

"Oh, sweetie!" Rebekah rushed forward and threw her arms around her. "I am so happy for you. Have you decided on a date?"

"We are hoping as soon as possible," Hope said.

Rose spoke up. "Henry is a minister."

"No," Hope gasped, turning to him. "You are?"

"In a former life," he said.

"But I thought you were in the British army?"

"I was a chaplain."

"Why, you sneaky bugger," Hope said. "Why did you stop practicing?"

"Are you kiddin' me, missy?" he said. "Do I look like I made a good minister of the Lord? No. Out of respect for God, I hung my collar up long ago."

"But you can still perform marriages, cannot you?" Rebekah asked.

"I suppose I can."

"Well, then, why not today?" She turned to Hope. "Or were you wanting a big ceremony?"

Hope shook her head. "Oh, no, no. Nothing elaborate." She turned to Conall. "What do you think? Are you really ready to marry me?"

"I think we'd better get it over with. I don't think I can last another day before I strip you naked and—"

Hope slapped her hand over his mouth. Her face burned in embarrassment. He scrunched his eyes in confusion and tugged her hand away.

"We *would* be married, Hope."

"You shouldn't talk about such things," she said.

He chuckled. "Let me get this straight. It's all right for a husband and wife to have sex, but we are never to talk about it?"

"Right," Hope said.

"I don't know about that," Rebekah chuckled. "Victor and I talk about it."

"Well," Hope said. "I guess it's all right in private conversation between husband and wife, but not in mixed company."

"That is a relief," Conall said.

"So, Hope," Rebekah said, "would you like to change for the ceremony? I have some lovely dresses Victor bought me in France last year that I think would look amazing on you. Would you like to try them on?"

"Could I?" Hope asked.

"Absolutely!" She turned to Rose. "Would you like to help?"

Rose's face lit up. "Sure."

Rebekah turned to Victor. "Dear, would you have Conall wash up? Oh, and ask Agnes if Conall is healed enough for her to remove his stitches. I would like to have the service this afternoon, if possible."

And just like that, they were preparing for a wedding.

* * * * *

Hope stepped out the back door with Victor on her arm and said, "I appreciate you stepping in for my father."

"It's the least I can do for all you've done for me."

A lump rose in her throat as she stepped into a lush garden filled with color. Conall stood between two towering trees, with Mr. Henry at his side. He wore the simple clothes she's sewn for him. They did not look quite right on him. He was a prince. He was probably used to wearing fine clothes and living in a castle. What was she thinking? She could not do this to him. Where would they live? In the tiny cabin? What would they live on? Would Conall, brother to the Elven king, become a lowly farmer? She could not ask it of him.

Turning to Victor, she mumbled, "I am sorry, this is a mistake. I cannot do this." She rushed back through the house, out the front door, and ran headlong into Conall.

"Mrs. Jones, are you trying to run away?" he chided.

She shook her head, tears streaming down her face. "I cannot do this to you. You are a prince, an elf, you deserve a better life than a simple farmer living in a small cabin on the edge of a rural human town."

"Who said anything about farming?"

"See," she said, her chin trembling, "you haven't even thought it through."

"Actually, I have. Vladimir has offered me a job with The Order. I will be paid handsomely. And yes, we may have to live in the cabin until a proper house is built, but I think I can handle that. I survived eight years lying in the dirt under the floorboards. I think I can handle a few months in a soft bed, with a warm fire and you sleeping by my side."

Hope shook her head. "You are sacrificing too much."

"Hope," Conall said, gently pressing under her chin to lift her head. "Look at me."

She blinked back the tears and raised her eyes to meet his.

"I love you. I love you more than I have loved any other living soul. I cannot abide the thought of leaving you. I am sacrificing nothing. Marrying you is a selfish act on my part."

"Are you sure you'll be happy?" she asked.

"There are no sure things in life, but I think finding happiness with you is a safe bet."

"I guess you have considered everything."

"I never walk into things unprepared. Now, Mrs. Jones, are you ready to marry me and make me the happiest man alive?"

Hope chuckled and wiped her tears away.

Minutes later, they were married.

There was no celebration. The town was in turmoil. The members of The Order left to search for Lavinia. Victor needed to make sure the townspeople were taken care of, and Rebekah was exhausted after her eventful day. They quickly ate some sweet cakes and went on their way.

There was one bright light on the horizon. Victor had given Conall the keys to a cute little cottage he'd acquired down the street. Hope's heart lightened when they stepped up the cobble walkway to an adorable, whitewashed home with glass windows. "It's beautiful," she gasped.

Conall chuckled. "You are going to be so easy to please."

"It *is* lovely!" He swept her up in his arms and said, "I am glad you like it." Adjusting her in his arms, he unlocked the door and they stepped inside.

"Oh, it's divine," Hope said, looking at the shiny wood floor and blue flowered wallpaper.

Conall said, "I should get a fire going." He set Hope down on her feet, and her heart pounded. She tried not to think about what tonight meant. It was too terrifying.

"I will get water for the basin," she said, "so we can wash up."

"Make sure you get enough for us to wash more than our hands," he said with a glint in his eyes.

Hope swallowed down the lump in her throat and nodded.

Stepping outside, she found the well and filled her first bucket. Walking back into the house, she made her way to the bedroom to find the basin. When she walked into the room, the first thing she noticed was the massive bed. Well, it was massive to her. She'd never slept in a bed large enough for more than one person. She found a basin wide enough to sit in and poured the water.

Fifteen minutes later, the basin was half full. Conall stepped into the room carrying a steaming cauldron. "I thought you might want warm water to wash in."

Hope's throat was so tight, all she could manage was a nod.

Conall poured in the steaming liquid and then swished his hand around in the water. "I think that is just right." Then he turned to her and raised his eyebrows. "Are you nervous?"

Again, she could not speak, but simply nodded.

Conall took her in his arms. "You have nothing to be nervous about. I will be gentle with you."

His words were the opposite of soothing as her heart pounded even more.

"Awe, love. I wish I could take your fear away." He sighed and held her until her heart calmed. "Would you like me to leave you while you wash?"

Hope nodded against his chest. He stepped back, looked down on her with concern in his eyes, and brushed a warm kiss over her lips. "I will be back in ten minutes."

Again, she nodded.

When he shut the door behind him, she stripped off her clothes, sat in the basin, and washed. "Oh, Hope. You are pathetic. We are married. There is no place for shyness between us." When she'd finished, she quickly toweled off and realized she had a major problem. She had absolutely nothing clean to put on.

"Hope," she chided herself, "you are being ridiculous. The marriage act does n-not require c-clothes." Oh, great! Now her

213

teeth were chattering. And she wasn't even cold. She was simply trembling so hard her teeth were knocking together.

Conall rapped on the door, and Hope's heart pounded.

"Hope? Can I come in?" he asked.

Hope could not find her voice. The tightness in the throat was so bad she was having trouble breathing.

"Hope?" he said. "I am coming in."

In a panic, Hope swiped up the blanket, covered herself from head to foot, and sank to the floor.

She heard the door open and footsteps coming toward her. She kept her head down, resting on her knees. A warm hand pressed down on her back.

"What are you doing here on the floor?"

Hope wanted to say, *Just waiting for you*, but she could not talk. She could barely breathe.

Conall sat down beside her and wrapped his arms around her. "Shh," he said. "It's all right. You can take as much time as you need. I am not going to rush you."

They sat there together for a long while. Eventually, her heart calmed, and she could breathe again. When she worked up the courage, she uncovered her face and looked at Conall. He looked truly worried about her.

"Are you all right, love?" He pressed a kiss on her head.

She nodded. "I don't know what came over me. I mean, I have always accepted that one day if I married, I would...you know. But the reality of it terrifies me."

"That is because you are missing the parts that lead up to it."

"And what is that?"

"It starts with a kiss." He leaned down, bringing his lips to hers.

Hope closed her eyes and sank into the bliss of kissing Conall. Her fear and trepidation melted away. Reaching toward him, she wrapped her arms around his neck. He made love to her with his mouth as a warmth lit in her belly. Minutes later, she was being lifted from off the floor and into his arms. She only gave her nudity a passing thought as she lost herself in his embrace.

From there, he led her willingly into a blissful journey. There was no room for fear or embarrassment—only gentle touches, waves of pleasure, and soft words letting her know how perfect she was.

Hours later, she awoke in Conall's arms. The morning light filtered in through the curtains. Hope had never felt so warm, safe, and completely whole.

Chapter 25

Life with Conall wasn't at all what she'd pictured. He was gone more than he was home. The Order was a demanding dictator that required him to drop whatever she and Conall had planned to go save the world. Well, it wasn't truly saving the world; usually it was saving some poor souls from a raving supernatural lunatic. And Hope knew he was needed. But still, she missed having Conall with her all the time.

When she suggested that she might want to join The Order so she could accompany him, Conall nearly went mad. Especially when Vladimir seemed to consider it. Conall would not even discuss it with her. He simply said it was too dangerous.

Washing her plate and silverware in the kitchen basin, she watched the children playing outside. She was so glad they'd been able to rent the cottage in town. Now that it was harvest season, school was not in session, and she had altogether too much time on her hands.

A light rap on the door had her smiling. It had to be Rebekah, it was always Rebekah.

The wail of a fussing child confirmed it. Hope opened the door.

Rebekah smiled at her as she walked in with little Constance on her hip. "Oh shush, that was not your father. He just looked like him."

Hope chuckled. "How much of that does a one-year-old understand?"

"You would be surprised. She's brilliant. Just like her papa. Oh, by the way. Let me show you what he bought her now. I tell you. She's going to be spoiled so rotten she'll be impossible to live with."

"With you as her mother? I would say her chances of being spoiled are next to nothing."

"I don't think it'll be enough. Victor is constantly buying things for her. If she looks at a toy in the shop for more than two seconds, he's convinced she cannot live without it."

Rebekah put her bag on the table and pulled out a pink ballroom dress. It was stunning, complete with lace and silk ribbons to tie around the waist.

"I have never seen a dress so fine."

"And he got me one to match," Rebekah said. "I told him I am happy to make her anything she needs, but he cannot seem to help himself."

Hope shook her head as she examined the fine dress. "Whoever sewed this was brilliant. Even I could not have done better."

"You are an amazing seamstress. Have you thought about starting on some baby clothes? You and Conall have been married for over a year now. You are sure to get pregnant before long."

Hope shook her head. "I dare not. Conall and I . . . well, being two different species, I don't even know if we can have children."

"Two different species? What nonsense is that?"

"It's not nonsense, it's science. Animals of different species do not cross breed. And they do not have offspring."

"The only difference between Conall and humans are his ears," Rebekah said.

"And the fact he can do magic," Hope said, "and shimmers in the dark. Oh, and lives forever."

Rebekah scowled.

"I had hopes in the beginning," Hope said. "But despite the fact we come together every night he's home, I am still not carrying his child." Hope's face burned. "I am sorry, that information was too personal, wasn't it?"

Rebekah shook her head. "Not at all. Victor and I did not conceive until a year after we married."

"Really?" Hope's heart lightened.

"Yes," Rebekah said. "Really. And I do think you should sew a few things. You know, start out with necessities."

"I will think about it," Hope conceded.

The sound of the backdoor opening lightened Hope's spirits.

"I am home, my sex goddess," Conall's voice boomed.

Rebekah chuckled. "Sex goddess?"

"Oh, shush. And don't you dare tell Victor what my husband calls me in private."

"I give no promises," she chuckled. "I think I need to leave the sex goddess alone with her husband." She was still laughing when she left out the front door.

Conall burst into the room and swept her up in his arms. His lips immediately found hers and he continued his way into the bedroom. Every time he came home from an assignment, he greeted her in the same way. And they would make love no matter the time of day. That was, unless she was teaching school, then he would ambush her as she came through the front door. It almost made it worth him leaving.

Almost.

An hour later, she was running her finger over the planes of his chest. "Do you ever miss Faery?"

Conall's eyes saddened. "There are things I miss about it. The lush green forests, the colorful flowers, and fruit on nearly every tree. But the thing I miss the most is no longer there."

"And what is that?"

"I miss my mother," he said, surprising her. He rarely spoke of his family.

"What was her name?"

"Talila."

"What was she like?"

"She was kind and so light-hearted, not like any other elven I know. Everywhere she went, she had a smile on her face and a spring in her step. She spoiled my brother and I rotten—much to the dismay of my father. But he could never get too upset with her."

"It sounds like you take after her."

"Actually, she's more like you, though you fret more than she ever did." He pressed his fingers lightly beneath her chin and gave her a scolding, yet playful look.

Hope narrowed her eyes as she suppressed a smirk. Her expression softened as concern crept in. "What happened to your mother?"

Conall's countenance darkened as he dropped his hand. "She died along with my father." His tone left no doubt in her mind that he did not want to discuss it. She did not press him; instead, she changed the subject. "So, what did Vladimir have you doing this past week?"

Holly Kelly

Months ago, he would have avoided answering her, but after her suggestion she accompany him on his assignments, he decided to open up to exactly what he did. She guessed he thought her worry was preferable to her rushing into a dangerous situation herself. He had confided in her that he feared if she joined the Order, she'd be dead within a year.

"He had me tracking a nasty creature called a wendigo. It ripped apart an entire settlement before I could get to him. He was annoyingly adept at camouflage."

"Did you arrest him?"

Conall shook his head. "We don't arrest things that kill dozens of humans. We destroy them."

Hope nodded, fear creeping into her heart. "Did it hurt you?"

"He was no match for me, love."

"So, what is a match for you? Is there something out there more powerful than you?"

"Oh, yes. There absolutely is. And it's close by."

Hope's heart took off in a sprint. "What is it?"

"It's a creature with beauty beyond compare, and eyes the color of nutmeg, hair so soft you simply want to spend every moment of every day running your fingers through it, and when she's in the throes of passion, she makes the most adorable squeaky sound."

Hope slapped him. "You ruffian."

"And when she's angry she strikes," he chuckled, turning over and straddling her.

Hope could not help but laugh. "So, what is your plan for this creature?"

220

"I plan to make love to her every chance I get and lay on so much affection that she can never think of leaving me."

"You had better be talking about me," she smirked.

"What?" he asked, feigning surprise. "What does any of this have to do with you?"

She raised her hand to smack him, but he easily caught it and leaned down to kiss her smiling lips.

*   *   *   *   *

Hope took her cloak off the coat rack and slipped it on. She stepped in front of the mirror and tucked a few stray strands into her bun. Conall's image came into view behind her, and his arms slipped around her waist.

"You know," he said, his voice low, his breath tickling her ear, "we could have more fun if we stayed home."

Hope tried not to smile. "My students are expecting me. the Fall Festival is a big deal."

"So, what, there will be music, dancing, and food?"

Hope nodded. "Uh huh. And that reminds me. I need you to help me carry the pies. I made a pumpkin and an apple."

"The festivals in Faery were a lot like the festivals you have here. Only the dancing was done naked. Maybe we should shake things up and take off our clothes to dance."

Hope laughed, shaking her head. "No, there will be no removing of clothes."

"Until after the festival." He winked.

She smirked. "All right, I will make you a deal. If you behave yourself, we can dance naked when we come back home."

"We have no music here. Can we bring the musicians with us? I will make it, so they remember nothing."

221

"No," Hope said. "No compelling people. It's not right to take away their free will."

"Have it your way," Conall said, "but I think it would be more damaging for them to remember. Your reputation will be in ruins. But you know what's best."

Hope held back a smile. "Sometimes I don't know why I put up with you."

"You put up with me because . . ." He leaned over and whispered in her ears, describing exactly what he did to her. His words were so unbelievably arousing, that she almost decided then and there that the festival was worth missing.

Shaking her head, she said, "Stop that. We have to go to the festival. That is all there is to it. Besides, I thought you liked festivals."

"I love festivals," he said.

"Then why are you—"

"I love you more," he smirked.

"Well, you can love me afterwards," she said, and pulled him down for a quick kiss.

Minutes later, they were walking down the path, following small lanterns lighting the way. Music filtered through the trees and a warm glow emanated from the grove.

"It looks like the party has already started."

"Good," Conall said. "I would hate to stand around being bored."

They weaved through the crowd of revelry and made their way to the food table. Hope's eyes widened. She'd never seen so much food in one place. This year's harvest was a plentiful one. She and Conall had already stocked up their stores. They had more than enough to last the winter. She'd even gotten honey, and a huge assortment of dried fruits. Between his salary and her meager teacher's salary, they were doing quite well for themselves.

Oh, and the fact that Conall was an amazing hunter did not hurt. In fact, the first time he left with his bow in hand, he came back an hour later packing an elk over his shoulders. Hope panicked when she saw him. Humans were not strong enough to carry a seven-hundred-pound elk by themselves. If someone had seen him, there would be questions to answer.

Now he slaughtered the animal where he shot it and packed the three hundred pounds of meat in one trip. Still impressive for one man, but it wouldn't raise any suspicions.

"What are you thinking?" Conall asked.

"How amazing a hunter, you are," she said.

"It's easy to hunt elk and deer. They don't hunt you back."

Conall took her hand and pulled her around to face him. "I think it's about time we liven this party up. Mrs. Jones, would you like to dance?"

Hope looked around. "But nobody else is dancing."

"Somebody has to be the first," Conall said. "We might as well be the ones to break the ice. How about we show them how elves dance?"

"All right, but we only do the tame dances."

"Now where's the fun in that?" he said with a glint in his eye, and then he pulled her into his arms and off they went—prancing and twirling to the beat. Almost immediately, others joined them in the clearing.

Minutes later, Hope was having difficulty breathing, and an ache in her side had her wanting to stop. Conall noticed her discomfort and led her to a chair.

"You don't look like you're feeling too well," he said, concerned.

Hope shook her head. "I'm just tired. I did not get much sleep last night."

"Are you sure you are not coming down with something?" He pressed his palm to her forehead.

"I don't think so," she answered.

"Why don't I grab you some cider?"

Hope nodded and Conall left. She was fanning her face when Dr. Porter sat down beside her.

"Having fun?"

Hope nodded. "Lots. I only wish I had boundless energy."

"Yeah," he said. "You are looking a bit pale."

"I am just tired."

Dr. Porter looked across the clearing at Conall. "It has to be nice having your husband back after thinking he was dead for so long. I never did hear, where was he all that time?"

Hope immediately felt defensive. "He was doing important work."

"He could not even send you a letter? You know, let you know he was alive?"

"It's complicated."

"I think I am smart enough to keep up."

Hope shook her head. "It's also a private matter."

"Oh." Dr. Porter frowned. "Well, I hope it never happens again."

Conall returned with her drink and Dr. Porter stood. "Good day, Hope. Mr. Jones."

Conall nodded politely.

When Dr. Porter was gone, Conall asked, "What did the good doctor want?"

Hope shook her head. "Nothing."

"You looked angry. Should I be sharpening my arrows? I can put one right through his heart."

"No, it's fine. Really."

"Hello, Mrs. Jones."

Hope turned to see young William smiling at her.

"Hello, William. How's the harvest going?"

"We are nearly done. I cannot wait to get back to school."

"Neither can I." Hope smiled.

William nodded and said, "I will see you next week," and then he ran to join his friends.

Rebekah squealed as she pranced forward, Victor following behind. "Have we missed much?"

"Nope, the party is just getting underway," Conall said, and handed Hope her cider.

She raised it to her nose, and her stomach took a turn. She must still be sickened by what Dr. Porter said.

And she thought he was her friend. Well, at least she knew that Rebekah and Victor were true friends. She turned to Rebekah. "Where's Constance?"

"My mother-in-law came to visit, and she abhors social events. So, she volunteered to stay home with Constance."

"How wonderful!" Hope sat the untouched cider on the table.

225

"How about we start a dance line?" Rebekah asked Hope.

"I am afraid Hope's not feeling too well," Conall said, eyeing her.

"Oh, no," Rebekah said. "I'm sorry. And at the Fall Festival, too."

"I think I'm just going to take her home and have her lie down," Conall said.

"And I think I'm going to stay right here and not spoil your fun," Hope said.

"Sweetheart," Conall said, looking down on her, "it's not possible for me to have fun while you are suffering."

"I can have fun while *you* are suffering," she said with a smile. "I don't see why you cannot."

"Liar," he said.

Hope smirked.

"And people think my wife is a saint." Conall looked at Rebekah and Victor and shook his head.

"I was until you corrupted me," Hope said.

"If anyone could do it, it would be me." Conall raised an eyebrow, his smile wide.

"Seriously, Conall," Hope said. "Go. Dance. Have fun. "He frowned at her.

"Just one dance," Hope said. "Then you can take me home."

He sighed. "I don't have a partner."

"I will be your partner," Rebekah said.

As the current song ended, couples filtered into the clearing. Conall stepped out with Rebekah's hand in his. They faced each other and waited. When the song began, they were off in a sea of dancers. Hope watched for Conall's pale hair—it was the best way to identify which dancer was him. She caught sight of him regularly and saw his smiling face on several occasions.

Good. He's having fun.

The song continued and Hope lost sight of him. She searched the crowd and didn't see him. So instead, she searched for Rebekah. And then she saw Rebekah coming toward them, her eyes were wide with worry as she bit down on her bottom lip.

Hope's heart sank like lead in her chest, and her stomach heaved. "He's gone," Rebekah said. "One minute he was there, and the next . . . he disappeared."

Hope turned and wretched the entire contents of her stomach on the ground beside her.

Chapter 26

Conall stumbled to a stop mid-step in his dance. All the dancers had frozen in place, like statues depicting laughter and revelry.

A low rumbling chuckle at his back had his heart sinking.

"Haryk," Conall said and turned to his brother.

"You had ten years with these humans, and you could not even show them how to have a good time?" He looked around. "This is pathetically wholesome. Though, perhaps these goodies taught you how to show respect."

"What are you doing here?" Conall asked.

"I came to put an end to your sentence, brother. You are free to return home."

Conall sighed. "I am grateful that you are no longer angry with me, but I will not be returning."

Haryk's expression hardened. "So, now you are angry with *me*?" he said, his voice rising. "You deserved what you got. You are lucky I did not execute you. If you were anyone other than my brother, I would have had your head."

Someone else beat you to that one. "I am not angry with you."

"Then why will you not return?"

"I've married."

"What?" Haryk was obviously taken aback. "Someone else is banished here? If you trust her, I am willing to lift her banishment."

Conall shook his head. "She's a human."

Haryk's eyes flew open wide as he shouted, "You married a rodent?"

Conall growled in anger. "You will never call her that."

"Oh, so now you are giving your king orders. I see my banishment has only made things worse." He looked around at the crowd. "Which one is she?"

"She's not here."

"Oh, I think she is. *You* know what we do to rodents. We poison them with nightshade." He drew his sword. "Or hack them in two with a blade."

Conall clenched his teeth to force himself not to speak. Anything he said now would likely make things worse. Hope's life rested on the fact Haryk did not know who she was.

"If you stay," Haryk continued. "I will stay too and root her out. No matter how long it takes, though I don't think it will take long." He strolled through the crowd. "Now who is beautiful enough to win your affections?" He paused at Rebekah. "Hm. She's pretty, but not enough to have you turn your back on your elvenkind." He continued to consider the women, one by one. "Too fat, too thin, too . . . ugly."

Conall dared not even look at Hope.

Haryk continued through the crowd for a long while. And just when he was about to turn to see Hope, Conall shouted, "All right, I will go with you."

Haryk whipped around in surprise. "You've given up?"

"Yes," he said. "But you have to promise not to go searching for my wife. You must give me your word you will leave her in peace."

Haryk narrowed his eyes. "What did she do to you? The Conall I know would never back down from a fight—no matter who would get hurt. Did you fall in love with a witch?"

Conall avoided the question. "Do we have a deal?"

Haryk shook his head in disbelief as he said, "Yes. I will leave her alone. Now let's go home. The stench of this place sickens me."

*   *   *   *   *

Hope spent the next two weeks in bed. Conall did not return. Hope knew exactly what had happened. His brother had come for him.

Her heart was so completely broken, she could not function. She ate little, and what she did eat came back up shortly after consuming it. She'd shed so many tears, she was sure there could be no more left, but each morning when she awoke alone, they would start falling again. She had no idea a heart could shatter so completely.

Rebekah came daily to care for her. She did her best to feed her and get her to bathe, but Hope saw no point in it. Bathing and eating were only for those who cared about whether they lived or died. Right now, she was in so much pain, she cared about nothing.

Stepping in the room, Rebekah said, "Your students want you to come back." She threw back the covers, sat Hope up, and stripped her filthy gown off her. She then brought the basin over and dipped the sponge in the soapy water and placed it in Hope's hand. Hope reluctantly obliged, but only because she knew if she did not do it, Rebekah would wash her herself.

"They haven't found a replacement for you yet," Rebekah said as Hope washed. "You can still return, though you don't have to worry about money. Apparently, Con—" Rebekah caught herself before uttering his name. Hope could not even think it without dealing with waves of pain. "Well, he paid for this house and set up a handsome trust to care for you for the rest of your life. I guess Victor was consulted and made all the arrangements months ago. I do wonder where he got the money. Regardless, I think it would be good for you to keep busy. And you love teaching."

Hope shook her head. "I cannot. Not yet."

Rebekah nodded and helped Hope stand up so she could put on a new gown. As she rose, her stomach took a violent turn, and she found herself vomiting in the water basin.

"This is just not normal," Rebekah said. "Even if you were sick with heartache, you still should be able to keep *some* food down." She paused for a few moments, and then said, "I wonder . . ." Her voice dropped off, and then she said, "Hope, I think you should see Agnes. She knows about healing." Rebekah's voice was more strained than usual.

Too weak to argue, Hope nodded and then laid back, not bothering to put on a clean gown.

"I will go get her right now." Rebekah's spirits seemed to be lighter. Why they would be, Hope had no idea.

Minutes later, Agnes sat on the bed beside her. "So, you are having difficulty keeping food down."

Hope nodded.

"Is your nausea worse in the morning or evening?

"Pick one," she said.

"Have you noticed any tenderness in your breasts?

Holly Kelly

This caught Hope's attention. Why would she ask such a thing? She pressed her hand to her bosoms and did feel a soreness. "They are a bit tender."

"And how long since your last bleeding?"

Hope's eyes flew open wide. She lay silent for a stunned moment and then she said, "You think I am pregnant?" Her mind raced. *How long had it been?* "Oh my gosh," she gasped when she did the math. "It was seven weeks ago. I am never late."

"Well, my dear. In my opinion, I would say that not only are you sick with heartache, you have morning sickness."

"Are you sure?"

"Well, there's one way to find out."

"How?" Hope asked.

Agnes took out a small cup. "I need you to urinate in this."

"And what will *that* tell you?"

"I will know by the smell if you are with child."

"Really?" Hope asked.

"It worked with me," Rebekah said.

Hope reluctantly took the cup. Three minutes later she was officially a mother-to-be.

Though she still felt sicker than sick, her spirits were lightened. She now had something more to live for—her baby. Conall's baby.

At that thought, tears slid down her cheeks. The tears accompanied mixed emotions. Her heart was still completely broken, but Conall had left a piece of himself behind, and that was a comfort to her.

"I wish I could tell what the gender is," Agnes said. "I usually can, but with your child—it's confusing. Must be the Elven blood in the babe."

"Did you know with Rebekah?"

"I did, but she made me swear not to tell her."

"Oh, I could tell you wanted to," Rebekah said. "I had to cut her off on several occasions when she almost slipped."

"I would not make you swear any such thing," Hope said. "I wish I knew what I was having." She sipped her raspberry leaf tea. The tea worked like magic, settling her stomach. She was even able to keep down a whole slice of bread and butter.

They continued to talk for a long while and made plans for the new baby. Rebekah retrieved yarn from Hope's chest, and Hope sat down to knit. Soon her eyelids were drooping.

"Hope?"

Her eyes opened as she jumped. "I am sorry. I must have dozed off."

Rebekah got up and stepped toward her. "You need your rest."

Hope took her hand and stood. The room spun a bit, and she closed her eyes to keep herself from falling down. "I guess I am still a bit weak and a little dizzy."

"That will improve once you are able to eat regularly," Agnes said.

Rebekah and Agnes made sure she was safely in bed before they left. Hope just had to do one more thing before she went to sleep. She rolled off her bed and onto her knees. Then, for the next twenty minutes, she poured her heart out to God and thanked him for his tender mercies. And then before she closed her prayer, she asked if he could find it in his heart to perform one small miracle—

Please bring my husband back.

*   *   *   *   *

The following Monday, Hope stepped up the wooden steps to the schoolhouse. The door creaked as she pushed it open. Everything looked as she had left it. Her stomach churned a bit, so she grabbed a couple fennel seeds from her pocket and chewed on them. Immediately, she felt relief. Thank heavens for Agnes and her remedies.

"Mrs. Jones?"

Hope turned to see little Martha running toward her. Hope braced herself as the girl threw her arms around her legs.

"I missed you so much," Martha said. "I was worried you weren't coming back."

"I am sorry to scare you," Hope said, stroking her hair. "I was feeling under the weather."

Martha turned her tear-streaked face up. "My mama was feeling under the weather once, and then she died. You are not going to die, are you?"

"No, sweetheart, I am going to be just fine." Hope said the words, but in the back of her mind, worry set in. Women died giving birth all the time. Could she be looking at her last few months of life?

"Stop fretting," she said, half to Martha and half to herself. "Go outside and play. I am sure Carolyn is waiting for you."

"All right, Mrs. Jones."

Hope watched the girl skip out to the play yard and caught sight of a man walking toward the school. She frowned as she recognized him.

Dr. Porter.

She had no desire to speak to the man. But seeing as how he was her superior, she would have to oblige him.

"Hello, Hope," he greeted, raising her ire. This wasn't the proper place for him to address her so informally.

She nodded. "Dr. Porter, to what do I owe this visit?"

"I heard your husband had to leave, once again."

"Yes, he was called away."

He looked down at the ground and nodded. "I was wondering . . ."

When he did not continue, she said, "Yes?"

"Have you considered an annulment?"

"What?" Hope could not hide the surprise in her voice.

"It's not unheard of in your situation. It is not right for a husband to abandon his wife, and yours has done it twice now."

Hope shook her head. "No, I have not. And I will not. You see, I am to have a baby come this June."

Dr. Porter's eyes widened. "So, you are pregnant?"

"That is usually how it is accomplished, but then you know that. You are a doctor, after all."

He gave a nervous chuckle. "Yes, I just . . ." he hesitated. She'd obviously caught him off guard. "Well, congratulations."

"Thank you."

He turned to leave and then paused, looking back at her. "I do wonder, though."

"What?"

"Why would a husband leave his wife when she's in a delicate condition?"

"He knows I have good friends to watch after me," she said.

Dr. Porter nodded. "So, you do." He looked as if he wanted to say more. Finally, he seemed to think better of it and said, "Good day, Mrs. Jones."

"Good day to you too, Dr. Porter."

Chapter 27

Conall stood on the balcony of his bedroom window high above a village lit up with lanterns and glowing pixies. Tucked between towering trees and foliage, small cottages with windows aglow with warm fires spoke of love and families having dinner and conversation. At one time, he would have relished the beauty of a quiet evening like this.

But not tonight.

Squeezing his eyes shut, he attempted to calm his rage. If he did not succeed, he would storm into his brother's room and drive a dagger into his heart. And that would not end well for him.

For the second time in his long life, he felt trapped. The first was when he was abandoned under the floorboards. But this was worse. Sure, he had riches, fine clothes, an opulent castle to live in, servants to see to his every need . . . but the truth was, he was nothing better than a prisoner locked in a dungeon.

A light knock at his door caught his attention. Who was it this time?

He opened the oak door, and a familiar face stood smiling at him. A heartbeat later, she threw her arms around him.

"Oh, how I have missed you, my love!" Seirye exclaimed.

"I have been back for days," he said, pushing her back.

"Yes, but *I* have been away!" she said, holding onto his lapel. "I haven't seen you in months."

It's been years for me.

"When I heard what the king did to you," she continued. "I was beside myself. I went a whole day without eating! Can you believe that? And entire day! I was too busy fretting about what would become of you in the human world."

"I thought you and Sontar were together now?"

"Him? Oh no! How could you think such a thing? He's so boorish and stupid."

"You did sleep with him."

"Stupid sprites and their loose tongues," she spat. "I simply got a little drunk and things got out of hand. You know how I get when I have too much wine."

Conall frowned down on the Elven girl. There was a time he thought himself in love with her. He'd chased her for decades, trying to get her to marry him. Why did he even bother? She was a filthy troll compared to Hope. Nothing in this world would ever compare to her. How much time had passed in the human world now? A week? A month? Had she moved on? Found another man to love?

Dr. Porter's face flashed in his mind, and his rage was back in full force. What was he doing while Conall was gone? Probably turning on the charm. The doctor had always had his eye on Hope.

What am I doing here? I belong by Hope's side.

"Conall." Seirye shouted, and he looked at her. "What is wrong with you? I had to shout twice to get your attention."

"I am sorry," he said. "I guess my mind was elsewhere. What were you saying?"

"I was asking you to take me to bed."

"You want me to walk you to your house?"

She barked a laugh. "Very funny. I want you to take me to your bed."

Conall shook his head and put his arm around her, leading her toward the door. "There's no room for you."

She gaped at him as he opened the door and shoved her into the hallway. She turned, a look of shock on her face. "But your bed is huge!"

"Sorry, Seirye. I neglected to inform you that I am married now. So, for future reference, I will not be available to satisfy your needs. I am sure you'll be able to find a replacement easily. Just go down to the pub, have a few drinks, and the possibilities are endless."

"Did I hear someone say something about going for a drink?" A deep voice came from the hallway.

Seirye narrowed her eyes at him. "You are making a serious mistake, Conall. If you apologize now, all will be forgiven. But if you don't, I won't be responsible for my actions."

"Goodbye, Seirye." Conall started to close the door in her face, but a meaty hand pushed it back.

"Hello, cousin." Dyffros smiled from around the corner, chuckling as he glanced at Seirye stomping down the hallway. "Looks like you angered your woman."

"She's not my woman anymore."

"Yeah, I heard. Your brother told me you married a human."

Conall turned back and stormed into his room. "I don't need a lecture. And I swear, if you insult her, I will tear your head off."

Whoa," he said. "You really are messed up about her. You do realize humans don't have an ounce of magic in them, and their life span is shorter than a pummerfly? I have to admit, some are nice to look at—for about a minute. And then they get old, leathery, and wrinkled." Dyffros shuddered.

"Dyffros," Conall growled. "I wasn't jesting when I said I would rip your head off."

Dyffros put his hands up. "I did not insult her. I am just stating the facts, Cousin."

"Well, how about these facts?" Conall sat down at a table filled with uneaten food. "I am not free to love who I want, I am not free to live where I want, and apparently my feelings mean nothing, as does my word. I promised to care for the woman I love for as long as we both live. But apparently I can only care for her as long as my brother says I can."

"You are being unreasonable," Dyffros said.

"And you are being an ass," Conall growled. "Visitations are over. Get the hell out!"

Dyffros shook his head and mumbled, "You are insane."

"If I am insane then lock me up, but don't expect me to pretend that everything is fine."

Dyffros glowered. "Your brother should have left you in the human world."

Conall slammed his palm down on his table. "Now that is the first reasonable thing anyone has said since I have returned."

Dyffros stepped to the door. "I will be back when you've had a chance to calm down and think rationally."

Conall scowled at his cousin.

Without a backward glance, Dyffros shut the door behind him.

Conall leaned forward, resting his head in his hand. He'd never shed a tear in his life—not one. But if he could, he would shed them now. His heart felt like dead weight in his chest. Hope was the one who brought life to his heart, and without her . . . there was nothing without her.

Searching in his pocket, he found what he was looking for—a lock of her hair. He always kept it with him. The smell of it comforted him like nothing else. Now it was all he had left of her. While his days in Faery crept forward, slow and painful, the days in Hope's world were flying by. Another month here, and she may forget him completely.

He pressed the curls against his nose and inhaled. Her scent was growing fainter, but it was still there. This time, it did not comfort him. Like the fading scent, Hope's memories would fade too. She would move on—forget he ever existed and eventually die. And then he would die too. He would see to it.

*   *   *   *   *

Hope sent the children home early on the last day of school. She simply could not handle standing one more minute. Her stomach was as big as one of Rebekah's oversized watermelons. Agnes assured her she was only carrying one child, but as large as she was, Hope wondered if the witch could possibly be wrong.

"Hello?" Rebekah called out from the schoolhouse doorway. She stood there, smirking.

"You can come in, you know," Hope said.

"I have a surprise," Rebekah said, and then a familiar figure stepped from behind her.

"Elizabeth," Hope squealed and waddled forward for a hug. "I thought when we parted at the inn, that I'd never see you again."

241

Holly Kelly

"Of course, we'd see each other again. I had ulterior motives when I sent you to my cousin. That way I'd know where to find you." She pulled away from the embrace and shook her head, smiling. "You look like you should have delivered last month. Are you certain there's only one in there?"

"I am not sure about anything," Hope said. "I only know I will be so happy when the time comes to have him. Though he's not due for another four weeks."

"So, it's a boy, is it?"

Hope smiled and shook her head. "I have no idea. I only know it doesn't feel right calling my baby an 'it.'"

"I know what you mean. I do the same thing, except I call mine a she."

Hope could not contain her surprise. "You are expecting?"

Elizabeth nodded. "I am only about four months into my pregnancy.

"Oh," Hope beamed. "I am so happy for you! And you thought you would not have any children."

"I know! I feel so blessed. And then when I received your letter telling me you were expecting, I thought it was about time I came to visit. I wanted to see you again, and I simply had to see Rebekah's new little one."

"How long do you plan to stay?" Hope asked.

"Until after you have your babe. I thought I could be a support. And it would give me a glimpse into what I will experience in five months."

Hope shook her head. "I hope everything goes well. I don't want—" Hope gasped as a crushing pain radiated from her back.

"Hope," Rebekah shouted as Elizabeth grabbed Hope's arm.

When the pain finally subsided, Hope was gasping for breath.

"Are you having labor pains already?" Elizabeth asked.

"I am not sure. I thought the pains would be in my belly, not in my back."

"Oh, no," Rebekah said. "Agnes discussed that with me. She called it back labor, and it's supposed to be more painful than regular labor."

"It's too early for labor. Though Agnes said I might deliver sooner than later."

"Maybe it was a onetime pain," Elizabeth said. "You haven't had another yet."

Rebekah shook her head. "It's only been a few seconds. And with as much pain as you were in, I think it's probably the real thing. Let's get you in the wagon."

"I am so sorry, Hope," Elizabeth said. "I should never have surprised you. If anything happens to your baby, I will never forgive myself."

*　*　*　*　*

The next morning, they sat in Rebekah's sunroom. It was wall to wall and ceiling to ceiling windows. It almost seemed as if they sat in the outdoors surrounded by trees. It was Hope's absolute favorite room at Rebekah's house.

"I am really glad it was a false alarm," Elizabeth said, taking a bite of her salad.

Hope smiled, grateful to have her two dearest friends close by. "Speak for yourself," Hope said. "I am so uncomfortable, I would be happy to have this baby today."

"Don't you dare wish that," Elizabeth said. "A month early is too much of a risk."

"I know, I'm sorry. I just feel as big as a house," Hope said.

"Hope?" Elizabeth said.

Hope turned to her friend, the trepidation in her voice making her anxious. "Yes?"

"I know it pains you to talk about, but what happened to your husband?"

Hope's heart clamped in her chest, and her hands trembled. She wanted to be able to tell her, but her emotions were so jumbled and raw she could not bring herself to. "I am sorry, I know you deserve to know, but I . . . I just cannot." Hope pushed her chair back and stood.

Pain hit—more severe than ever. She bent over and groaned, unable to focus on anything but the agony. When it finally subsided, she was gasping for breath. Warm fluid drenched her legs and splashed the floor beneath her skirts.

"Is that what I think it is?" Elizabeth asked.

"That is no false alarm," Rebekah said. "We need to get Agnes."

"I am so sorry, Hope," Elizabeth sobbed. "This is my fault."

"This is not your fault," Hope said between gritted teeth. "When a baby decides to come, there is no changing it. And when he is not ready, there's no coaxing him."

"But—" Elizabeth protested.

"We'll be fine," Hope said, trying to put on a brave face. Inside she was terrified. What if this was too early? What if Conall's baby did not make it?

Another contraction hit, and Hope doubled over in pain.

On the way home, they stopped outside Agnes and Mr. Henry's cabin. Rebekah leapt out and knocked on the door. Mr. Henry opened up just as Hope let out a wail.

"It's time, is it?" he said, and then turned and shouted. "Agnes, love. Hope's gonna be needing your midwifery skills."

"Already?"

"I told ya, Rose said she'd probably deliver early."

"Yes, but this is even a little early for an Elven child."

Agnes rushed out the door with a bag in her arms. "You sure this isn't a false alarm?"

Rebekah shook her head. "Her water broke."

"Well, that cinches it."

Hope squeezed her eyes shut as another pain washed over her.

"Did Agnes say an Elven child?" Elizabeth asked.

"Oh, no. That is just what she calls babies that are impatient. You know, like a child who tries to spy elves on Christmas Eve," Rebekah said.

Hope might have been impressed with how fast Rebekah could come up with a plausible story to explain Agnes's blunder if she wasn't in so much pain.

Hope's cottage came into view, and she experienced a mixture of feelings: glad to be home, but dreading having to walk the distance to make it inside. Elizabeth held one arm and Rebekah held the other as they helped Hope into her house, stopping only once when she had another contraction. Finally, she was able to lay her down in her bed. Hope turned to Rebekah. "Can you bring me the crock from behind the kitchen door?"

"Oh, sure." Rebekah stepped into the next room. "Is it the one with a big rock on it?"

"Yes, please."

Rebekah stepped into the room with a small crock in her arms. Hope took off the lid and pulled out a white, collared shirt.

"Is that—?" Elizabeth began and then hesitated, looking at Rebekah before saying anything more.

Rebekah nodded.

Hope held it under her nose and took in a deep breath. She could still catch Conall's lingering honeysuckle scent. Tears sprang to her eyes. It almost felt as if he were in the next room.

"Elizabeth, can you help me in the kitchen for a moment?" Rebekah asked.

"While you are in there, get a large pot of water on to boil," Agnes said.

The two women left, and minutes later Hope heard Elizabeth say, "Where is Hope's husband?"

Unfortunately, the house had really thin walls.

"He had to leave."

"He abandoned her?"

"No, no. It's not like that."

"Then why didn't Hope go with him?"

Their voices were drowned out by Hope's groans as another contraction hit. A few minutes later, Elizabeth returned from the kitchen.

"Rebekah is getting the water on. She said it was too heavy for me to help."

"That is all right, dear," Agnes said. "I can use your help right here."

Fourteen hours later, Hope did not think she could last a minute longer. She'd been pushing for a full four hours. She felt as weak as a drowned kitten and could barely put any effort into pushing her baby out.

"I just cannot do it," she rasped.

"Nonsense," Agnes said. "You are doing fine."

Hope shook her head as tears rolled down her face. "No, I am not."

Hope took a glance at Elizabeth and Rebekah. Their downcast expressions said it all. Hope and her baby were in serious trouble.

"Here, sweetheart," Agnes said. "This'll help." She brought a cup to Hope's lips. "Now drink deep."

Heat scalded Hope's throat as she took in a gulp of fire. She knocked the cup from Agnes's hands.

When she finally stopped coughing, she asked, "What did you give me?"

"Cayenne tea."

"Are you crazy?" Hope shouted and coughed some more.

"See." Agnes turned to Rebekah. "Just look at her color now. And her energy is back."

"Were you in on this?" Hope asked Rebekah.

"You needed it," she said simply.

Hope continued to scowl and then she had to push again. Her energy level truly was better as she pushed with all her might. This time, it felt like she made progress.

"Ooh, good work, Hope," Agnes said. "Your baby is crowning. It won't be long now."

And it truly wasn't. Just minutes later, they lifted a wrinkled, bloody baby up and sat it down on Hope's bare chest as it cried and wailed. She looked down on the tiny face, and her heart completely melted. "Is it a boy?"

"Not unless he lost something in the womb, dearie," Agnes said.

"Oh," she smiled. "A girl."

"Yes, and she's perfect," Agnes said. "Just look how pink she is."

Hope nodded, blinking back tears as she kissed her baby's bald head and mumbled against her skin. "Look at what we did, Conall," she whispered. "We have a daughter."

"Elizabeth," Agnes said. "Use the terry cloth and the water to wipe the baby clean, and then we'll get her diapered and wrapped in a blanket."

Elizabeth got to work gently toweling her off. As she was wiping the baby's head, she froze. "What's wrong with her ears?"

"Her ears?" Hope said.

"Oh, that happens," Agnes said, waving it off like it was no big deal. "They must have been pressed against the side of the womb."

"Wow," Elizabeth said. "They look pointed. She almost looks like a Faery baby." Her eyes widened as she darted a look from Rebekah to Agnes. "Or an elf?"

"Very funny." Rebekah chuckled uncomfortably. "She's perfect."

"That she is," Agnes said.

Elizabeth's concern melted away, and she heartily agreed with them.

"So," Rebekah said. "What are you going to call her?"

Hope had put off deciding on a name. She'd hoped Conall would return before the birth, and they could decide together. But that hadn't happened. There *was* one name she thought he might be happy with, and it would honor her Elven side.

"Her name is Talila."

"Ta . . . lila," Elizabeth said. "What kind of name is that?"

"Um, well . . ." Hope began.

"It's a Celtic name," Agnes supplied.

"But you are not Celtic," Elizabeth said.

"No, but Conall is," Hope said, proud she could say his name without a breakdown into tears.

"Oh, well. I think Talila is a beautiful name," Elizabeth said.

"Thank you," Hope said, her eyes drooping as exhaustion seeped into her bones.

"You had best hurry and suckle your baby before you fall asleep," Agnes said. "She'll need the nourishment."

Hope nodded and followed her instructions. She fell asleep with a smile on her face and warmth in her heart.

Chapter 28

Being the mother of a new infant was exhausting. Hope got no more than two hours sleep at any one time. Talila was up throughout the night demanding to eat. Hope might have thought she wasn't producing enough milk, but the rolls of fat on her two-month-old said otherwise.

Today she had to go to the market. She needed fresh eggs and milk. She'd run completely out and could not put it off any longer.

Putting a knitted cap on Talila, Hope covered her ears. She tied a knot to secure it to keep her babe from pulling it off. She had to be extremely careful to keep her uniqueness hidden from others. Hope worried about her daughter's future. The ears could be easily hidden. To those who had ingested thyme, the soft glow from her skin was a bit harder to mask—especially on a moonless night. Too bad thyme was a popular herb to grow in the area.

Pushing the carriage out the door, she squinted against the bright sunlight. The wheels bumped over the uneven road as she made her way. Her heart skipped a beat when she noticed a figure in the trees near the road ahead.

It was a woman, staring at her. Hope did not pause but kept walking. Something in the way she watched her made Hope uneasy. When she was only a few feet away, the woman smiled. Her face was dazzling—her teeth as white as pearls, her eyes too large for her delicate face. She was beautiful, though in an otherworldly way. Could she be Elven?

Hope mentally kicked herself for not drinking her thyme tea this morning. If she had, she would know for sure.

"Hello," the woman said, smiling. She stepped forward and looked down on Talila. Her eyes narrowed. "What a lovely child."

"Thank you."

"She practically glows, doesn't she?"

Hope swallowed uncomfortably. "She's a little angel."

The woman laughed. "No, not angel. She looks more like an elf."

Hope's heart pounded. "Who are you?"

"What?" the woman looked up in mock surprise. "Conall did not mention me?"

"And who are you to Conall?"

"Why." she raised an eyebrow. "I am his lover. We've been lovers for over a century. Though his banishment put a kink in our relationship for a while, but now that he's back, things are better than ever. I have hardly had a moment's sleep—not that I can complain." She winked.

Hope felt her heart sink. *No. It's a lie.* "You mean you 'were' his lover."

The woman smirked. "If it makes you feel better to tell yourself that."

"It's the truth. Conall would never betray me."

The woman laughed out loud. "Oh, you humans are so trusting. And I suppose you think he was taken back to Faery against his will?"

Hope pressed her lips together and narrowed her eyes. She would not waste another breath on this woman.

The woman laughed out loud. "You did, did you not? No, my dear. His brother lifted his banishment, and he is free to come and go as he pleases. Looks like he's grown tired of you and is looking for lusher fields to plant his seeds in."

Hope shook her head. "You're lying." She pushed her carriage, attempting to get past the vile woman.

She stepped into Hope's path. "Oh, you think you're special? That somehow you are different from every other lowly human? You might be beautiful now but wait ten years. He will not be able to even look at you without cringing at your wrinkled skin and yellow teeth." She looked down at Talila and brushed her fingers over her cheek. "And as for her...she won't last a decade before she's ridiculed, beaten, and finally killed. Humans cannot abide anything supernatural."

Hope took a menacing step toward the woman and growled, "Get away from my daughter."

The woman turned a furious eye on Hope. "I do not take orders from swamp rats." And then she spoke in an unearthly voice, words that Hope could not begin to understand. Dancing lights swirled around Hope until they gathered together and floated toward her face. She wanted to flee, or even cringe away, but she could not. She found herself frozen in place.

The lights sank into her forehead, bringing warmth just before they numbed her senses.

The stunning creature before her strolled up and stopped when they were nose to nose. "Now, rat, I want you to tell me your deepest, darkest secrets."

A cool breeze raised goosebumps on Hope's arms. She stood alone in the shadows of a grove of trees, far from the village. There was a definite chill in the air. Talila's cry rent the air.

"Oh, my sweet baby, why are you crying?" Hope rushed forward and lifted her child from the buggy. She felt cold to the touch. Fear sliced through her. They'd only just left the house. Why were they both so chilled? And what were they doing deep in the woods?

She looked up, and her heart skipped a beat. It was high noon when they'd left the house, but now it appeared to be late afternoon. How could she lose hours from her day; not to mention end up so far away?

She pushed the buggy over the uneven ground and rushed home as she cradled Talila in her arms. Perhaps she was having a breakdown.

It was possible.

After all, she'd had so little sleep lately—not to mention that when she did sleep, it was fitful. She would see Agnes tomorrow and find out what she could do to help her rest.

The remnants of something she could not quite put her finger on tickled her mind, as if she'd forgotten to lock a door or douse a campfire. No. It felt like it was something much more important. Still, she could not recall what it was.

Talila let out an ear-piercing wail. Now was not the time to figure it out. She needed to care for her baby.

Chapter 29

"You simply must come!" Rebekah said for the hundredth time.

Hope rubbed her temples in an attempt to ward off a headache.

"It's the biggest celebration of the year."

"It's also the anniversary of the day I lost Talila's father." At times, Hope still had a difficult time saying Conall's name. Today had been especially difficult. "Besides, Dr. Porter will be there."

"And that would be a bad thing?" Rebekah raised her brow. "He is wealthy, handsome, and completely smitten with you."

"I am a married woman." Hope shook her head in disapproval.

"I hate to state the obvious, but Conall is gone, and you said yourself that he'd mentioned if his brother came for him, he would likely never be allowed to return."

"Him living somewhere else does not mean our wedding vows are no longer in force."

"No, but you could get a divorce. Abandonment is grounds for one. Dr. Porter said—"

"Oh, great." Hope raised her hands in the air. "And now he is talking to you. I don't know what he's playing at, but I am weary of his attempts to subvert my marriage."

"He is simply worried about you," Rebekah said.

"I am a grown woman, I can take care of myself. I don't need a champion."

"I know. Still, I really wish you would reconsider coming to the festival. Your students have missed you since you left to care for Talila. I am sure they'd love to see you."

Hope nodded, melancholy. "I will think about it."

Minutes later, Hope sank into a kitchen chair and propped up her chin with her hand. Talila lay asleep in her cradle. Should she go to the festival? Rebekah said she could drop Talila off at her house to be watched by her sitter.

Hope truly did not feel like going, but then, she hadn't felt like celebrating anything since Conall had disappeared. And it had only gotten worse.

In the past month, she had woken up in a cold sweat every night with remnants of a nightmare she could not seem to recall. But she was sure Conall was featured in each one.

Will he ever come back? Her heart ached whenever she considered the possibility that he would not. Surely, he could convince his brother to let him leave.

But maybe she was fooling herself. Perhaps Conall had found forgetfulness in the arms of a beautiful woman with eyes almost too large for her face and a sweet, melodious voice. The image of an Elven woman flashed in her mind.

Hope shook off her thoughts. "Hope, this is not healthy for you, and it's definitely not healthy for Talila—to see her mother forever pining after a man she cannot have."

For the next hour, Rebekah's word kept replaying in her mind. Standing up, Hope pushed back her doubts and fears. "All right. You've mourned enough. It's time to start living."

It was well past sundown when Hope dropped off Talila and stepped away from Rebekah's house. Crickets chirped in the thickets, and an owl hooted from nearby. Her heart thumped in her chest. She'd rarely walked about unescorted at night. Still, what could happen to her in Tarrytown? It was a peaceful place—well, at least it was now that the Horseman and the town's evil witch had vanished. Still, walking in the moonlight with only the shadows and eerie silence for company gave her an ominous feeling.

She did not waste time but rushed forward, her heart pounding with every step. "What are you so afraid of, Hope?" Her voice filled the silence, making it just a tad more bearable. "There is nothing in the darkness that is not there in the daytime."

The snapping of a twig had her jolting to a stop. She did not step on a twig. So, who did?

Hope broke into a run. The sounds of music and laughter of the festival filtered through the trees and made their way to her. If only she could get there, she'd be safe. A sharp pain shot through her foot, and she flew toward the ground. When she hit the dirt road, there was more pain—mostly in her hands. Laughter billowed around her. Her heart slammed against her chest. That laughter was too close to be from the celebration.

Hope scrambled off the ground and ran headlong into something hard. Her heart stopped when a familiar voice said, "Hello, wife."

She shook her head. "You are not my husband."

A group of rough men stepped from the trees into the road carrying a lantern. The flickering light fell on her would-be husband. The shadows stretched over his face drove chills down her spine. The smell of sweaty men mixed with the scent of fall leaves.

Hope turned her eyes toward the glow of the festival. Should she cry out for help? Would anyone even hear her with all the music and revelry going on. Probably not.

He chuckled again. "We made vows until death do us part. Do either of us look dead?"

"You annulled our marriage."

"Who told you that?" he growled.

"A friend."

"And does this friend have a name?"

Hope shook her head. She would take that information to the grave. She would give this man nothing that would put her friends in harm's way.

He raised his hand and she cringed away. When he did not strike her, she took a shaky breath and asked, "What are you going to do to me?"

"I am not going to do anything to you."

She looked up. She'd hoped she'd find some hint of compassion in his eyes; instead, she found nothing but malice, cold and hard. "Now the constables with me, they have orders to bring you in dead or alive."

"And what is my crime?" she asked, jutting her chin out.

"You know very well what you did."

"The only thing I did wrong those many years ago was to agree with my father that I would marry you."

"And then you shot him. Not a very loving way to treat the man who raised you."

"That is a lie. I would never raise a hand to my father."

"I have eight witnesses that say otherwise."

"I thought it was only three? Have you paid a few others for their testimonies?"

He narrowed his eyes. "Those eight men are honorable men. They would not lie about a crime so heinous. And the judge thought so too. He condemned you regardless of your absence."

"Your definition of honor and my definition of honor are two very different things."

"Says a murderess."

"I did not kill anyone."

"We've already been over this. Now, I don't blame you for being upset. If I were about to be hanged, I might be upset too. But I do have a deal I can broker with you."

"And what deal would you be able to offer?" she said as a sick feeling settled in her stomach.

"I hold your life in my hands, Hope," he said. "The judge in Boston has given me, as your husband, the right to choose your fate—life or death. There is a jail in Ipswich that would hold you for the duration of your life. There you will receive food and a bed to lay your head. In exchange for this leniency, I would visit you from time to time."

"And why would you care to visit me?" She narrowed her eyes.

Eli laughed and then leaned down and lowered his voice. "It pleases me to see you are even more beautiful than I remembered, and it pleases me even more that you are still so innocent. I will take great pleasure in ridding you of that innocence, my sweet. In the end, you will beg me to come to you. I can promise you that."

"I will never beg you. And I would rather die than lie in your bed."

At those words, his hand flew, striking her on the cheek. Hope was knocked back, hitting the hard ground. Dazed and in pain she choked back a sob.

"If that is your decision, then I will arrange it," he said. "I will give you until sunrise to decide otherwise. If you still refuse, you will hang." He turned to a circle of men who approached. "Tie her up and put her in the wagon."

Rough hands pulled and wrenched her arms around her back. Hope cried out for help as coarse ropes lashed around her wrists.

"Keep her quiet," Eli said, and her screams were cut off when they stuffed fabric across her mouth and tied it at the back of her head.

A large man lifted her up and dropped her over his shoulder. His sour odor wafted up to her and had her swallowing bile. He dropped her like a sack of potatoes into the wooden bed of a wagon. Before this was over, she'd have bruises from head to toe. She squeezed her eyes to keep her tears from falling.

No. She would not be bruised. She would be dead.

There was no way she would sell her virtue for her life. There was a small comfort in knowing Talila would be in good hands with Rebekah. But Conall? Her heart broke all over again as the hope of his return extinguished in the reality of her dire situation. If she died, she would never see him again.

Hope lay in the bed of the wagon with nothing to cushion her. Each bump, each divot in the road caused shooting pain in her shoulder and hip. Not to mention the cloth in her mouth was soaked through with saliva and tasted of mud and grit. The riotous jeers and the sickening tales of her captors made Hope's stomach sour. Still, she wished their journey would never end. She did her best not to think about what would happen once they stopped but trying not to think about it only made it that much harder not to. Truly, there was no one to save her. No one who even knew where to begin to find her.

When the sky took on an orange glow, she knew her time was nearly up. Blinking back tears, Hope propped herself on her elbow to peer over the side of the wagon.

They entered a clearing with no buildings in sight. When the driver pulled on the reins and the wagon stopped, Hope's heart sank. Was this the place? Hangings usually occurred in town squares.

Eli gave orders to unload the lumber and assemble the gallows. A group of ten men worked quickly as Hope's heart sank. This really was it. This was the end.

Rising to her knees, she bowed her head and opened her heart to the heavens.

God, please help me. I have lived a Christian life. Though I have not been perfect, I have tried my best. Can you not find it in your heart to deliver me? If you choose not to save me from these wicked men, I will still be true to you. But there is one thing I beg of you. Please, watch over my family, and if it be Thy will, let Conall and Talila find one another. Please God, grant me this one request, and keep them safe.

Laughter brought Hope back to the stark reality before her. She opened her eyes and looked up.

A man with dark, curly hair and a scraggly beard sneered at her. "You think God hears you?" He looked up and shouted, "Obadiah, this criminal thinks God listens to the likes of her."

"God don't hear you, missy," Obadiah said, strolling up to her, his eyes tinged yellow. "If He answered prayers, I would have been struck down years ago. I have had many a man and woman pray for deliverance from me. And yet here I am, without a mark to show for it, while they lie in their graves."

Hope considered warning him that death would come soon for him. The yellow in his eyes meant his liver was failing. She held her tongue. He'd find out soon enough.

"Your best bet is to take up Eli's offer. Bedding him has got to be better than the gallows there yonder." Obadiah turned to the first man. "I don't know why he don't just take her and have his way with her."

The man shook his head. "He said he won't unless she begs him. Put the noose around her neck, and I gander she will."

They thought she'd change her mind when faced with death? They did not know her very well.

Hope turned her back on them. She would not waste the last moments of her life looking at such filth.

She spent the next hour pouring her heart out to God. This time, she did not kneel. Spending her time praying accomplished two things: it helped her prepare to meet God, and her prayerful thoughts drowned out the crude conversations of the men.

She smelled the overpowering scent of sandalwood before she saw him. If Eli thought drenching himself in cologne would make him more appealing, he was completely wrong. It turned her stomach.

"Get her out of the wagon," Eli said, facing her.

The two men dragged her out and put her on her feet. After lying so long on the wooden planks, Hope stumbled a bit before she righted herself.

"Have you considered my offer?" Eli asked, stepping around to untie the fabric from her mouth.

Hope attempted to spit the grit from her mouth.

"No," she rasped, wiping her mouth off. "I haven't given it a second thought."

At those words, his eyes narrowed, and blossoms of red blotched his face. "I should beat you to an inch of your life before putting the noose around your neck."

Hope's heart took off in a sprint. She'd been preparing for a quick death. She felt faint at the thought of being beaten first. Still, she tried to put on a brave face. She would not die sniveling and cowardly. "You can do what you wish. I have made peace with my Maker."

His chest rose and fell as the thin set of his lips relaxed. He took Hope by the arm and led her toward the gallows. She looked down as she stepped up the wooden stairs. When she reached the top, she saw the noose hanging—the course rope looked thick and strong. Hope was surprised by the length. It seemed a bit short— though, truth be told, she'd not been to many hangings. She found them too barbaric.

He looped the heavy rope over her head and looked down at her. "I will give you one last chance," he whispered. "I don't want to see you die. I have always cared for you, Hope. Loved you since the moment I laid eyes on you. I lied when I said I had our marriage annulled. I did no such thing. You are my wife, and I will deny you nothing. If you now beg for your life, I will grant it. Beg for me to make you mine, and I will take you. I will worship you both body and soul. You don't even have to live in a prison the rest of your life. We can return to England; I still have friends and allies there. You can live a life you've only dreamed of. Just say the word, and I will save you."

Hope stood in silent resolve, refusing to look at him. *He would save me? He is the one threatening my life.* She realized at that moment how sick he was—it was a sickness of the mind and spirit that afflicted him. She felt his anger building at her silence, gathering strength. She prayed for God to have mercy on his soul.

"Answer me!" he roared.

Hope finally looked at him. "There is only one word I can give you, Eli. And that word is 'never.'"

"So be it," Eli snarled, and he cranked the lever.

The floor dropped from below Hope's feet. Her thoughts filled with images of Conall, Talila, her friends, and students as a myriad of emotions swirled in her mind. Her descent was much slower than expected. Though her thoughts and emotions were poignant, she was still acutely aware of the sensation of falling. It was not unlike the feeling of jumping from the high branch of a tree into a pond. But instead of cool water greeting her, pain like a vice snapped around her neck. A cheer rang out and faded into deafening silence.

Chapter 30

Conall buttoned his royal tunic and strapped his bow and arrows to his back. His brother had finally allowed him weapons. It had taken time, but he was slowly regaining the king's trust. Looking at himself in the mirror, he was satisfied that everything was in place—he looked every bit the part of a royal prince.

Minutes later, he joined his friends and relatives in the hall. The jovial mood was apparent, and Conall put on a smile as he greeted the others.

"This will be the grandest festival yet," Dyffros said, clapping him on the back. "And I have arranged for a beautiful escort for you." He winked.

Conall shook his head. "That is really not a good idea."

"Of course, it is," Dyffros said. "How are you to move forward, if you cannot enjoy a woman from time to time?"

"Yes, brother," Haryk said, putting his arm around him. "And this woman will not get you banished if you take advantage."

Conall frowned. If he had any hope of making his way back to the human world, he would need his brother's permission. And he would not gain his permission if he raised his ire.

"Are you in on this?" Conall asked Haryk.

"I was consulted, and that is all. Your love life is your own. I want no part in it."

Conall bit back a retort. His brother wanted no involvement in his love life, yet he was keeping Conall from the only woman he ever truly loved.

The king mounted his horse, and Conall followed on his own steed. All but the servants in the castle left as they made their way to the equinox festival. Conall's heart sank when he thought about what this day meant. Though it seemed he'd only been away for two months, an entire year had passed for Hope. Was she safe? Was she happy?

The smells of the festival were carried on the wind—roast pig, fruit pies, sweet cakes, and though he could not smell it, there would be ale enough to fill a river.

Scattered tents were seen amongst the tall trees, and lights hanging from branches everywhere filled the forest with a warm glow. Music played, and laughter filled the air.

When they arrived, Conall dismounted and tied off his horse. He started for his tent, wanting to sit for a bit before he joined the revelry.

"Cousin," Dyffros said. "Where do you think you're going? The party is this way. You can return to your tent after we find your lady."

Conall frowned and then turned to follow his cousin. When they reached the clearing, he was surprised to see such organized chaos. Men and women drinking and dancing in various states of undress. Uproarious laughter and riotous revelry everywhere.

Conall shook his head. And these creatures thought humans were vile. How could he have once found enjoyment in this?

"Ah," Dyffros said. "There she is."

Conall followed his line of sight, and his heart turned cold. "Seirye."

She gave him a full smile and rushed into his arms. He pushed her back.

"If I had known. . .."

"What? Am I really that repulsive to you?"

A tear glimmered in her eye. The show of emotion shocked him. Was she really broken-hearted?

"I just don't know what I did," she sobbed. "You once loved me. You once wanted to marry me."

Conall shook his head. "It's not you, Seirye. I just . . ." he paused, not wanting to talk about Hope. Whenever he brought her up, his words were met with ridicule and disgust. He could not abide one more condescending remark about his wife.

"How about a dance?" Seirye asked. "I will not ask more of you."

Conall nodded and took her hand.

The dance started out awkwardly but as the music filtered through, he pushed back his reservations and depressing thoughts and focused on the melody. It was lively, and his heart lightened as he remembered why he so loved to dance.

They stopped to have a drink, and his mood lifted even more. He might even go so far as to say he was having fun.

Hours later, he laughed as he twirled his way through the crowd. Seirye jumped into his arms, and he twirled her around. Her body was warm, and she smelled like peppermint. When her lips met his, he kissed her back. As he deepened the kiss, the wrongness of her sickeningly sweet taste hit him like a club to the back of his head.

What am I doing? He pushed her back, berating himself for his betrayal. What would Hope think of him? How could he forget her—even for a moment.

"Conall?" she said as he turned his back and stomped into the woods.

Seirye rushed after him, trying to pull him back. "What have I ever done to you to make you hate me?"

"I don't hate you, Seirye. I hate myself."

"Is this what human love does to you? Makes you hate yourself? She's the problem, isn't she? Your beloved Hope."

Conall's heart froze in his chest. "Where did you hear that name?"

"Oh, um. You mean, where did I hear the human's name? Haryk must have mentioned it."

"I never told him her name." Anger burned the iciness in his heart away as fury built. He hid his anger, knowing she would not tell him a thing if she felt threatened.

"I don't remember." She avoided his gaze.

"Seirye," he pressed.

"What does it matter? She's nothing. Don't you see? She's a human with a pitifully short life span. For all you know, she could be dead already."

Those words got his heart pounding. "What have you done?" His voice was low—just above a whisper—but there was a hard edge he couldn't mask. "Tell me."

Her eyes widened as she shook her head. "I-I did not do anything. It was the humans that wanted her. They're the ones threatening her."

Conall sickened, knowing exactly what she was talking about. It was the reason Hope had to flee to Sleepy Hollow in the first place. "And you led them to her, didn't you?"

"No. I didn't mean to."

"You must think me a fool." He let her go. "You knew exactly what you were doing."

267

"And what if I did? What of it? She would die anyway." She turned a hopeful eye to him. "And now there is nothing to keep us apart. Conall, I don't know what happened to you in the human world, but you need to forget it, forget her."

He looked away, bitterness and anger threatening to overtake his reasoning.

"Is she still alive?"

"Yes, but she's as good as dead. They're hanging her at dawn."

Conall's heart pounded in his chest. How much time did he have? Seirye was his best hope at saving his wife. "Is there anything I could do to convince you to stop them?" he asked. "I am sure you could—"

"And why would I? So, you can keep pining after her?"

"But if I—"

"No, forget it. There is nothing you can do or say to convince me to save that filthy rat. Even if you hate me forever, I will not lift a finger to help her. I am glad she'll be dead. Food for the buzzards, that is all she's good for."

Conall drew his sword and thrust it into Seirye's chest. Her eyes widened as she slumped forward. Conall caught her in his arms and pulled his blade from her body.

She turned to him and hissed. "Why?"

Warm blood drenched his shirt as he held her. "I will destroy everyone and everything that threatens the woman I love." He lowered her to the ground. "But you are not dead yet, my sweet. This wound will heal if you receive care quickly, so you still have a chance. Tell me how to get back to the human world, and I will take you to the healers."

She shook her head and coughed. Blood trickled from her mouth. "Never."

"Are you willing to die?" he asked.

"It's you who has a choice. My life, or Hope's."

He shook his head. "There's no contest. Just tell me where she is."

"Why is she so important to you? What does she have that I don't?"

"My love."

"You once loved me." A tear slipped down her cheek.

"I did not know what love was until I met Hope."

"No," she shouted. "I curse your human, and I curse you too. I am the only woman who has ever loved you."

"What you feel for me is not love, Seirye. Love is putting someone else's wants and needs above your own. If you truly loved me, you would want me to be happy."

"I want you to suffer. I want you to suffer as I have suffered."

"Please, Seirye. Just tell me how to find her."

"Never."

Conall continued to plead with her, but to no avail. Her desire for vengeance was greater than her desire to live. The light extinguished from Seirye's eyes. Her head dropped forward as her heart stilled.

She was gone.

A shadow fell over Conall's shoulder. "What have you done?" Haryk growled.

Conall turned to see his brother and his guard and said, "I have lost the only woman I ever loved."

"Oh, so you've decided you love Seirye after all. It's your blade that is stained with her blood. Why did you kill her?" he said, incredulous.

"She went after my wife in the human world and set things in motion that would assure her death."

Haryk sank down beside him. "You love a human enough to kill the woman you pined after for more than a century?"

"I love a human enough to kill even you if you threatened her, brother."

The guards drew their swords and took a step toward them. Haryk raised his hand to stop them. "At last. You understand."

Conall looked up in surprise.

"You understand why I banished you. You were lucky to get away with your life after what you did to my Edwina."

Conall sighed. "Yes, I understand."

Haryk gestured to Seirye. "Still, I cannot let this go unpunished."

Conall nodded, feeling utterly defeated. "Do what you will. I don't care. I cannot save Hope, and I refuse to live in a world without her. My life is worth nothing now."

"We'll see about that." Haryk stood, scowling intently at Conall. He turned to his men and shouted, "My brother is guilty of murder. He has admitted to his crime, and now he will pay for it."

Haryk hesitated, and then said, "I decree that Conall, Prince of the Elven court is, as of this moment, stripped of his title. He is no longer a prince. No longer my brother. And he is banished from Faery for all time. If he attempts to return, he will die." Despite his words, his brother put out his hand and lifted him from the ground. Haryk embraced him. His brother slipped something into his

270

pocket and whispered so that only Conall could hear, "This stone will allow you to travel anywhere you want to go. I only ask that you don't return here. I can't begin to understand why you would choose a human over your Elven kind, but I will fight you no longer. You are free. The safest place for a human and elf to live in peace is in the 'between'—the realm between our worlds."

Conall said, "Thank you, brother."

"Don't thank me. One day you will regret what you did here. Now go and save your human."

Chapter 31

Darkness descended, and the air grew chill. The familiar scent of Tarrytown filled his nostrils. Conall's heart raced. He'd done it. He was back.

And he had until dawn.

Looking up, he saw Victor's house with the lights still blazing. He ran to the door and pounded on it. If anyone knew where Hope was, they would.

Victor opened the door, and his jaw dropped. "Conall! I am so relieved to see you!" He looked behind Conall. "We were so worried. Where is Hope?"

"I was hoping you would tell me," Conall said.

"She's not with you?" Victor said, his eyes widening.

He shook his head. "I don't have time to explain, but Hope is in danger. Where is the last place you saw her?"

Rebekah rushed forward, her eyes red and swollen with tears. "We found her hat trampled on the road to the festival, but we haven't been able to find any other sign of her. Elizabeth told me about her former husband. I fear he's come for her."

"Take me to where you located her hat."

He and Victor dismounted their horses minutes later, and Conall searched the road. There were tracks from a wagon, and the dirt was trampled by no less than ten men. From the looks of it, she'd fallen twice before they dragged her away. Conall had to force back his fury. He needed to keep a clear head if he hoped to find her in time.

"I will go on from here," Conall said to Victor.

"I am coming with you."

Conall shook his head. "I don't want you implicated in what I plan to do to those men. You've got Rebekah and your baby to worry about. My only concern is Hope. If she dies, I will not hold back. I will slaughter each and every one of them."

Victor nodded. He put out his hand, and Conall took it. "Godspeed. And if you ever need a place of refuge, our home is open to you."

Conall nodded, grateful to have such loyal friends.

He followed the tracks for a long while. His Elven eyes could see what no man could in the darkness, but he still nearly lost the trail a couple times. When the light of morning brightened the forest around him, he drove his horse harder.

He broke into a wide clearing. A crowd of men in the distance gathered around—

A cheer rang out just as his eyes landed on Hope. The rope around her neck snapped tight as he roared. Fury washed over him like a tsunami. Hope hung lifeless, swinging from a hangman's noose. Pulling an arrow from his quiver, he took aim at the cord. It flew true to its target, and Hope dropped to the ground.

The men turned in confusion. Conall narrowed his eyes as adrenaline rushed through his veins. None of these men would make it out alive.

Eli's eyes narrowed as he locked gazes with him. He pointed to Conall and shouted, "Kill that man."

Conall notched two arrows and took aim, hitting two men simultaneously as they mounted horses. The others rode toward him with their muskets raised. Conall drove his horse forward, releasing arrow after arrow, taking out four more.

273

The remaining men slowed, some of them turning away. One fired his weapon, the musket ball whizzing past him on the right. Undeterred, Conall dispatched the shooter and another man who was fleeing—striking the shooter in the forehead and the other in the neck, slicing through his spinal cord.

In minutes, the only man left alive was Eli. When he saw his hopeless situation, he raced behind the gallows. Conall finally reached the scaffolds and leapt off his horse at a run. He skidded to a stop when Eli stepped out from behind the planks with Hope's lifeless body in his arms. The soon-to-be dead man pointed a pistol at her head.

"You are threatening the life of a woman who is already dead?" Conall growled as he shook in fury.

Eli shook his head. "She's not dead. I made sure the rope was too short to break her neck."

Conall's heart skipped a beat. *Could it be true?* "You are lying."

"I promise, she's alive. And she'll stay alive if you put down your weapons and surrender to me."

Conall examined Hope, searching desperately for any signs of life. The rope was so tight around her neck, it was misshapen. There was no movement from her, and she looked as white as death.

There was only one way to find out if the man was telling the truth.

"Alright," Conall relented, raising his hands. "I will do as you say. Just don't hurt her." He lowered his bow slowly to the ground and then shrugged off the straps holding his quiver and squatted to set them down. As he rose, his hand brushed over his boot, and he caught the pommel of his dagger. Like a whip it flew. Eli did not even have time to look surprised when the blade sliced through his eye socket.

Conall flashed himself behind Hope and caught her before she could fall. He lowered her gently to the grassy ground and laid her down flat. He wanted so much to gather her in his arms, but feared, despite what Eli said, her neck was broken.

He loosened the rope from around her, and a wheeze of air escaped her throat. He knew better than to read too much into it. He brushed her hair from her face and felt for a pulse. If she were truly dead, there would be nothing he could do. But if there were any signs of life, he could save her.

And there it was. A gentle thrum of a pulse. Conall blew out a sigh of relief. She was still there. "Oh, baby, thank the gods, or is it your God who is responsible? I don't care, I am just glad you are still here."

Conall gathered all the magical energy he could from himself and the air around him and poured it into Hope's body. He concentrated on the most vital parts—her airway, veins, arteries, and spine. He felt the healing energy pouring from him.

His heart flew when she took in a heaping gasp of breath. Weakened from using so much power, he fell back, barely able to remain sitting. Blinking, Hope seemed confused as she searched around her. Her eyes widened when they landed on his face.

"Conall?" she rasped and attempted to sit up.

He moved toward her and gently pushed her back. "Don't try to sit up yet, love," he said, breathless.

"Am I dead? Oh, please, don't you be dead too."

"You are not dead. And neither am I. I have come back."

At those words, Hope broke down in tears, sat up, and threw her arms around him. Conall cradled her head against his chest, still fearful of her condition. She held him tight, her body trembling against him as she sobbed. He swallowed the lump in his throat and blinked back tears. For the first time since he'd left the human world, he felt complete. His shattered heart was whole again, and he was home.

Despite the dangers of both his world and hers, they were together. And he would see to it nothing would ever threaten her again.

Finally, her cries quieted, and she pulled back, blinking back tears as she studied his face and lifted a shaky hand to press against his cheek. "I have missed you."

Conall blinked back his own tears. "I have missed you too." And then he kissed her—taking care to be gentle. He took his time savoring her, worshiping her with his lips. Finally, he pulled away, and her breath hitched. Fresh tears fell down her cheeks.

"I cannot believe you are back."

He nodded. "I will always come back for you."

She nodded.

"But now, I need to take you somewhere safe."

"Can't we go home?"

"I am afraid I may have made things worse." He looked around and her eyes followed. She gasped when she saw Eli at her feet with a dagger protruding from his eye. And then she looked farther. Bodies were strewn across the ground.

"You killed them all?"

"Yes, and don't pray for my forgiveness. I don't feel the least bit sorry."

Hope shook her head. "I will never stop praying for you, but I think the Lord understands you were trying to save me."

Conall did not contradict her, though this was not an act to save her life. He'd thought she was lost to him. This was an act of pure vengeance. Though her delicate spirit did not need to hear such brutal realities. He would make it his life's mission to protect her mind, body, and soul from the harsh realities of life.

"Though noble your act may have been," she said, "Eli had orders from a judge for my execution. And now . . . well, I am afraid you'll be a wanted man too. We'll need to find a place to hide you from the authorities."

God, how he loved this woman. Even now she only thought to protect him—and this while she still had the bruises from her own hanging. "I know just the place." He smiled.

"But first, we need to go back to Tarrytown."

Conall shook his head. "It's too dangerous. That is the first place they'll look. It's best if we don't give them a fresh trail to follow. Vladmir will help us get what we need to relocate."

"You don't understand. We *have* to go back."

"Why?" he asked, frowning at her.

"Because, my dear, sweet husband, we need to get our daughter."

Conall felt as if someone had knocked the wind out of him. Breathless and feeling a bit faint, he said, "What did you say?"

"I said, we need to get our baby girl. Rebekah has her."

"You . . . you had a baby?"

"*We* had a baby. I was pregnant when . . . when you . . ." she could not seem to get the words out. His heart broke when he realized how much pain she'd endured when he'd been taken from her.

"It's all right, love." He pulled her into his arms. "I will never leave you again."

"But what about your brother? Will he come back for you?"

"No. I am afraid I did not behave myself when he took me back. He's banished me from Faery forever. I will never have to leave you again."

She chuckled softly, surprising him.

"What's so funny?" he asked.

"I have never been so grateful for a harsh sentence," she said, and then grew quiet. "But, what will you do when I die? You'll still be trapped here."

"I won't let you die."

"But—"

"If I have to use every ounce of power I hold to keep you with me, I will."

"You could do that?" she asked.

"No. I *will* do that."

"Enough talk of my mortality. I am in an excruciating amount of pain."

Concern darkened his eyes. "Is it your throat? Do I need to heal you further?"

She shook her head and pressed her arm to her chest. "It's been far too long since I have nursed our child. And you have no idea how painful that is."

A smile softened his features as he removed the stone from his pocket and wrapped his arms around his wife. "Then I guess it's high time we go get her."

Hope gasped when he transported them to Victor's house.

"Hope!" Rebekah shouted over the wailing of a small babe. She rushed toward them. "I am so glad—oh dear heavens!" She looked at Hope's neck. "What did they do to you?"

"I don't want to talk about it. It's enough to say that Conall got there in time."

"I did *not* get there in time. You are lucky to be alive."

Agnes walked in the room with a crying infant in her arms and said, "She has refused to eat since you've been gone."

Conall could not take his eyes off the baby in the old woman's arms. She was the most beautiful child he'd ever seen. Her face glowed with magical energy, her cheeks were round and healthy, and her cry was strong enough to fell trees.

Hope gathered her in her arms and sat down. The others left the room, allowing them to be alone. Hope quieted her baby's cries as she suckled her. Conall sat down beside her and brushed his hand over the infant's soft baby skin. "She's so tiny."

Hope nodded. "But she's still a force to be reckoned with. There's no calming her once she gets riled up. She gets that from her father." Hope's eyes sparkled when she winked at him. "And that is not all she got from you." She untied her bonnet and pulled it off her head, revealing the most adorable pointed ears.

He shook his head. "She'll never pass for a human with ears like that."

"And that is why we keep her bonnet on her head," Hope said.

"We?"

"Rebekah and Agnes have been my guardian angels. They've been with me, helping me from the start."

Conall's heart saddened. "I am sorry I wasn't here for you."

"You could not help it. But I have to say, if you ever leave me again, I will never forgive you."

"You could never hold a grudge, my sweet. You are far too forgiving."

"For you, I would make an exception."

"Then I guess I will have to stay." He leaned forward to kiss her. Hope tasted so sweet that his heart filled to bursting.

A tiny squeak came from between them, and then his hair felt as if it were being pulled from its roots. He groaned as he broke off the kiss and looked down. His daughter had a fistful of his hair. He smiled and pried it from her chubby fingers.

"What did you name her?" he asked.

"Talila," Hope answered. "I hope you don't mind."

"No. It's perfect. My mother would have been honored to have her granddaughter share her name."

Hope nodded, smiling at his approval. "How long before we need to leave?"

"The sooner, the better. I can shield us with glamour while we are here, but I would say we should be gone by tomorrow."

Hope stood, turning toward him. "Would you like to hold her?"

Conall's heart pounded. "I don't think I should. I would probably break her."

Hope laughed. "She's sturdier than she looks. You'll do fine." She leaned down and placed the tiny babe in his arms.

Conall's heart swelled in his chest as he held his daughter. He'd thought he could never love anyone as much as he loved Hope, but this tiny thing . . . she won over his heart completely. He leaned down and kissed her head. She smelled like primrose and jasmine mixed with the lavender scent of Hope's soap. She scrunched her nose and made a tiny squeaky sound. He smiled at the bead of milk at the corner of her mouth and said, "She looks satisfied."

"I wish *I* were," Hope said, raising a brow and smirking at him. She then reached for Talila, "May I?"

Conall nodded and reluctantly relinquished his child to her mother. Hope lay her in a nearby bassinet. She then turned back, put her hand on her hip, and gave him a disapproving look. "Husband, it's been a long time. . .."

Conall suppressed a smile as his heart rate picked up. He took a step toward her. "Far too long." He turned to look at Talila. "Will she be all right sleeping here for a while?"

Hope nodded. "She should sleep for an hour or two."

"Hmm," he said, frowning and wrapping his arms around Hope's waist. "That is not near enough time, but I guess it will have to do." He lowered his lips to hers and transported them home.

*　*　*　*　*

Rebekah stepped back into the living room. "I can watch the baby if you want to be . . ." her voice dropped off when she noticed the room was empty. She chuckled and then finished her sentence. "...alone."

She stepped forward to see Talila sleeping soundly in the crib. Beside the cradle lay a pile of clothes on the floor. She

281

recognized them as the clothes Conall and Hope had been wearing just minutes ago. She looked around the room, half afraid of finding them in an embarrassing predicament. When she was satisfied they had left, she gathered up the clothes up for Agnes to wash.

She looked down at the sleeping angel and whispered, "I am so glad your mommy has your daddy back. And soon, you'll know just how lucky you are too."

She left the room, humming a tune.

Epilogue

Sixteen Years Later

Hope stepped into the backyard of her two-story clapboard home carrying a basket of damp clothes. The sun shone warm against her face in the small clearing of a thick forest. Pixies fluttered around the perimeter, lighting up the shadowed forest like fireflies. One by one, Hope hung the clothes on the line to dry.

"I can see the appeal you held for my brother."

Hope whipped around to see an elf standing regally behind her. His dark hair was pierced by pointed ears and hung well past his shoulders. His eyes were the most striking shade of indigo. His shoulders were broad, and he had a jeweled crown sitting on his head.

"You *are* quite a beauty," he continued.

"You must be Haryk," Hope said, as she attempted to calm her heart.

"Yes, though most would not address me so informally."

"I apologize. Conall only has ever called you Haryk.

He waved off her comment. "It doesn't matter. My kingdom lies outside this realm."

"I'm sorry, but Conall is not here."

"I didn't come only for Conall. I wanted to see you."

"Me?"

"Yes, I couldn't contain my curiosity. I had to meet the woman who had captured my brother's heart so completely that he would forsake his home, his kingdom, and his family."

"I never expected him to." She hung a blouse and then stooped down to the basket, her brows pressed together.

"No. I'm sure you didn't. My brother is not one who is easily controlled."

"No, he isn't." Hope pulled a small shirt from the basket and lifted it to the line.

Haryk eyed the garment. "Does that belong to Conall's son?"

Hope nodded. "Yes, we have two children, a daughter and a son."

"How old are they?"

"Our daughter is sixteen and our son is two."

Haryk's eyes widened. "Sixteen?"

Hope sighed. "Talila was born several months after you took Conall from me."

"I'd apologize, but I still think my brother would have done better to remain with his own kind."

Hope raised a brow. "Shouldn't that be his decision to make? Though I guess it doesn't matter now; he's been banished."

"Yes, he has."

Hope hung the last of the clothes and picked up the empty basket. "I appreciate you making the trip to visit. Conall should be returning soon. Would you like to come in for some refreshments and wait for him?"

"I have a feeling he would not want to see me."

"And why would that be? He is your brother. Family is important. I'm sure your mother would not have wanted this distance between the two of you. I can tell you, as a mother, my heart would break if my children ever estranged themselves from one another."

Haryk's brows pressed together. "I thought of all people, *you* would be the one who would not want me in his life."

"I want Conall to be happy. I know it pains him to not see you."

"It does?" His brows raised.

"He doesn't talk about it, but I can tell that he misses you."

Haryk regarded her with doubt, clouding his eyes. "I do regret how we parted. Though, I don't see how it could have ended differently. He was determined to return to you, it seems at all costs."

"The past is gone. There is no changing it. I think it better we focus on the future."

Hope reached out her hand to him. He hesitated before taking it.

"I would like you to come and meet your niece and nephew." She led him into the house and then into the living area. "Would you perhaps like some apple pie and a glass of milk?"

"No, thank you."

A gentle tug at her skirt was soon followed by a small voice saying, "Mamma, who is that?"

Hope looked down to a little a white-haired little boy with pale, blue eyes.

"Jonas, this is your uncle Haryk."

"Uncle?"

Hope nodded. "Yes."

"I've never had an uncle before."

"No, sweetheart," Hope said. "Haryk has always been your uncle."

Haryk studied the boy in wonder. "He looks so much like my brother."

"That he does," Hope said and then turned to Jonas. "Where is your sister? Has she returned?"

Jonas nodded.

"Where is she?" Hope asked.

Jonas didn't speak but pointed out the window.

"She's outside?"

Jonas nodded, not taking his eyes off Haryk.

Hope stepped over to the window and looked outside. The yard was wide and lined with trees broken by a cobblestone path leading from the house into the forest. There was no sign of Talila. "I don't see her."

"No, mamma. She is up."

Hope frowned. "What do you mean, 'up'?"

Jonas's feet padded against the wood floor as he stepped up beside her. He squinted as he looked through the window. His eyes searching—

Hopes' heart dropped.

He was searching the sky above the trees. "Oh please, no," she said and then gasped when she saw a speck in the distance. It looked like a strange bird with a blue cape. It swooped down giving her a better picture of what she was seeing. Hope squealed as she raced to the front door.

Leaping off the porch, Hope shouted. "Talila! What under God's heaven are you doing?" She pressed her hand against her chest as her heart pounded.

"How could she tame a beast like that?" Haryk asked, coming up behind her, gaping at the sky.

"You would not believe me if I told you."

As Talila got closer Hope could see exactly what she was riding. It was a white horse with wings as wide as a barn. "Talila, you get down here right now before you fall!" she shouted.

The winged horse continued its descent as Talila's laughter rang out. Hope could feel the vibration as the hooves met the ground. "Mother, I was perfectly safe. Ichabod would never let me fall." She leapt off the back of the horse, her dark hair billowing out behind her as she landed gracefully to the ground.

"Ichabod?" Hope asked.

Talila shrugged, "It's a name."

Hope shook her head and mumbled disapprovingly. "Your father and his fireside stories."

A familiar menacing voice snapped, "Get away from my wife."

Hope turned to see Conall with his sword pointed at his brother's throat.

"Conall," Hope screeched. "What are you doing?"

Conall searched their faces, assessing the situation and then his eyes landed on Hope's. "You were afraid. I could feel it."

"I was not afraid of your brother." She rushed forward and tugged at his arm as it continued to hold the blade. Finally, he dropped his sword.

He turned a disapproving eye on Hope. "Then what were you afraid of?"

Holly Kelly

"Your daughter was riding that winged creature through the clouds." She gestured to the horse as it grazed on their grass. "She could have been killed."

Talila rushed forward. "Father, I was perfectly safe."

"We'll discuss this later," Conall said and then turned to Haryk. "I need to speak to my brother."

Conall pulled Hope into his side and pressed a kiss down on her head. "Can you take the children into the house, luv?"

"I'd be happy to," Hope said, tugging him down to brush a kiss against his lips. As he began to pull away from the embrace, Hope held him fast and whispered, "Be nice to your brother."

*   *   *   *   *

Conall watched his family walk up the path. Talila and Jonas both eyed Haryk curiously. When Hope pulled the front door shut, Haryk said, "Your wife is an amazing woman."

"You have no idea how much of an understatement that is."

Haryk chuckled, "I don't doubt you."

"I'm sorry I threatened you, brother," Conall said.

Haryk shrugged and said, "It was a misunderstanding."

They stood in silence for several moments before Haryk spoke again. "How long have you been linked to your wife?"

Conall frowned, obviously not happy with the question. Regardless, he said, "Since the day I returned to her."

Haryk nodded. "Does she know what that means?"

"She knows that I keep her from aging and falling ill."

"Ah, you did not fill her in on all the details. You know that if she is killed…"

"I die."

"Is she worth your life?"

"She is worth so much more than my life."

Haryk nodded and stepped away. "Truly, I had hoped things had soured between you and your human. I planned to petition you to return, but now I see that it was a fool's errand."

"I could never leave them," Conall said. "Besides, I've been banished for all time."

"The realm of Faery is in turmoil," Haryk said. "There are many calling for you to return, but now I see that it is impossible."

"Yes, it is."

Haryk lifted his hand and a portal appeared, shimmering in the air beside him. "Tell your family I'm sorry I couldn't stay."

Before his brother could leave, Conall said, "Don't stay away so long next time."

Haryk's eyes widened. His surprise melted into a smile. "She has changed you."

"In more ways than you could ever know."

"I have to admit, I may have been wrong about humans. Well, at least I was wrong about your human. And I think mother would be pleased with your daughter's name. It's a fitting honor for her."

Conall bowed his head in agreement.

"May the gods watch over you and your family, brother," Haryk said.

"Thank you. And may the gods watch over you also."

Haryk smiled as he stepped into the portal. And then he was gone.

Conall turned back to his home. Through the window, he could see Hope busying herself in the kitchen. The sound of her singing made him smile. His heart filled with a love so powerful,

Holly Kelly

he wondered how he could have existed without it. Now that he'd found Hope, he would never let her go. His family was his life, and it was of more value than all the riches and power in this world or any other world. And at that moment, he vowed he would never take them for granted.

The End

About the Author:

Holly Kelly is a wife, mom to six, English teacher, freelance editor, voracious reader, Kenpo black belt, Halloween prop maker, and art enthusiast. Oh, and she writes books in her spare time–at 4:00 AM every morning. Who needs to sleep, right?

Holly has written many novels, six of which have been published. All of her books have been best-sellers, but her most popular series, *The Rising Series*, has sold nearly 200,000 copies worldwide and has been on the best-seller lists in several countries, making it an international best-seller.

You can find all of Holly's books at **HollyKellyBooks.com**, along with updates on new books she'll be releasing soon.

Want to read more from Holly Kelly?
Try the #1 Best-Selling Rising series.

Xanthus is the most lethal warrior to rise from the sea. He has a simple job~kill a woman in a wheelchair. Sara is a crimimal. Her crime? Being born. She's a half-breed, an abomination, and it's his job to rid the world of her. If only she weren't so beautiful, so innocent... Will the warrior do his duty or will the executioner become the protector, and the hunter become the hunted?

Made in the USA
Las Vegas, NV
05 September 2022

54739351R00164